Seaside Cowboy's Best Friend

Book 2 in the Seaside Cowboys series
By Alexa Verde

About *Seaside Cowboy's Best Friend*

A strict, career-minded lawyer, an easygoing flirtatious cowboy, a mysterious disappearance, and a mischievous puppy... Can childhood friends with opposing personalities become more?

.

Back in her small coastal town, divorced and heartbroken lawyer Marina Helms is a fish out of water helping in her mom's seafood restaurant kitchen. Then Marina lands in hot water when she agrees to help her best friend, Kai Lawrence, find the brother he didn't know he had. She just needs to keep her crush on Kai under wraps until she goes back to her demanding job and lackluster life.

.

A part-time cowboy, a part-time pirate impersonator, and a full-time player, Kai wanted Marina to spread her wings. But his protective instincts flare up when he inadvertently leads her into peril. He can't walk away now. And he can't put a lid on his feelings, either.

.

Will their dangerous search unite them—or lead to disaster?

.

Welcome to Port Sunshine, a small coastal town where a family of cowboy brothers discover the treasures of love and uncover the mysteries of their pasts.

Dedication

In loving memory of Clydene Martin.

Chapter One

Marina Helms winced as something clattered in the restaurant kitchen's opposite corner. How exactly had she gotten herself into this situation? She was used to things being organized and everything in order. This was chaos.

"What happened?" she yelled.

"I dropped a pan," her only remaining sous-chef yelled back.

Hopefully, not with the food in it. They were behind on the orders already.

She breathed in the scents of baked fish, garlic, and spices, doing her best to smooth her raw nerves. She was no cook, but how difficult could it be to flip a few steaks? Easy-peasy, right?

Minutes later, she was looking at charred steak. Apparently, not easy at all.

Her sister, Saylor, who was chopping a salad right now, grimaced, then turned up the air-conditioning, sending a wave of cool air through the kitchen. "Yes, the customer wanted their steak well-done, but not burned."

"What an astute observation." Marina groaned and started a new one with a jolt of envy toward her childhood friend, Skylar.

Skylar was on her honeymoon now, in bliss with the guy she'd always loved. No matter the years apart, Marina had reconnected with her friend recently and was happy for her. She really was.

Skylar had found her passion again in many senses, and she'd deserved it, especially after everything she'd gone through. Marina didn't intend to get married again. One heartache and failed marriage was enough. More than enough.

She glanced with longing at the beautiful cerulean sky beyond the window and the calm waves touching the sand, then returned her attention to the skillet. Hopefully, the steak was good enough.

Her mother was on a cruise, and this was Marina's first day working the restaurant without her. She could handle it fine. But for various reasons, several staff members had called in, unable to come to work today.

At least, the day couldn't get any worse, right?

One of her remaining waitresses, Jan, rushed into the kitchen. "I'm so sorry, but my babysitter just called. My daughter is unwell. I have to go."

Marina sighed. She stood corrected. It just got worse. Still, she nodded. "Of course. I hope your daughter feels better."

Then she placed the steak on the plate with rice and green beans. She'd have to deliver it herself. And while she didn't like asking for help, she was in too deep now.

"Thanks, Sis." She did her best to stifle the resentment souring her stomach like acid as she hurried to the dining hall carrying the tray with the plate, a bowl of the salad Saylor had made, and a basket with biscuits emitting a mouthwatering aroma.

Saylor had stayed to help and was much better at cooking than Marina had ever been. But the rest of their sisters had returned to their busy lives in the city after Skylar's wedding. So unfair.

Yes, Mom had only asked Marina to help in her absence because Marina was the eldest and therefore the most responsible one. Why did the firstborn child always have to be punished for arriving first?

The buzz of voices in the dining room met her together with a few curious glances. One of those glances sent a jolt of awareness charging through her.

Kai. Her secret crush. So secret it had taken her years to realize it herself. Her heartbeat increased from his mere presence.

Distracted, she stumbled, and her arms flailed in her desperate attempt to catch herself. Food flew in different directions. One of the biscuits landed in someone's tea.

Oh no!

She held onto the plate and the basket.

Kai rushed to her and steadied her. He wore a white pirate shirt with long sleeves, and now he also wore a steak, a few rice grains, and green beans with long pods. One of those beans even ended up in the loop of his earring.

The steak skidded on the floor, and the rice and green beans plopped behind it. Except for the pod that stayed in the earring as a statement to her clumsiness.

"I'm... I'm so sorry." She gave out a sound close to a hiccup but not quite.

"Hello, Marina." He smelled of something musky and exciting, sending her pulse into overdrive. "It's okay. Are you all right?"

"Hi. Yes. No. Yes. Of course, I'm all right." Even if she realized she wore some rice, too, and probably had a green pod stuck in her hair.

She stepped back from the enticing heat of his arms. Because now he wasn't the flirtatious boy with twinkles in his brown eyes she'd become best friends with. He was a man with a broad chest and muscles chiseled by outdoor labor. But just as before, he was off-limits. Even more so now.

She tore her glance away from him and surveyed the damage. "We'll get that tea replaced right away," she said to the woman who now had a biscuit in her iced tea.

A few biscuits landed in a corner and one on a man's lap. But nobody was wearing the salad. Whew!

Overall, Kai had endured the biggest damage. She gasped at the large grease stain spreading on his shirt. "I... I'll pay for dry cleaning. Or... or I can try to remove it now."

"Yeah, why doesn't he take off that shirt?" A woman in a bright marmalade-hued dress with a wide white belt called out.

Heat crept up Marina's neck.

Thankfully, Kai didn't pay attention to the comment. "It's no problem." Then he stooped to gather the mess on the floor with napkins. "Don't worry. I'll clean this up."

"No, I'll take care of it." She placed the juicy steak back on the tray, which was far from a good idea, but she couldn't think straight in his presence.

Why was this happening again? She was supposed to get over her ridiculous crush many years ago. She had. She'd even fallen in love with someone else. Someone who'd felt safe. Who'd been his total opposite.

Well, the joke was on her, wasn't it?

"I'm so sorry about the steak, sir," she apologized to a bald sixty something man in gray slacks. "I'll get another one ready immediately." She didn't know how, but she'd have to figure it out.

She'd helped at her mother's restaurant before, but mostly by waiting on tables. She'd never made anyone wear food then.

"You're understaffed today, aren't you?" Kai's tone turned unusually serious.

She nodded. "Yes." And she needed to get back into the kitchen instead of staring into his eyes. Oh, and mop up the floor before anyone slipped.

"You're doing great. Looking great, too." He winked.

Yeah right. He'd paid compliments to everything in sight, one of the secrets of his popularity. Usually, she was well-put together, but today, her apron was stained and crooked, her hair probably a mess—or did she forget to take off her hairnet? She'd be grateful if she didn't have sweat stains under her armpits from all the heat in the kitchen.

"Any day now." The woman pointed at her tall glass of iced tea with a floating biscuit in it. Then she gestured to the biscuits near the wall. "And you're just inviting roaches with bread on the floor. Not to mention, I've been waiting *forever* for my order."

Now Marina would have those stains from all the heat she was getting *here*.

"Right. Sorry about that." Her stomach clenched while she picked up the biscuits. She didn't like apologizing, either.

Twin boys at a nearby table started fighting, so their screams mostly drowned her words.

She squared her shoulders as she marched back into the kitchen. She was a confident, successful woman now. Not a shy geek who'd been mercilessly teased until Kai found out and put a stop to it.

She could do this.

"Help! My daughter fell into the water!" The cry from the patio made her run there.

Just in time to see Kai dive into the ocean.

KAI MET THE COLD ONSLAUGHT of the water as he jumped into the ocean.

With broad strokes and held breath, he surfaced and dragged in the precious air.

Keeping himself on the surface, his heart beating frantically, he glanced around for the child. His stomach clenched when only calm waters met his gaze.

"Cody! Cody! Where are you? I can't see her! She's only six years old! She can't swim!" The woman screaming on the dock was hysterical, loud enough for him to hear despite the water filling his ears. "I only looked away for a second!"

Lord, please keep this child safe! Please help me find her.

Somewhere in the background of Kai's mind, it registered that Marina was calling 911 before he took a deep breath and dove under.

The friendliness of the sparkling surface could be deceitful. He pumped his legs and arms as he dove deeper into the darker, colder waters, holding his breath. Growing up near the ocean, he'd learned to swim fast and hold his breath for some time, but that couldn't be said for the poor child.

Lord, please!

The next moment, he spotted a sandy-blond head and salad-green shorts.

Yes! Thank You, Lord!

The girl's hands and legs flailed, and her eyes were huge. But she seemed to be conscious, which was a blessed relief. With wide strokes, Kai made it to the girl who first fought him, then tried to climb him, dragging them both down. A typical terrified response to a rescue attempt.

One couldn't talk in the water, so Kai wrapped one hand around the child while he worked with his other hand and kicked with all the energy he could muster to propel them to the surface. The pressure built inside, and his ears rang. It must be much worse for Cody.

A distant, unclear memory assailed him.

The salty spray of the ocean and the lilt of a woman's laughter. A gently scolding voice. He'd never remembered how he'd ended up at the beach alone as a child or what happened before that. But snippets of memories reached him in the most inopportune moments, like now. That female voice calling him "baby." Or a whiff of a scent. Jasmine, maybe?

Well, right now, it was all about saving this little girl. Not the memories Kai didn't know he even wanted.

He shoved the child to the surface, and to his shock and enormous gratitude, she coughed and sputtered. The sounds played like clichéd music to Kai's ears.

"She's breathing!" He shouted once he could get precious air into his own lungs. He gulped more and more oxygen. "Keep breathing, Cody. Keep breathing. It's going to be all right. It's going to be fine." At least, he hoped so.

"Cody! Oh, my sweet baby!" The woman who must be Cody's mother cried from the dock.

The wail of a distant ambulance reached him.

Thanking the Lord, Kai looked at the child. "I'm going to get you back to your mom right now. But you've got to help me, okay?" What he received in response was somewhat of a nod, and he sure hoped the girl understood him.

Indeed, Cody didn't attempt to drown them in her panic anymore. Kai propelled them forward with his right arm and both legs while he supported Cody with his left arm, his movements fueled not only by practice but also by a huge adrenaline surge.

The crowd on the dock cheered. Ignoring them, he swam with Cody. Kai's mother had said he'd taken to it like the proverbial fish to water, literally, since the first time she'd brought him back to the beach. After all, that was where she'd found him.

His heartbeat increased, more from seeing Marina there than from exertion, as he approached the dock. She did show up, though most likely she came because of the commotion in her mom's restaurant and her worry for the child, not because of Kai.

While he was desperate to save an innocent child from drowning, he'd partly jumped in to show off in front of her. He'd done such things as a teen to impress her. He'd impressed plenty of other girls, but Marina, with her nose in a book more times than not, hadn't seemed to care about his heroic deeds. Which had only made him try harder.

It was high time to grow up and forget this crush on his childhood friend. And he had, mostly. Until she showed up in their hometown again, this time for weeks.

Once the water was shallow enough, he stood on the sand and carried the crying Cody to her mother, who ran into the water, letting it soak her skirt as she reached for the little girl.

"Cody! Oh, my darling baby!" She howled as she cradled her daughter, her shoulders shaking. Kai had never seen the woman before, so most likely she and the girl were tourists.

"Sowwy, Mom." Cody's small face scrunched up. "I shouldn't have sneaked away. I just wanted to look at the fishies."

"Here. This will help dry her." Marina gave the woman towels, which she wrapped around her daughter. Then Marina offered her a bottled water.

His wet clothes seeming to weigh a ton, Kai sloshed onto the sand and then onto the steps to the dock, water pouring from his white pirate shirt and matching slacks. At least, he'd taken off his shoes before jumping in. The crowd met him with applause, but he didn't care for the attention.

And where were the paramedics? The girl—and probably her mother who still seemed to be in hysterics, not that Kai would blame her—needed to be checked.

As if to answer his question, the wail of an ambulance neared. He'd go guide them, but now that the adrenaline was gone, fatigue took its place. He couldn't just collapse onto the sand, though.

"Clear the way, please! Clear the way! The paramedics need room to get through." Marina's commanding voice urged the crowd back.

A frown marred her forehead as she disappeared into the crowd again, leaving him with an irritating and irrational sense of disappointment. The main thing was that the child seemed to be okay. Why should Kai care that Marina hadn't even given him a second glance?

"You saved my little girl!" The woman sobbed, rivers of mascara leaving furrows on her cheeks. "I can't thank you enough!"

"You don't have to thank me." Heat rose inside him, which was a good thing, considering how the wet clothes stole his body temperature fast, making him shiver.

The woman shook her head, sending her tangled almond-hued hair flying. "You're still a hero."

His cheeks flushed. "Seriously, I'm no hero."

But the crowd seemed to agree with the woman because everyone erupted in cheers again. Everyone except Marina.

She was making her way through the crowd, guiding the paramedics as they towed a gurney, her brows still drawn together. "This way, please."

Good thinking about the paramedics. Kai and Marina would make a good team, even if she didn't seem to think so.

Saylor handed Marina a bunch of towels before disappearing inside the restaurant.

The paramedics took over, one of them putting the girl on the gurney, then giving oxygen and taking vital signs while another spoke to the child's mother.

Kai suppressed a grimace at the bunch of cell phones the onlookers pointed at him. Did people seriously film that stuff? Those videos better not end up on social media. Well, he wouldn't hold his breath. Just like he'd stopped waiting a long time ago for Marina to pay attention to him and had settled for being her friend.

"I said you should've taken that shirt off!" The same unfamiliar woman who'd made a similar comment in Bay and Basin shouted. He didn't know her, so she must be a tourist. Still, he cringed at the comment but didn't say anything.

"Would you like this to dry yourself?" Marina handed him the towels.

"Thanks." He rubbed one against his hair, then draped the other over his shoulders.

"Great job, man!" One of the paramedics slapped Kai on the shoulder after closing the door behind the mother and her daughter.

"I just hope Cody and her mother are okay." He meant every word.

Many tourists came to their small town every summer for the sunshine and ocean. And while he was grateful for the business it brought to Port Sunshine and he loved the ocean itself, those welcoming, peaceful waters could turn deadly if one wasn't careful.

As the ambulance drove away, the sound of its motor fading, he sent up one more prayer for the girl and her mother.

"I can get you hot tea and some hot crab soup." Despite her caring words, Marina's gruff voice grated as her brows stayed furrowed.

Argh. Was she still worried about the child? That made sense, yet Kai sensed he himself was causing her irritation. But why? And he wanted to be the reason she smiled, not frowned.

"No, I'm good." Though hot soup could be helpful.

Despite the warm day, his wet clothes clung to him like a second skin and siphoned the warmth from his body, so more shivers wouldn't be far behind.

Not that he'd let her see him shivering.

She averted her gaze. Well, this was getting better and better. She didn't even want to look at him.

He plastered on a smile and tried to lighten up the mood. "If I drowned, would you save my life and give me CPR?"

"This isn't a laughing matter." Marina rolled her eyes, the way she'd reacted to what she called his antics when in their teens. "Can you ever be serious?"

I'm serious about you.

He kept those words to himself.

"I'd give you CPR!" Several women from the crowd volunteered in unison.

His cheeks flamed up, and Marina's face reddened. Her gaze traveled over his torso before snapping back to his eyes, and her cheeks now matched the color of the broiled lobster in her mom's restaurant. She looked adorable when she blushed.

His temperature increased despite the chilling wet clothes. He feigned offense. "Huh? You wouldn't save my life?"

She pulled her shoulders back. "I need to get back to work." She glared at him as if *he* were to blame for the unnecessary holdup. Seriously? Then she spun around and stormed inside the restaurant.

Chapter Two

A familiar voice behind Kai startled him and he turned to his brother. Concentrating on Marina, he hadn't noticed Austin join him.

Austin shook his head. "After all the years of knowing you, I still can't figure out if adventures find you or you find adventures."

"It's a bit of both." Now a shiver went through Kai's body, and he slipped his feet into his shoes, then gestured to Austin to accompany him to the car. He always kept a spare change of clothes and an extra pair of shoes in his vehicle because, as Austin had put it, adventure did find Kai rather often.

Austin followed him. "No kidding, huh?" Of all their siblings, Kai was closest to Austin and suspected he had an adventurous streak as well, though he didn't show it often.

"And here I thought that, as a doctor, you'd appreciate me making sure that the child was okay," Kai teased as they walked along the parking lot.

"I do appreciate it, though I'm an animal doctor." Austin spread his hands. "Anyway, Mom's arrived at Bay and Basin to help. More of our brothers should pitch in soon, as well. History repeats itself, doesn't it? Marina, as the eldest and the most responsible of the Helms, has to, well, take the *helm* of family responsibilities again?"

"Yup." Anger at the unfairness bubbled under Kai's skin. "And they're understaffed today to boot."

"Where am I going to be more useful, cooking in the kitchen or waiting tables?"

Austin was much better at treating animals than chatting up customers, but no need to mention *that*. Kai clicked on the fob to open his car. "Kitchen. Please help Mom with whatever she needs."

Mom and his siblings drove trucks, but Kai opted for a small chocolate-brown sedan. He'd always stood out in the family and in some ways even in their small town, so he'd never attempted to fit in.

He could either resent it or accept and own it. He chose the latter.

He changed into dry shoes and locked the car again. Then he pinned his brother with a stare as he carried his dry clothes back to Bay and Basin, intending to use their restroom. "Marina can't know I asked you all to help her. Understood? This conversation never happened."

Austin blinked at him. "What conversation?"

Kai smiled.

What would've happened if he hadn't been adopted into such a wonderful family as the Lawrences? He wondered that often. Okay, Mr. Lawrence wasn't wonderful at all, but the rest of them were a great bunch, though by no means perfect.

Minutes later, in blissfully dry clothes, Kai moved among the restaurant patrons with a tray. He'd done odd jobs here and there since he'd reached the legal age to work. He'd learned to adapt fast.

His family and the locals in town had never made him feel like an outsider, even knowing his history—or actually, his lack of it. His mother had reported finding the boy to the police, and the research had been done. It appeared he wasn't born in a local hospital.

So rather than others making him feel like an outsider, a feeling he'd harbored inside insisted he was different. Not worse, of course, just different. Of course, he didn't look like his brothers, but his eyes weren't just brown compared to their baby blues. His eyes had a different slant, as well. And while most people didn't realize it, they still could erect a slight subconscious barrier toward those who were different from themselves.

Even if it was all in his head, he'd learned early on to give an extra smile, along with an extra sweet remark or an extra helpful gesture. If people saw kindness in someone's eyes, then it mattered less that those eyes had a different cut from their own—right? He didn't think he should dial down on being courteous even after he'd felt welcomed.

Now, he paid compliments to adult customers, making smiles bloom on their faces, then distracted fighting twin boys with a pirate impression. He was genuinely interested in people, but smiling and showing he cared was also how he'd thrived. And he believed in complimenting people. If it was sincere, it wasn't flattery, right?

Everyone wanted to be liked. Everyone wanted to feel accepted. He knew that better than most.

However, there was a thin line leading to the territory where people—okay, women—might perceive he was making advances. So he kept his compliments lighthearted as he moved among the tables delivering food orders and taking new ones.

From time to time, he made jokes, careful to keep them inoffensive. People had different senses of humor. One thing he didn't like was how the news about the near-drowning incident spread fast and everyone was complimenting him on his heroic actions.

"I'm not a hero," he said for the thousandth time as he swallowed hard. "Anyone would've jumped into the water to save a child."

"But you were the only one who did." Austin stepped out of the kitchen to give a hand delivering a new order.

"You did great." Mom hugged Kai as he stopped by to pick up another Fisherman's Catch in the kitchen.

"You sure did," Darius said from the stove. He wore a frown as often as his Stetson—in other words, nearly all the time. So, he went to work in the kitchen instead of serving the customers. Though he now had to wear a hairnet instead of his Stetson.

Dallas was on his honeymoon with Skylar, or he'd have joined in, too.

Marina still didn't say much. As if copying Darius, she seemed to have donned a permanent frown along with her apron today. Kai's spirits fell a little. Her opinion shouldn't matter so much to him, but it did.

"Everyone is talking about you, Kai." Saylor paused from chopping up another salad, glanced at him, then at Marina. Then an understanding smirk curved her lips. "Didn't Kai do great today, sis?"

"Just fantastic!" Marina cut the cucumber with such force and speed she barely missed her finger. The cutting board shook, and the table did, too.

"Um, thank you. Anyone would've done it in my place." He picked up his spirits together with the plates ready for delivery and hurried toward the dining room. Before that knife could fly in his direction for some reason.

"Not me!" Saylor said after him. "I swim about as well as this frying pan."

Behind him, the knife thumped into the cutting board again. Maybe he should offer to chop the salad? Because at this point, he worried about Marina's fingers.

Thankfully, he heard Austin speak up. "Marina, how about I cut those vegetables, please?"

Awesome, Austin!

Kai did a mental fist pump to his brother as he brought the tray to a family of four, including two surly teenagers on their phones.

His phone pinged in his pocket with an incoming message, and he stepped aside to check it in case it was some emergency at the ranch.

The text was from Austin.

Would you like to trade places and cook beside Marina? Or is it getting too hot in the kitchen for you?

Kai chuckled. The jerk. But then, they were used to brotherly teasing. His finger slipped to his social media, and a private message from an unknown person popped up.

I believe I know your brother. You look as alike as two drops of water.

Must be some weird prank. Or phishing. He shrugged and slipped his phone back into his jeans pocket.

He almost physically felt when the restaurant's stressful atmosphere changed. It became... softer, maybe. More amicable.

"Mrs. Rafferty, don't you look beautiful today." He grinned at the new customer, who happened to be Skylar's grandmother. Skylar was his childhood friend and once Marina's best friend, as well as her only cousin. "But then, you look beautiful every day. You make the world a more beautiful place. I'll be your humble server today. What can I get you? Hot tea, perhaps?"

"Oh, you." The white-haired woman rolled her eyes behind thick glasses as she patted his arm. But her lips curved upward, so she was pleased. The seashell bracelets her artistic granddaughter had made were wrapped around her wrist and even adorned her hair.

He told the truth. The kindness shining from Mrs. Rafferty lit up her face and made the world a better—and yes, more beautiful—place.

"I'll have the seafood soup and hot mint tea." Mrs. Rafferty responded without looking at the menu. She was a regular.

"One has to admire a woman who knows her mind." He marched to the kitchen, not just to drop off the order but also to steal a glance at the woman who made *his* world more beautiful.

Even if she never realized it.

Marina was torturing—ahem, cooking—steak as he approached her. Another thing he'd never tell her, either. And people called him outspoken. A blush scorched her cheeks, but she looked determined, so those steaks would surrender eventually. He placed the order with his mother, but he couldn't look away from Marina.

Flustered, she peered over her shoulder as if she felt his intense focus. Weirdly, he was drawn to her even when she was rushed and irritated. She had an adorable habit of sticking out the tip of her tongue when she concentrated on something, or twirling the tip of her hair. Because her sun-kissed hair was gathered under a hairnet, she couldn't do the latter, but the tip of her pink tongue appeared between oh-so-kissable lips, sending a low hum through his body. As a teenager, he'd sometimes sneaked into the school library just to watch her study.

At that time, she'd thought he'd been having difficulty with physics and offered help. For several weeks, she'd tutored him on things he'd known already. He'd enjoyed it, letting the sweet sound of her voice and the scent of the mint gum she'd pop in her mouth "to help her think" wash over him.

But now, knowing how overworked she'd been with her study load and helping her siblings, he winced at a stab of guilt. Yet he still loved simply looking at her.

His heart shifted. Even more so now.

"Do I still have food on my face?" She grimaced.

"No. Why?"

"Oh. You were staring at me." She frowned as she spoke. She must be too preoccupied with Bay and Basin to guess his real reason for staring. "How is it going in the restaurant?"

That probably wasn't an idle question. She was worried about her mother's business. She was always the most responsible one in the family.

"People seem happy." He smiled, grateful he'd had a small part in that.

"Meaning Kai charmed everyone from the age of two to ninety." Austin brought in a tray and emptied dishes into the dishwasher.

"Not true." Kai bumped his brother. "I believe the age of our customers today capped out at eighty-nine. And I wouldn't ask a woman about her age to start with."

Marina sighed. "You're incorrigible."

Here we go again. Using big words he'd have to look up later. But he'd always found intelligence incredibly appealing.

She turned to his mother. "Thank you so much for coming through for me and asking your sons to help. You saved me today."

Kai nearly held his breath as his mom sent him a sidelong glance. She wouldn't betray him, would she?

"Um, thank you, Marina. I mean, you're very welcome. That's what friends are for." Mom wiped her hands on her apron.

Thanks for covering for me, Mom.

He said the words with his eyes, not his lips. Aloud, he said, "I love you, Mom. You're awesome." He'd hear from Mom about this later, and the words might be much worse than the mysterious "incorrigible." Mom didn't enjoy taking someone else's credit.

"Yeah. I'm awesome. But one of my sons better start to figure things out soon." Mom placed her hands on her hips.

Uh-oh. "I'm sure he'll figure it out, whoever that is. Later, gators! New orders await. We must feed all these hungry people." He rushed back into the dining room, though he'd rather stay and stare at Marina.

Several hours and an uncountable—because he didn't count them—number of orders later, Marina stopped him before he was about to leave the kitchen with a tray. "You should take a break. You've been working nonstop. Not to mention you took that stressful swim in the ocean."

His insides warmed and not just because the kitchen was indeed much hotter than the dining room. Did she care? He'd started losing hope, considering her brusque attitude today. "Uh, thanks. I'm good. Glad you're not upset with me anymore, though."

Austin nudged Saylor. What was so funny?

Marina's lips pursed as she returned to cutting onions. "I *wasn't* upset with you. Why would I be?"

"Um, you frowned and your voice was gruff. And you were looking to the side instead of at me, and—"

"I was worried about you, okay?" Her eyes glistened. Must be the onions.

"I'm telling you, it's getting hotter and hotter in the kitchen." Austin chuckled as he fried fish. Sometimes his brothers could be a little *too* helpful.

"Yup. I feel like I need to fan myself." Saylor smirked again.

"Sis, come on, we have an air conditioner for that." Marina blinked fast. Then she concentrated on cutting onions again, never one to stop working or abandon a task.

"Hold on. Hold on. You *worried* about me?" A wide grin stretched up his lips. "But you know I swim well."

"I do, but there are undercurrents. And... and... and I worried about the child, too, of course. And... and... what if there was a shark?"

Kai didn't often roll his eyes, but he did it this time. "We haven't seen a shark here since 1999, and even then, it was seen by a tourist who had too much whiskey." He studied her as his heart made a strange movement in his chest. "So you worried about me, huh? A lot."

Could her reaction mean something? Or did she just worry about him as a friend?

"Looks like something is burning here." Austin tsked.

"Yeah, your fish!" Mom pointed to the skillet.

"Well, almost." Austin flipped the fish fillets and added spices. The peppery scent spiced the air.

Then Mom shooed Kai out of the kitchen like in childhood when she'd make a batch of cookies and he'd be the first to try to steal them while still hot. "Didn't you say we had a lot of hungry people to feed? Someone's order is getting cold."

Many hours later, when it was time to close the restaurant, he stayed to mop the floors, clean tables, and put up the chairs on the tables, not in that order, of course.

Soon, it was just him and Marina. Even Saylor and Austin had left with a wink at Kai he'd pretended not to understand.

Marina closed the cash register and moved a chair that looked a little crooked on the table. Then she looked at him and twirled a strand of her hair. Free from the hairnet, it cascaded over her shoulders in soft waves. "I hope I didn't sound unappreciative earlier. I do value your help."

"And I'm happy I could be here for you." He stepped closer, wanting to say so many things.

But her beautiful features looked exhausted, and her feet must be killing her by now. "We should get going," she said, confirming his thoughts.

Fatigue settled in his bones, as well. "You're right." He chuckled. "But then, you're always right. Even teachers learned the lesson fast that it was best not to argue with you."

She shrugged, and then her shoulders slumped forward a bit. "I just happen to have a good memory and do good research. Plus, I had a demanding father who would leave me without dinner if I got a low grade."

Compassion stirred, as well as desire to comfort and protect her.

But the next moment, she pulled her shoulders back as she marched to the door. "But it's in the past. I'm successful and independent now."

After they locked the front door, he walked her to the car in the dim lantern light. The air was humid and cooler than before, and he wished he had a jacket to offer her.

He'd heard about her divorce two years ago, of course, but it was difficult to imagine that a beautiful woman like her would still be single, unless she chose to be. He hadn't heard anything about her dating life through the grapevine, but it could be because she'd guarded her personal life.

A burning question slipped from his tongue. "Are you seeing anyone?"

Her head snapped up. "No! Absolutely not. I've had enough of deceit and betrayal and hurt feelings. I'm not interested in romance whatsoever. Some men don't get it, so I have to spell it out for them."

His heart tumbled onto the asphalt, and he swallowed hard. "I'm so sorry that guy hurt you." He raised his arms to hug her, but then he didn't want her to think he was making a pass at her like other guys. His arms dropped by his side. They reached her car and stopped.

She clicked on the fob, and he opened the door for her. But she didn't get inside. "I guess I shouldn't ask you if you're seeing someone." She chuckled without mirth. "You were *always* seeing someone."

Did he imagine bitterness tinted her voice?

"I'm not seeing anyone now." Because the woman he truly wanted to be seeing was right in front of him.

"Oh. Really? That's unusual for you. Good night." She slipped into the car.

Disappointment ripped through him, but he followed her and then watched her run to the porch. She glanced back and waved to him, then disappeared inside her childhood home.

Hours later, sleep evaded him, so he daydreamed about Marina. Then he decided to check his social media. A strange message made him raise an eyebrow. It was from the same person as before, and again, the name didn't say anything to him.

My friends think you might be his brother, too.

He chuckled. The entire town probably knew his brothers. Minus tourists, of course. If this was some scam, it was a strange one. Then he checked the sender's profile.

Huh. Two states away. Now that was weird. The next message made him frown.

He'll be in contact with you soon.

Chapter Three

Two days later, Marina stretched in her bed in the early morning.

Her body hummed from tiredness even after sleep. She'd promised herself she'd keep working on her depositions while on vacation. But so far, she hadn't read a sentence. Every day, she'd been falling off her feet. Every day, her mind refused to cooperate after a long day.

Today was the day to do it, though. Today, Bay and Basin was closed.

She stretched, enjoying the luxury of extra time in bed for the first time in what seemed to be an eternity. Her mornings, even on weekends, had been rushed. She hadn't taken a vacation in forever. Some people called her a workaholic, but those people didn't know what it cost to make a career in a man's world. Or to have a father who'd expected a lot of her, then a husband who was the same.

Thinking of Travis brought her heart a painful thud, even all this time after the divorce. She'd never thought she'd be happy to revert to her maiden name, but she'd been as eager to erase his mark on her as she'd once been to leave behind her father's last name. Now, though, she was ready to take the helm of her own life.

Saylor was supposed to occupy the room she used to share with Gale as children, but Saylor had decided to go to the beach early. So Marina had the house to herself. Someone must've made coffee first, though, as the faint aroma drifted from the kitchen.

Then her bed shifted from a bump as a furry bundle landed on her stomach.

"Harrumph!" She half laughed, half groaned at the tiny puppy.

Her cousin Skylar's dog had puppies, so Marina nearly had to shove her cousin out on her honeymoon as she had worried about the pets. Golden retriever mixes, but with what neither Marina nor her friend's family had determined yet. Skylar had a list of guesses, though.

It was difficult to look at the puppy without a smile, and Marina pushed away thoughts about her ex and the reason she'd never look for another romance. Even with Kai.

Especially with Kai.

"Aren't you adorable? Yes, you are!" With a childish language she rarely used, she hugged Buttercup and stroked her soft fur.

The puppy barked in response and licked Marina's face, her little tail wagging with tons of enthusiasm. It was... it was pleasant when someone was happy to see her in the morning, even if the reason wasn't completely altruistic.

"Are you hungry, darling?" Marina loved on the puppy some more, tenderness filling her to the brim.

Neither Skylar nor Marina had even a plant since they'd concentrated on their work, much less a pet. And now look at Skylar. Honeymooning with a great guy, adopting a dog, getting a puppy, and even talking about her and her husband expanding their human family, as well.

Wistfulness stirred Marina, but she pushed it down fast. She'd chosen her path, and she was going to stay on it. From her childhood to her job to her personal life, every marriage she'd seen—and some she'd felt deeply—had failed. Well, hopefully, Skylar and Dallas's would be the exception.

Dallas with his quiet insistence had persuaded most of his brothers to take a puppy each. Skylar had kept a puppy for herself, unable to part with all of them, but while she'd taken her dog with her, she'd been worried the puppy wouldn't handle travel well. So Marina volunteered to take care of Buttercup while Skylar was on her honeymoon. Kai had offered, too, but wasn't sure how the puppy and his parrot would get along.

Kai. A heat wave rushed through Marina as the image of him emerging from the ocean the day before yesterday accosted her. His wet clothes clinging to him, exposing his muscular torso. Chiseled by many years of work outdoors at the ranch and frequent swims, he wasn't the teen boy she'd once known anymore.

Oh my.

She sat up in bed, throwing away the covers. She needed to crank up the air-conditioning here. Or like Saylor so eloquently put it, she needed to fan herself.

She'd been irritated yesterday because Kai made her worry—no, the correct word was *freak out*—for him. But she'd been irritated even more by how much he meant to her, by her growing attraction.

"We're just friends. We've known each other our entire lives." She told Buttercup, who was a great listener. "That's the way it's going to stay."

Buttercup barked something, which Marina took for full support. The gorgeous golden-yellow hue of her fur caught the sunlight. Then the puppy licked Marina's cheek, the little rough tongue causing a bubble of laughter again. "Oh, stop! Or not. I wish people had this unconditional love of yours."

Marina always had to earn love, especially from her father. From Travis, too, for that matter. But never again. Constant rejection had hurt too much.

Would Kai reject her, as well? He'd seemed to fall in love a lot in high school. But after some time, he'd lose interest. Well, often it didn't even take much time.

Look at you. You don't even know how to have fun. You're bland and boring. What man could stay attracted to you for long?

Travis's words hurt deeper than knife cuts.

Though Kai was different, if she allowed things to happen between them he'd get tired of her quickly, too.

"Don't get me wrong. I don't just like Kai for his physique." She paused, heat pooling in the pit of her stomach. "Though there's that. There's an aura of fun and... and merriment around him. He makes me smile. He makes me laugh. But then, I'm not special. He does it for everyone. He makes people around him happy." She recalled the way he was with horses and more recently with the puppies. "Animals, too. Even plants. Mrs. Lawrence says her garden grows much better since he started tending to it."

Such a difference from her home life growing up, when her father could make everyone gloomy simply by showing up. Pets hadn't been allowed, and no plants had survived in that atmosphere, despite Mom's feeble attempts.

Marina scowled but changed her expression when Buttercup stopped wagging her tail and tilted her head as if half curious and half frightened. Her family members all had to walk on eggshells around her father, and Marina most of all, as the eldest and therefore responsible for her siblings.

But she was used to operating with facts now, not auras and feelings. She also had lots of willpower, and her crush on Kai would dissipate.

"It should, right?"

The puppy wiggled out of her embrace. Even Buttercup didn't want to listen to Marina talk about her romantic life or rather the lack thereof. Booooooring.

Buttercup slid from the bed onto the floor together with the thin cover, then scampered to the kitchen, barking.

"You're hungry. Got it." Barefoot, Marina followed the pet, the smooth tile cool under her feet. She passed Saylor's room, now open and indeed empty.

In the kitchen, the coffee aroma drew her, and Marina eyed the coffee pot. But first things first. She filled one teal ceramic pet bowl with fresh water, which Buttercup successfully splattered all over the floor. "Did you get to drink any?" Marina filled the second bowl with puppy kibble, this bowl a soft hazelnut hue and stamped with brown paw prints. Then she wiped the tile with paper towels.

Buttercup munched a little, then wobbled to the front door. Oh. She knew to go outside to do her business, and Marina appreciated the lack of puddles to greet her first thing in the morning.

"Okay, okay. I know what you need. We'll go outside in a minute."

She glanced at her pajamas with puppy imprints. Mom's gift before she'd left on the cruise. Usually, Marina slept in a T-shirt and loose pants, but she'd promised Mom she'd wear her gift.

In court, Marina had dressed in strict black or navy-blue jackets and matching below-the-knee pencil skirts. Her colleagues would laugh at her if they saw her in these pajamas. But her colleagues weren't here.

"Darling, wait a minute! I need to change."

Based on the sound, Buttercup scratched on the front door, clearly impatient, then howled. Uh-oh. They might not have that minute. No time to change, and no need to make the little one wait.

"I guess I could make a quick dash in the yard," Marina muttered.

Probably nobody would see her at this early hour anyway. She slipped her feet into indigo-hued flats, opened the door, and let Buttercup out. Buttercup squealed, taking a higher note than most singers Marina had heard before, and tumbled down the porch, then to the nearest tree.

Marina *didn't* tumble down the porch, but her stomach did. Because she stumbled on Kai who carried a large box.

"Oh, hi!" He smiled sheepishly as if he didn't expect to see her, either. The scent of his exotic cologne drifted to her, mixing with the scent of grass. "Nice outfit."

"Hi. Um, thanks. Buttercup inspired my mom to buy it." She knew he meant his words and wasn't being sarcastic like other people would be in his place.

Still, her cheeks flushed. She wanted to look good for him, and almost every time she'd encountered him since her return, she looked ridiculous. Either with food or a fishnet—okay, hairnet—as hair decoration. And now her hair resembled a bird's nest, probably. And what a classic combination—flats and puppy-print pajamas. Not!

Buttercup was now exploring the yard and sniffing the next tree.

"We've got so many chew toys and biscuits for the puppies that we figured we'd share some with you. I was just going to leave it at your front door." He pointed at the door.

Just great. She suppressed a grimace. Her childhood friend who knew her better than anyone—except for realizing her crush on him—didn't even want to see her and was going to sneak out if she didn't happen to open the door.

Most likely, his kind mother had asked him to drop off the toys for Buttercup. That reminded her. "I'd love to thank your family for all they did to help me at the restaurant. Could I buy you all some pastries or something?"

"No need, but we'd love to have you for lunch." He grinned. That grin could melt an iceberg.

Buttercup abandoned her research and rushed to Kai, nearly getting entangled in her paws, too large for her little body.

"I'd love to. And I'll pick up pastries on the way." Marina's legal documents wouldn't approve, but how could she pass up the chance of time with his family?

And not only because he would be there, though she had to admit that was important. Hearty meals at the Lawrence ranch were always a noisy, fun affair, especially since the patriarch wasn't there any longer. Mrs. Lawrence had a heart as big as her home state—Texas, of course, to which she'd done homage with several of her boy's names, such as Dallas, Austin, and even Tex.

Marina's mother had tried to provide a good home for them all, she really had, but it wasn't easy with Dad's frosty attitude making the atmosphere just as frosty. Mom had started pouring her energy into Bay and Basin where the atmosphere was warm and welcoming. Meals at home were a quiet affair with strict rules when Marina and her siblings were afraid even to chew the wrong way.

She squared her shoulders. That was a long time ago.

Buttercup's tail wagged like a mini propeller as she raised herself on her hind paws, her front paws clutching to Kai's slacks. "Would it be okay if we take Buttercup with us? I don't want to leave her behind for long."

He scooped Buttercup up and raised her in the air, eliciting another puppy squeal. "Of course! How could we leave this beauty behind?"

How could we leave this beauty behind?

Her heart fluttered. Well, this was getting better and better. Now she was jealous of a dog. Buttercup's tail wagged so fast now it was nearly invisible.

He studied Marina, growing serious again. "I have something I'd love your advice on. Do you have time for a stroll on the beach?"

Like in the old days. He didn't say that, but he didn't need to.

"Sure," she said without thinking, which she rarely did. Okay, she did have to think fast on her feet, but most of her words these days were prepared and measured. "I've always been honored by your trust."

Nothing about Kai was prepared and measured, though. That spontaneity bordered on recklessness, and she'd often berated him for it in the past. But now, she realized it was one of many things that had attracted her to him.

"Great." He grinned again, causing that familiar flutter in her chest. He'd always been the bright spot in her childhood.

"Just let me change first, okay?" And do her hair, and put on makeup.

As a teen, before Kai had found out and put a stop to it, she'd been bullied for her geeky appearance, glasses, and the short bowl-cut hairdo her father had insisted on. She'd had acne, probably from all the pressure, but she'd never been allowed a smidgen of makeup to cover it.

These days she wore contact lenses. Her blonde hair was cut in a fashionable style, her skin was flawless due to years of treatments, and her makeup subtle but elaborate—that was, when she didn't tumble outside first thing out of bed. But she was still sensitive about her appearance.

Well, nobody liked to be ridiculed, right?

"Sure," he parroted her word back to her as if it were a ping-pong ball. "Buttercup and I will just hang out here. Right, Buttercup?"

The puppy barked as if in agreement. Marina suppressed another wave of envy. Buttercup behaved as if she was Kai's dog and not Marina's—or, well, Skylar's dog.

Buttercup squirmed in his hands, and he placed her on the ground.

Good dog. Marina nodded as she hurried inside. In her bedroom, she stepped out of her shoes and changed into a sleeveless latte-hued top and white slacks.

Then she hurried into the bathroom and gasped. Her stylishly cut hair indeed resembled a bird's nest—*if* the bird wasn't particularly skilled in nest building or didn't care what neighbor birds thought.

Good thing Kai had never considered her anything more than a friend. She snorted. Right. A small consolation. She brushed her hair fast. Then she brushed her teeth just as fast, the mint flavor refreshing. No need to subject him to her morning breath any more than she already had. Hopefully, she'd stood far enough away that he'd missed that.

Also, a good thing he didn't try to kiss her. Argh. That didn't feel like a *good* thing and was a small consolation, as well.

No time for elaborate makeup, but she dabbed on her cherry lip gloss and a few drops of her perfume. It wasn't overbearing and had a fresh scent to it with a hint of mint and sage.

This would have to do. It wasn't like she was going on a date. She wished!

Stop it.

What did he want to talk to her about? Curiosity unraveled as she slipped back into her flats. Not the best footwear for the beach, but they went with the outfit better now. Yes, she was honored by his trust, but she didn't harbor illusions. She wasn't the only one honored with his trust. Therefore, it must be something he'd rather not discuss with his family.

She shot out the door, her enthusiasm unnerving if she thought about it. So she *didn't* think about it. The air smelled of a mix of the grass nearby and the salty ocean farther away and, as she approached Kai, the spicy, exotic scent of his cologne.

He leaned down and petted the puppy, whose tail became a propeller again. With his muscular frame—though slightly less than that of his brothers—he looked like a giant near the tiny furry bundle of paws and ears.

He and Buttercup were like best buds. The picture was endearing enough to make her smile. But familiar wistfulness tugged at things inside her.

Growing up as a studious geek, she'd often felt on the outside of different groups, looking in but not exactly there. Then there'd been an age gap between her and the rest of her siblings at home. In school, she wasn't sociable enough to fit in with the popular groups even if her appearance had been better. Even with the Lawrence brothers, she'd felt out of place. Skylar had been more than a cousin and a close friend as well—that was until she'd started hanging out more and more with the guy who was now her husband.

Being an introvert didn't help. Marina had been called stuck-up on numerous occasions. Told she'd thought too much of herself.

In reality, she didn't know how to fit in. She'd chosen studying over socializing not only because her father had pushed her, though there was that, but also because books had never made her feel rejected.

Neither had Kai. And because of that, they had to stay just friends. Because even if she'd glimpsed interest in his eyes a few times, if they became more, he'd move on to someone else sooner or later. Her heart would never recover. If just looking at him made it thud, how would it feel to lose him forever? This way, she still had the best friend she'd always had. He was the best thing that had ever happened to her, and no way would she risk losing that.

Kai smiled up at her, sending her heart into somersaults with that lopsided grin. "Look, Buttercup, Marina is back." He moved Buttercup's paw as if to wave at her.

Marina couldn't help chuckling. No wonder he'd played the pirate in the school play in their teens, and now at the pirate ship reenactment for children. Something was innately mischievous about him. Intriguing even. At the same time, he'd been the only person with whom she'd felt like she'd fit in, welcomed and appreciated no matter their differences. But then, he'd done so for everyone.

He straightened out, his brown eyes appreciative. "You look stunning."

A pleasant feeling spread through her, but she waved it—and his words—off as she started walking toward the beach. Not too fast, though, so Buttercup could keep up. "Oh please. Don't think I don't know you say that to everyone."

He fell into step, giving her a whiff of his spicy cologne. It suited him, though she could never place which scent notes it had. Intriguing and mysterious like the man himself. Nobody knew his origin, and that included Kai himself. "No. I tell many people they are beautiful because they are. You're the only person I call stunning."

"Thank you." The pleasant feeling intensified, but she couldn't allow it to. So she latched onto the closest distraction available. "What did you want to talk to me about?"

His eyes dimmed, maybe at her question or her businesslike tone or both. Unlike his brothers, who all had baby blues, his were chocolate brown. Rich dark chocolate. Her favorite.

He kept quiet as if gathering his thoughts. Or wondering if he should tell her anything. Regret pushed against her sternum. What was she doing? He wasn't here for her to cross-examine him. And his serious expression, so unusual for him, meant it must be something important.

They moved forward slowly, stopping a few times as Buttercup didn't leave a stone unsniffed or a bug unexamined.

The sparkling silk of the ocean rippled in front of them. She'd always found the whisper of the waves soothing and had studied at the beach often while growing up. It was the most beautiful library in the world. Unlike many people, the ocean had been kind to her.

Just like Kai.

Finally, he said, "Someone contacted me via social media, saying he saw the video of me fishing Cody out of the sea. He thinks he might be my brother."

Her eyes widened. "Wow."

This was huge. He might find his parents and siblings, find out where he'd come from. He'd never complained, but it must've been difficult to be the only person around with a blank page for their background.

Okay. She drew a deep breath of salty air, her mind at work. She always believed in examining the evidence first. Things could often be presented in favor of the presenter. In fact, they usually were. She exploited that in her job, or she wouldn't be good at it. "Did he provide any proof?"

"Just that he looks like me." He chuckled and lifted his arms in mock surrender. "Yeah, I know what people might say. But he's willing to take a DNA test once he gets here."

That could be admissible evidence. She nodded, then stopped as Buttercup met a hermit crab and plopped on her behind, studying it. In turn, Marina studied Kai before she asked the possibly painful question. "Does he have any idea what happened to you?"

"Blake was adopted." Kai's Adam's apple bobbed. "His biological mother didn't want to have contact with him or his adoptive parents. There was no father's name on his birth certificate."

Her stomach dipped, but she wouldn't make it far in her profession if she gave up easily. The crab dug into the sand and burrowed in, and Buttercup ran to her, whining as if complaining the crab didn't want to make friends.

"That could've ended even worse. Those pincers are tiny but could still hurt." She lifted the puppy to comfort her. "Not everyone you meet will want to be your friend." Something Marina knew very well.

Buttercup stared at her, clearly perplexed, perhaps wanting to say, "But I'm so cute!"

And many people had their agenda. Marina's mind set in the work mode again. "Can your PI brother, Barrett, run a background check on this person? I'll be glad to do some research if you'd like me to, as well."

"That's kind of you." Kai's lips curved, but the smile slipped. "Blake's arriving tomorrow."

Huh. That was fast.

She lifted her chin, then placed the squirming puppy on the sand again. Buttercup wobbled toward the ocean, and Marina followed.

"Then it's a good thing I have the day off from the restaurant today." She still had to look over the menu for the week and ensure they had enough products for everything, but she was no stranger to working late into the night.

"That said, I'll be glad to pay you your regular hourly rate," he added.

"No need." It was best not to mention how high that rate was by now. Her social skills might leave a lot to be desired, but she was astute enough to know money and friendship didn't mix—besides, she was good at research. "Please send me a text or email with everything you know."

It could also be a fake social media account, but she didn't want to disappoint him without studying it first. Buttercup dipped her paw into the water, then crawled back. Then she ran toward Marina, barking, as the tide moved toward her.

"It's the ocean, darling." Marina lifted the puppy but didn't cradle her against her chest this time to avoid wet paw prints. When the puppy wriggled in her hands again, Marina chuckled. "You want to go back, don't you?" She placed Buttercup back onto the wet sand but watched the tide, ready to scoop her up again if a wave came in too high.

As a wave ebbed away, she glanced at Kai.

"You haven't told your family yet." She should've framed it as a question, but it came out as a statement.

"No. I... well, I want to be sure before I tell them anything." He stared at the horizon, his gaze pensive. "It's not that I don't appreciate them. I do. I love them with all my heart. But... it would be nice to know where I came from, you know? I just don't want to say anything before I'm sure. It could be some scam." He shrugged. "Or it could be for real."

Though he was more optimistic than she was, he might share the same suspicions. She was right. This was the reason he'd come to her—he couldn't talk to his family about this. The second reason might be that she didn't gossip.

She was used to him laughing and making jokes. To compensate for it, she bumped his forearm playfully. "It's going to be all right. It might be good news, after all."

"I hope so. I've dreamed of finding my biological family. And now... now it feels weird." He touched her arm. "I'm glad you're here. And not only because you're great with research."

A warm wave spread inside her. "Me, too," she whispered.

But then another, not-so-warm wave reached her shoes, and she uncharacteristically squealed and picked up Buttercup.

The puppy shook in her hands, sending generous droplets onto Marina's hair, face, and clothes. "Buttercup, no!"

"I believe it's too late for that." Kai laughed, took out a handkerchief, and dabbed at her face, causing her to look into his eyes.

Delicious tingles went over her skin at the contact.

So much for her elegant top staying intact. Her heart shifted as she stared into his chocolate eyes far longer than she should, her pulse picking up speed. So much for her heart staying intact, too.

Chapter Four

Kai brought a new carafe with lemonade and poured it into several glasses, then took his place again. Lunch was yummy and the company great, but his gaze kept returning to one particular person over the ranch dining table where the roast with potatoes and vegetables emanated a delicious aroma.

Marina.

She used to stoop and duck her head as a teen, as if trying to curl into herself and attract less attention. Now her back was straight and her chin raised. Sophisticated and classy, she wore a sleeveless cornflower-blue cowl-neck top that made her eyes stand out. Well, they always stood out. She paired that top with black slacks and a long necklace made from tiny green quartz that matched her dangling earrings. The earrings caught the sunshine spilling into the large dining room windows and danced every time she moved her head. With her honey-blonde hair swept up in a chic updo, a few wisps dangled free to frame her lovely face. Her makeup was subtle, and a faint cherry scent emanated from the cherry lip gloss that made her lips shiny.

His heart skipped a beat. Not that he should be looking at her lips in the first place.

She could've arrived for lunch with royalty in a palace, not with their cowboy family at a ranch. With the rest of them in T-shirts and worn-out jeans, she stood out like a diamond among pebbles.

He'd never admit it, but while they were growing up, her mind and perseverance had intimidated him a little. Now her looks did, as well. He suppressed a grimace. He should've taken his shot while he had a chance. It was too late now.

"You're not going to make a joke about my mishaps?" Austin bumped Kai's elbow, bringing him back from his musings.

Kai blinked and took a sip of his iced tea. "What mishaps?"

"Your head must be out to sea today." Austin winked, then looked pointedly at Marina.

Oh, please!

Kai wasn't one to blush, for several reasons, but heat crept up his neck. "I have a lot on my mind."

Which was true. Besides Marina's temporary return, he had a possible upcoming meeting with a brother he'd never known existed. Or someone pretending to be his brother for unknown reasons.

But Austin was right. Usually, Kai joked, winked, bumped elbows, and overall carried the conversation at family lunches and dinners. As chatty as his gorgeous parrot who, by the way, still hadn't unlearned those curse words a tourist at their uncle's store taught him.

Today, Kai was the equivalent of a turtle.

"It's okay." Mom sent Austin a stern glance as she helped herself to more potatoes, then turned to Marina. "How are the things at the restaurant going?"

Marina brightened. "Better than I hoped they'd be. Thank you so much for all your help. And your family, of course."

Mom's eyes narrowed at Kai, but she didn't tell on him. *Thanks, Mom!*

Hmm. A premonition tightened his gut. He already had a great family, gentle teasing included. Dare he risk connecting with a family that might not turn out so great?

"And my sister Gale is coming to help." Marina twirled a free lock of hair around her finger, the gesture Kai had always found adorable. But now it sent apprehension through him as it brought his attention to the tender oval of her face, then to the plump glossy lips again. "After, um, several insistent requests on my part. I'm not off the hook by any means, but it'll help. Plus, we were fully staffed yesterday. It's still chaotic, but I don't feel I'm going to run Bay and Basin into the ground while Mom isn't here."

He was glad for her. Truly, he was. But a part of him—okay, the whole of him—enjoyed helping her. Even if she didn't realize it. Or maybe precisely because she didn't realize it. Besides enjoying her company, he savored a sense of justice in that. She'd helped others a lot, and it was only fair he'd give back.

Then, of course, this pesky attraction simmered under his skin now like a beef stew would simmer in Mom's kitchen. Tired of the teasing aroma as a child, he'd put a lid on the stew. It had only made it bubble over and, well, redecorate the stove top. If he tried to put a lid on his growing feelings for Marina, would it make them bubble over one day, too?

His feelings for her were more mixed up together than those stew ingredients. And unlike Marina, he'd never been great at analyzing things. He tore his gaze away from her before he could get another elbow nudge from Austin.

Not that Kai complained. Most of his siblings had silent, sometimes brooding personalities. Austin had the personality of Skylar's golden retriever, goofy, cheerful, and energetic. Kai had felt the closest to Austin while they'd been growing up.

He smiled. "Mom, remember you used to say Austin and I were close 'like two peas in a pod'?" Two very different-looking peas. "At first, I heard it as two peas in a pot. Like in soup. I couldn't get it because peas in a soup aren't very close."

That brought a smile to Marina's face. Good. Kai tore his gaze away from her. Uh-oh. The bread basket was near empty. "I'll bring more bread." He headed to the kitchen, refilled the basket with heavenly-smelling biscuits, and brought it back.

"Thank you. I'll have one." Marina reached for a biscuit the moment he placed it on the table, and her fingers brushed against his.

A simple touch shot straight to his heart. Oh boy. He muttered, "My pleasure." Literally. What was he thinking? He nearly groaned. Would this sweet torture ever end? Did he even want it to?

Her eyes widened, and her breathing quickened as she plopped the biscuit on her plate. Great! The touch affected her, as well. He took his seat again.

Despite all his experience with women, he could never read Marina, could never figure her out even after knowing her all this time. Maybe that was part of the attraction. He'd been much more curious about the treasure trunk in her mother's attic after trying to open it and finding out it was locked. Why did it have to be locked? He'd even attempted to pick that rusty lock with Mom's pins, though unsuccessfully. And then her mom had decided to store the trunk in Skylar's grandmother's place. Weird, wasn't it?

There was some mystery about Marina, as well. She'd been generous with her time, but she'd guarded her soul, keeping it all inside. And the more he knew about her the more he wanted to know. He'd been honored to be her friend, to be closer to her than she'd let anyone else. His heart stuttered. The issue was, he wanted to be more.

Okay. Earth to Kai. Her glass was near empty, so he reached for the lemonade carafe. "Would you like some more?"

"I'd love it." She smiled again.

Growing up, she'd smiled rarely, especially after she'd started to wear braces. He'd made an extra effort to make her smile and especially laugh. Cliché or not, her smile had brightened his day. Now it set his heart ablaze.

"Happy to do it." He got up and refilled her glass, earning a whiff of her perfume as it mixed with the cherry scent and her breath touched his face. Her perfume was as complex as the woman herself, though he recognized the chords of sage and maybe mint, but the rest was a mystery. The only thing clear was that the scent—and the woman herself, of course—wreaked havoc on his senses.

After lunch, he and Marina carried the dishes into the kitchen and loaded the dishwasher. Usually, his brothers would help, but today, they made themselves scarce. Even Austin. Kai could guess the reason. They'd wanted to give him a chance to be alone with Marina.

He took a deep breath of air tinted with that sophisticated perfume. "Would you like to hang around a bit longer?" Uh-oh. Was he too obvious? He didn't want to spook her. The day he'd helped her in the restaurant she'd mentioned she wasn't looking for romance ever again. Thankfully, he had a legitimate reason for wanting her to stick around. He lowered his voice. "I'd like to go over what we learned about my biological brother."

"*Alleged* biological brother." She straightened after putting a plate in the dishwasher.

"Right." He placed the carafe with the remaining lemonade in the fridge, cold air hitting his face for a moment, then brought out his secret weapon. "One of the horses foaled the day before yesterday. I need to check on them. Would you like to see the little one while we talk?"

She paused, then nodded. "I'd love to."

"You hesitated."

"I did not!"

"You did, too!" He laughed, reminded of their childhood banter. "I miss the days when we argued. Okay, that didn't sound right."

"I know what you mean." Her lips curved up. She tore off a paper towel and wiped down the counter. "Arguing with you was one of the best parts of my childhood. And yes, I know that doesn't sound right, either. I miss it, too. I–I missed you."

As a profound longing surged through him, he stepped toward her. Close enough to see the tiny navy dots in those cerulean eyes of hers. Close enough to breathe in her enticing scent. Close enough to reach to her and brush the strand of her stunning hair—liquid gold!—behind her ear, causing her a sharp intake of breath, causing himself an electric jolt of the heart.

He couldn't have been wrong about attraction in those eyes, could he? Or was it his wishful thinking? Frankly, he wasn't thinking. His gaze slipped to her plump shiny lips, and his pulse skyrocketed.

"Marina, I—" His voice came out husky.

But before he could say anything else, she pivoted around him. "Let's go see the little one."

"Yes. Right. Sure. Yes." He followed her from the kitchen into the hall and then outside, still in a mental fog from the near kiss.

"I got it on the first yes."

"Right. I mean... I don't know what I mean." He raked his fingers through his hair as they strode to the stable.

She seemed to have a much better presence of mind than he had. Or was he wrong about the attraction he'd glimpsed in her eyes? Or like she'd said, she wasn't ready for romance after the heartbreak with her ex. Or maybe she didn't want to ruin their friendship. His bruised ego wanted to choose the latter, but it was probably all of the above.

To get some oxygen to his fuddled brain, he breathed in, savoring the scent of freshly cut grass. Sunshine and birdsong in the oaks greeted him. Though disappointment cut deep, if he stopped to analyze, which he rarely did, it was for the better. She'd be leaving soon anyway. That sent another stab of disappointment, but he'd always wanted her to spread her wings, not clip them.

The stable smelled of straw and hay. The foal was having her kind of lunch—milk from her mother—when Kai and Marina approached.

Marina squealed. "She's soooo adorable!" Then she cleared her throat. "Please don't tell Buttercup that. I want her to think she's the most adorable, the most beautiful in the world."

"I won't. But I believe *you* are the most adorable, the most beautiful in the world," he whispered, meaning every word.

She rolled her eyes. "Would you please stop? I know giving compliments is second nature to you. But I'm not your next conquest. It's just me, your best friend."

He hadn't minded his reputation and was rather proud of it. Until now. He straightened his spine, standing tall as if she could see him standing firm on his words. "I do mean it."

But she narrowed her eyes, and he backed off.

The foal finished her meal but stayed close to her mother. Then she made a few wobbly steps forward on long squiggly legs. Austin had declared her healthy, and Kai was grateful.

"She has a white star on her forehead like her mother," Marina whispered, awe in her voice. "She's her Mini-Me."

"True." He quirked an eyebrow. "By the way, I never heard you squeal before, and now it was twice in a row."

She raised her chin. "I did *not* squeal."

He knew where this was going. "You did, too!"

"I did not! It was a much more dignified sound. Okay, maybe I did squeal a little, but who wouldn't looking at this baby?"

He'd liked her since they'd been teens—braces, glasses, and all—because none of that had ever mattered compared with her curious mind, sparkling light-blue eyes, and strength of character. She'd been a star to him long before her legal career had started shining, long before she'd changed her appearance.

Though of course, he was glad to see her blossom. Her newfound beauty wasn't just about her gorgeous hair or fancy clothes or braces-free teeth or even flawless skin, though they played a role. Makeovers in the movies where a girl took off her glasses and changed her hair and was immediately considered beautiful always puzzled him. With Marina, it was about the inner confidence with which she carried herself now.

He suspected her father had wanted to create his own Mini-Me in her and also someone who'd fulfill his dreams. He'd told everyone who'd listen that he would've had a legal career if he hadn't settled with a wife and children.

It all wasn't right, and it wasn't fair to Marina. But she'd been guilted into it first simply by being born and then by showing signs of intelligence higher than her peers.

"Would you like to go horseback riding?" he asked her as he checked on the rest of the horses, then got them fresh water.

"I haven't done that in forever. I'll need a very slow horse. Would you be okay with that?" She walked to the wall with the tack.

Okay with that? His eyebrows shot up. He could just breathe near her and be the happiest human alive. But he refrained from expressing a compliment. He'd given her compliments as a teen, as well, and she hadn't brushed them off as much as she did now. Maybe because back then he'd complimented her mind and her accomplishments instead of her looks.

"I'll get you a slow horse. That's totally fine." He saddled and bridled two horses who had a calm demeanor. Then he led the horses outside and debated bringing the mounting block for Marina. That would be a sensible thing to do. Nah. It was much more fun to lift her, so he did. Feeling her in his arms made his blood rush faster.

Her lips parted, but then she seemed to recover enough to get in the saddle. "Um, thank you."

"My pleasure," he muttered as he mounted his horse. His entire being woke up to life from having her close, and his heart thudded. It shouldn't be like that. They were just friends, remember?

Misty Morning neighed as if hearing his thoughts and mocking them.

"Okay, let's see what we know about Blake Park at this point." Just like her to go straight to business.

Still, Kai settled in, giving a go motion with his posture, and Misty Morning plodded forward.

Marina did the same, her face taking on that concentrated look of hers. "It's difficult to say for sure, but he looks like a real person and not a fake account. I have some IT friends who can track it down better than I could. Is it okay for me to ask one of them?"

That was another thing he liked about Marina. She'd never felt superior in her knowledge. If she didn't know something, she wouldn't hesitate to ask for help. "Sure. Would you like to go to the beach?"

She rose in her stirrups, staring at the horizon. "No, let's go into the fields. The flowers are blooming. It must be gorgeous." In a surprise move, she removed the pins from her hair and slipped them into her pocket, then shook out that gorgeous hair of sparkling gold—at least to him. It fascinated him.

"It is," he said while looking at her but again refraining from any more compliments.

He guided Misty Morning toward the fields, and they rode side by side. The emerald-green fields with splotches of magenta, violet, and gold provided a colorful contrast to the turquoise sky. And on that majestic backdrop was Marina with sunshine hair flowing over her shoulders. He took a mental snapshot to remember it forever.

While he preferred to gallop, he didn't mind going slowly because it allowed him to look at her.

Instead of lighthearted chitchat, she went back to the matter at hand, like he knew she would. "Blake is a doctor. An orthopedic surgeon."

He searched his word database, which was much smaller than hers. "That's someone who deals with bones?" *Here we go again.* He had to ask her to clarify things, just like in high school. She seemed to carry an encyclopedia in her brain, while his was more like the comic pages.

"Correct." She leaned and patted her horse.

They reached the most beautiful part of the ranch during the most beautiful part of the year. Well, if Marina stayed here and became part of the family, *she* would be the most beautiful part of the ranch.

Wow! What was he thinking?

He must've shifted back because Misty Morning stopped, then took the opportunity to graze. He was about to tap his heels when Marina said, "Let's stop here. It's perfect." She breathed deeply, taking it in.

Her horse stopped, as well, preferring to graze than to run in the field.

He opened his mouth to say what or rather *who* was perfect, then closed it. No compliments, right? "Sounds good to me."

Misty Morning neighed as if to confirm she agreed. He dismounted, then stepped to Marina.

"Hmm, the ground seems so far from here." She raised herself in the saddle.

"I'll make sure you won't need an *orthopedic* surgeon any time soon." Ha! He even used that big word.

"I'd appreciate it. I don't want *that* to be the reason I meet your alleged brother." She swung her long leg to the side of the horse.

He held her for a few seconds more than he should have, reluctant to let her go. He'd always been reluctant to let her go. His breath caught in his throat as he stared into her baby blues, the endless sky and endless possibilities reflecting in them. Her breathing seemed to go shallow, as well. Was it possible his attraction wasn't one-sided?

Lord, what am I supposed to do here?

Then Misty Morning neighed, breaking the moment, and he placed Marina on the grass. That must be the answer. He was supposed to set Marina aside and forget his attraction. The latter was easier said than done.

"Th–thank you." She stumbled back as if puzzled, surprised, but then her expression became serious and controlled again.

Yup. He'd been the one who carried his emotions on the surface. She never had. Would she ever?

He led both horses to a lonely tree and tied them to the thin trunk. Even calm horses could get spooked, and while he could run, he couldn't run fast enough to keep up with them. He picked up a blanket and spread it over the grass. She sat down gracefully, but then she did everything gracefully.

He was about to say they should make it a picnic next time, but would there be a *next* time? She was going to be busy at the restaurant for the rest of her stay. Taking up her rare day off was already selfish.

He sat near her, taking in the wildflower scent. The breeze moving her sunlit hair gave him a nearly irresistible urge to run his fingers through it. How he ached to touch the gentle outline of her face, to kiss the tiny birthmark alongside her mouth, then move to her lips and drink them in...

His heartbeat shot up just from the thought.

He leaned on his elbows, forcing himself to stay in place. He remembered every tiny birthmark on her face, every freckle, every one of her expressions and what they meant in the moments she'd forgotten to keep them controlled. They all were his map to something fascinating and forbidden.

Being near her and making himself stay away was pure torture, and he looked away, at the vast open space that had become his home. He might not know where he'd come from, but he knew where he wanted to stay. With whom, too.

"Remember how we ran through these fields as children, chasing each other?" Her voice turned nostalgic.

"Of course." His brothers and her siblings and cousin had been part of their big company. "And how we played hide and seek in the forest."

Now she seemed to play hide and seek with his heart without realizing it. He plucked a few flowers, making a humble bouquet.

"Thank you. I forgot how amazing it could be here." A ladybug landed on her hand, and she lifted it. Then she chuckled. "Buttercup would've loved it here."

"You miss your puppy already."

She shrugged. "I shouldn't, because how can you miss someone who was never yours to start with?"

His heart shifted. He knew the feeling.

"Okay, let's keep it on topic." She raised her knees to her chin and hugged her legs. "Blake might be your elder brother. Two years older. He married right out of high school and was divorced two years ago. One child, a fifteen-year-old girl. He doesn't post much on social media, and his accounts are private to start with. But his daughter is a typical teenager and posts multiple times a day. And her account was public." Marina pursed her lips, clearly disapproving of the latter.

"What were the posts about?" He rubbed his temples. How about that? He might have a niece. He still couldn't wrap his mind around it all. He checked on the horses, but they placidly turned grass into digestive matter.

"Mostly photos with her friends. Updates about her favorite boy band. Selfies in new outfits. Selfies at the mall. Selfies in new outfits at the mall. But some of them were at a café with her father, then at a concert." Marina picked several flowers and started weaving a wreath.

Fascinated, he watched the fast movements of her elegant fingers surrounded by wildflowers. But then, she could sneeze, and he'd find it fascinating. "Did he go to see the boy band?"

"He sure did." Her lips curled up. "Wore the band T-shirt and everything. He seems like a good dad, involved in his daughter's life." Her wistfulness threaded around the wreath she wove as she added more flowers. Her father was nothing like that.

Kai's rib cage tightened. He didn't know his biological father. To think about it, he never knew his adoptive father well, either. While the Lawrences had officially adopted him, Mr. Lawrence hadn't been involved in his life. Kai should be grateful, considering how the man had been involved in his other sons' lives.

Long-suppressed anger and guilt surged to the surface, but he pushed it down. The man had taken him in. But he'd also hurt Kai's mother and brothers—and yes, Kai considered them his mother and brothers even if they didn't share the same DNA.

"I believe in the found family because mine was great." He stumbled. "Except one person. Also because it's the only family I've got."

"Until now." She raised a finger, the flower wreath dangling. "Allegedly."

He should be excited about this new prospect. Hadn't he dreamed of this? Instead, his rib cage tightened even further. The pot roast soured in his stomach. Did he want to go through with this? Some unknown things were fascinating. But other unknowns were scary. Was he ready to risk having his world turned upside down?

She finished one wildflower wreath and crowned him with it, sending a different wave through him. Her fingers tangled through his hair. Once again, their gazes met and held, and once again, breathing became difficult.

Then she scooted away and started on a new wreath, and disappointment jolted through him. "Now, about Blake's adoptive family. His father was a doctor before retiring, which might explain his professional choice. His mother was a stay-at-home mom and now dedicates most of her time to different charities. The family is prominent in the city's social life. Blake has one sister who is an actress, not a famous one."

"My brother said Blake and his relatives checked out so far. Nothing suspicious in their past. Well, except for a few parking tickets, but I wouldn't call that suspicious." Kai kept silent for a few moments. "Are we going too far with all this?"

"If I wasn't in the profession I am in, I'd probably say we were. But having seen and heard so much, I say better safe than sorry."

Right now, his heart wasn't safe, though part of it was sorry. *Sorry things couldn't be different.*

Her eyes darkened. "Would you like me to go with you when you meet him?" Then she gulped. "I mean, for moral support. I'm also a good judge of character. Or... would it be too awkward?"

"I appreciate your offer." And he did. It wouldn't be dangerous for her, would it? He couldn't see why, but still, best to be prepared. He'd go in armed, and he wouldn't be surprised if Blake was armed, as well. His uncle had taught them all how to shoot, and Kai was a quick draw. Most likely, Blake had background checked Kai and his adoptive family before contacting him. "If you don't mind, that would be great. I'll let Blake know to make sure it's okay with him."

Once done with her wreath, she got up and walked to his horse, then placed it on the horse's head. The Appaloosa moved her head up and down, then stared at Marina as if not understanding what her meal was doing on her head.

"Now my horse and I wear matching wreaths." He chuckled.

"Yeah. Oops." She reached as if to remove it.

"No, it's okay. It looks beautiful." Though he'd prefer it on Marina's head. "And you know I'm up for different headwear, be it a bandanna or a Stetson. Or flowers, in this case."

Then he had a mischievous thought. She'd always been competitive, and he hoped to play up on it. "Let's see if you learned to run faster than you used to. I'm sure it won't take me long to catch you."

She sighed demonstratively. "Seriously? We're not seven any longer."

"Hmm. Giving up already?"

She glared at him, then got up.

He did a mental fist pump. "One, two, three—"

"Go!" She took off.

He gave her a few seconds lead before chasing her, but soon regretted his overconfidence. She ran faster now than in childhood, so he had to pump his legs in earnest.

They were both laughing by the time he caught up. He swept her off the ground and whirled around. "Got you!"

"You make my head spin!"

Then his blood surged faster for a different reason than exertion. His heartbeat went into overdrive, and the scent of her mysterious perfume—mint and sage?—made his head spin. They stopped laughing. He placed her down awkwardly, the joke on him.

Because he hadn't "got her" and never would. Friendship was all he could count on with Marina, and that was valuable in itself. It should be enough, right?

"We'd better get home before it starts to rain." She gestured to the clouds.

He didn't want this day to end, but reasonable as always, she had a point. And he'd been so concentrated on her that he hadn't even noticed heavy clouds gathering. "Right. We should."

Were thunderstorms going to appear in his life, as well? Premonition tightened his rib cage again.

Chapter Five

The next night, Marina was so tired she felt her arms were about to fall off. Her legs, too, for that matter.

"How did Mom run the restaurant all these years by herself?" She asked Buttercup since Saylor was already asleep in another room.

Hearing her name, the puppy lifted her head, then returned to destroying yet another chew toy Kai had brought. Better than furniture, though the nightstand had suffered a little. Marina grimaced as she glanced at its legs. "You and I will have lots of explaining to do when Mom comes home."

Buttercup didn't even move an ear, which meant Marina was on her own.

"It's a good thing Kai brought so many chew toys." Her insides warmed from recent memories.

How he'd held her when he'd helped her dismount. How he'd scooped her up and whirled her around when they'd been running through those wildflowers, stealing her breath. She flushed.

No, she was reading too much into it. He was raised right, so of course he'd help her dismount from a horse. And then they'd just replayed their childhood experiences. They'd both been nostalgic. That was all.

"Anyway, I'm not going to leave my job in the city. I worked too hard for it. And one failed marriage is more than enough, right?"

The puppy abandoned the toy and tilted her head. Then she barked as if to say she knew nothing about marriage. Or maybe to say she was hungry or thirsty because then she ran to Marina's bed, chewed on the cover a little, and wobbled into the kitchen, clearly expecting Marina to follow her.

Buttercup was right because Marina leaped out of bed and walked into the kitchen, the tile cool against her bare feet. She filled the food bowl with puppy kibble and then put fresh water into the water bowl. Buttercup lapped up water—or rather splashed it all around the bowl again. Way more water ended up on the tile than inside the puppy.

Marina didn't like messes, but she just chuckled and wiped the tile with a paper towel. "You gotta be more careful."

Then Buttercup froze as if on high alert, her ears standing at attention.

"What's happening?" Marina tensed and lowered her voice. "Did you sense somebody?"

Buttercup dashed back into the bedroom, barking. Somehow, Saylor still slept through it all. It was dark outside, and Marina stared at the thick curtain hiding the window.

Okay, the barking didn't sound like a warning but more like joyful barking. Then something clattering against a window made her pause.

"Oh, you gotta be kidding me." She rushed to the window, a familiar excitement bubbling under her skin.

She pushed the heavy curtain aside and opened the window before the next pebble had a chance to hit it. "You can't be serious. You know you can go through the door now."

Kai grinned at her. "But isn't this more fun?"

She was a good girl. She hadn't sneaked out of the house—except for a few times with Kai. And she didn't really leave the house per se, because they'd stayed on the roof. Okay, maybe not technically *in* the house but on it, but not outside its perimeter, either...

"Would you like to go on the roof?" That lopsided grin of his did strange things to her heart. "We can stargaze from there."

"Seriously?" She rolled her eyes. "With as many times as I roll my eyes at you, they'll soon be permanently stuck in the back of my head."

"That wouldn't be a good look on you. And I'd miss your eyes too much. Even more than the stars."

"You never take anything seriously." Despite her words, a pleasant wave swept over her.

"Part of my charm." He spread his arms.

Riiight. He probably used that line about missing their eyes more than stars on many women. And she'd already had her heart broken by a man who'd turned out to be a player. Her fingers wrapped around the windowsill with too much force, the outline biting into her flesh. "We can watch the stars from the porch." And she'd better get out there before all this talk woke her sister.

"But the sky is closer from the roof." His smile turned deceptively innocent.

Well, she wasn't going to succumb to his charm like others. At least, he'd never hidden the fact he wasn't going to settle and enjoyed dating. Her ex had pretended to settle—with her. Many years into marriage, she'd discovered he'd dated other women while married to her. More than just dated them. She swallowed the hard lump in her throat.

But Kai was her best friend. It had been years since she'd spent much time in her hometown. Most likely, after this mini-vacation, she wouldn't see him again for years.

"What am I going to do with you?" She sighed for more reasons than one as she snatched up her purse. Not that she'd need it, but she believed in being prepared for everything. Somehow, having it with her made her feel more secure.

She couldn't be sure, but she thought Kai muttered, "Don't make me answer that question."

Buttercup wobbled after her, but Marina wiggled her finger at the puppy. "Oh no, you don't. There's too much chance you'll fall."

She grabbed a couple of cans of juice from the fridge and put them in her purse along with a flashlight, then went outside. Just like when they'd been teens, Kai helped her climb on the relatively safe part of the roof. The exotic note in his cologne struck a chord with her heart, and his touch made heat pool in the pit of her stomach. She jerked her hand out of his, missing it immediately.

His eyes dimmed—or did she imagine it? It was difficult to see without sunlight.

"I've brought a blanket." He pointed to the blanket he'd already spread for them.

For some time, they sat staring at the stars. She offered him a can of apple juice from her purse, then sipped from hers, enjoying the sweet taste.

His proximity did a number on her, so she started naming constellations to distract herself. But then she did need to talk to someone about the things she'd carried inside for so long. And Kai had always been her trustworthy listener, especially after one of her sisters blurted out Marina's deepest secret at school. She placed the empty can into her purse to throw away later.

"Aren't you going to ask me why my marriage failed?" she whispered without looking at him.

Instead, she stared at the black velvet of the sky where stars sparkled like diamonds on display in an upscale jewelry store. Her ex had taken her to such stores and insisted she choose whatever she liked. As she'd later discovered from his credit card charges, she wasn't the only one he'd done it for. The diamonds were genuine. His feelings apparently weren't. Maybe she shouldn't have brought up her marriage, shouldn't have ruined the beautiful night. But she'd kept it inside for too long, and it hurt more instead of less with time.

"I figured if you wanted to, you'd tell me." Kai's voice grew quiet.

"I discovered his infidelities. Lots of them." As anger surged to the surface, her fingers fisted.

It had rocked more than her faith in her husband; it had shattered the Christian faith she'd been raised with. The first she'd never be able to get back. But could she ever return to the other? Find God again? And trust Him completely as she'd once trusted Him and her husband? Argh! She'd never mention *that* to Kai. "How could I be so blind for years? Where was my famed mind then?"

"Trusting the man you love doesn't make you look bad. Betraying your trust makes *him* look bad. He wasn't worth you."

Her stomach clenched. "Travis said I was too boring for him. Bland. He had to find someone more exciting."

Kai turned to her, the movement sudden. "Are you kidding me? You're never boring. You're so bright in so many senses. You're the shining star. What was that bright star you told me about? You're the North Star. What was it called?"

"Polaris." She hid a smile but found it easier to breathe.

He'd always known how to make her feel better about herself and the world. He had the amazing ability to calm her and make her feel more excited, all in the span of minutes. She'd always sensed he cared. Not because of the things she could do for him, like with nearly everyone else in her life. But because she existed.

"I remember you told me how to find it in the sky." He craned around. "Um, I could use help here."

"Sure. First, you find Ursa Major. It's Latin for 'great bear.' We call it the Big Dipper." She pointed to the sky. "See those five stars?"

"Got it! And then we find the little bear and draw the line between them, right?"

"Ursa Minor, or the 'smaller bear,' but basically correct. And now see that bright star? That's Polaris."

"Yes! I see it! Thanks." He puffed up, appearing as pleased with himself as when she'd tutored him in physics and he'd figured things out.

"Polaris was often a guiding star," she added as she mentally located more constellations in her mind. The sky wasn't as clear as in her childhood due to light pollution and satellites, but still, it was fascinating. "People used to travel following it in the sky ages ago."

"Right." He nodded. "You're like my guiding star, too. You set my course, the helm and rudder I steer by. When I'm not sure what to do, I ask myself, 'What would Marina do?'"

"And then you do what I would do?" She couldn't fight a smile. It was impossible not to smile in his presence. When they'd been teens, sometimes he'd made her laugh so much her cheeks would hurt.

He cleared his throat. "Well, not always. But often enough."

Warmth rose inside her, and she didn't look at the sky any longer. In the starlight, his eyes looked darker, pupils dilated, and a delightful shiver of attraction rushed through her. "I—I'm still flattered." This time, she cleared her throat, trying to shake off that untimely attraction. "By the way, several planets are visible in the sky tonight. Venus, for example."

"Venus is about love, right?"

"It's about love, indeed." But she wasn't thinking about the planet as she leaned closer to him.

Nooooo. She had to force herself to look away.

This side of the roof connected with a steeper part to create a sort of alcove, something she'd told herself was somewhat safe. Yet climbing on the roof with him had been one of the most reckless things she'd ever done. Of course, if she'd fallen for him, *that* would become the most reckless thing she'd ever do. Her heart fluttered the same way her hair did in the breeze.

"Cold?" He took off his jacket and draped it on her shoulders.

"Thank you. I'm good now." She snuggled into the warmth and the comforting yet enticing scent of his spicy cologne, breathing it in, holding it in. She didn't want to admit it, but that was the reason she'd often skipped her jacket on their outings. She'd wanted to wear his, and he'd always obliged, though she'd never asked for it.

How come she could name the constellations in the sky, but couldn't hush the feelings he'd been raising in her?

"The stars are mesmerizing, but your eyes are even more so." His whisper was hot on her skin, the words lingering in shimmering light, illuminating a simple truth like a falling star. She was falling, as well.

For him.

His gaze unnerved her while sending currents of longing through her body. The magnetic pull to him was so strong she could barely breathe. But this wouldn't do because she'd never be a satellite again, orbiting someone who'd never even fully commit to her. She'd survived a broken heart once, but it had cost her. The next time, she'd become a supernova.

Besides, her star could never shine in her hometown.

"I could stare into your eyes forever," he whispered.

"Oh please. I have the same retinas as other people." She made herself look away. "Let's see if I can find another constellation." She knew the history behind them. How they were named and why, and she listed a few.

She didn't even notice how she placed her head on his shoulder as she stared at the sky as if she were going to find the answer there in large white letters. Yup, constellations would just spell it out for her.

Her fingers moved toward his, but this time, she caught herself. His was right near her, and yet the distance between them was like that from Earth to Mars.... Probably longer. If she got too close, she'd get burned the same as she would too close to the sun.

Yet she craved his presence with a force of a thousand—no, a million—stars, even while he was still here. She latched to the nearest distraction. "When is your alleged brother arriving here?"

"Tomorrow morning. Blake wants to get settled, then meet us in the afternoon." He winced, and she felt it. "He rented *that* cottage for a few days."

"What?" With a jolt, she sat up straight, jostling her position on the roof, and blinked at him. "Did you tell him about its history?"

"Of course." His brow furrowed. "But he said the hotels were fully booked during the tourist season, and he wanted a secluded place."

She grimaced. "I'll still go with you."

"I appreciate that. I did try to change his mind." He spread his arms. "I'll try to entice him to a walk on the beach instead of staying in *that* cottage."

Yup, she nearly rolled her eyes again. "No kidding. You could entice a ghost crab out of its shell if you wanted to."

"Good idea." He snapped his fingers.

"Huh? To get crabs out of their shells?"

He laughed. "No. Let's go see the ghost crabs."

She blinked. "Right now?"

"Well, it's much easier to spot them in the sand at night."

She studied him, but couldn't read his expression in the moonlight.

He'd probably devised this plan all along and now passed it off as her idea so she'd agree. She'd done the same plenty of times when she led people to think what she wanted them to think with carefully placed questions to the witness.

"What do you say? Remember my brothers and your siblings used to do it, but you stayed at home."

She'd been an obedient daughter and an overworked one. Maybe too obedient and too overworked. She flinched from the sting. All those sacrifices for her father, and they were barely talking to each other now.

Kai had always been spontaneous, while she could prepare PowerPoint presentations for family meal discussions. But for a few days or at least for a few minutes, she could allow some unplanned things. She squared her shoulders. "Let's do it."

"Great. We need a flashlight, though." He helped her down from the roof, and his touch sent delicious tingles along her skin once again.

Her mind became cloudy in his presence, but she forced herself to think. "I have one in my purse. I'm going to leave a note for Saylor in case she wakes up. And talk to Buttercup and explain I'll be right back."

The slow grin made its appearance again. "You're talking to your puppy."

"I saw you talking to your horses." She turned up her nose. "So don't judge."

"I talk to my parrot, horses, and now a puppy." He lifted his arms in a mocking surrender. "Sometimes I talk to Mom's plants. They like it. No judgment here. It just didn't sound like you."

Yeah, she might be getting a bit defensive. "What about your blanket?"

"I don't talk to it—just so you know."

She almost rolled her eyes again, but he hurried to add, "I'll place it in the car—without talking to it—while you're talking to your puppy."

Once inside Mom's house, Marina explained the situation the best she could to Buttercup, but the puppy still scowled at her with an offended stare. Marina would probably return to more gnawed furniture. She put several chew toys in front of Buttercup, but the pup turned away and covered her head with her paw as if she didn't even want to look at Marina. Marina sighed.

"Okay, okay." She scooped Buttercup up. "You have me wrapped around your little... paw, and you know it, right?"

Buttercup just licked Marina's nose in response.

As Marina slinked into the hall, she stumbled into Saylor. "Ouch."

The puppy barked half-heartedly, but it was probably more out of caution not to get squished between two humans than in warning.

"Well, well, well." Saylor chuckled. "It used to be me sneaking out at night. Now it's you. And why are you sneaking out?" At least she didn't add "as if you were twelve."

"I didn't want to wake you up."

Saylor folded her arms on her chest. Her flamingo-hued silk pajamas, just as cheerful as her personality, suited her, and Marina didn't mind the ribbing. Besides, Saylor had been the one to help the most when they'd been growing up, and she'd been the only one to show up now, as well. "That doesn't answer my question, sis."

Marina studied the tile as if she'd been caught by her parents the way Saylor had been more than a few times. "Um, Kai is waiting for me outside. We're going to the beach to look for ghost crabs."

"Oh." Saylor chuckled. "*That's* what it's called these days."

Heat crept up Marina's neck. Then she pursed her lips. Why was she behaving like a teen caught, well, sneaking out? "You don't have to believe me."

"Ooooh, someone is getting cranky. Or should I say *crabby*?"

"Bye!"

Her sister's laughter trailed Marina as she fled the house with Buttercup in her hands and walked down the white porch passing the swing. Hmm, Kai and Saylor would make a great couple. Both were upbeat and easygoing while Marina had struggled to find a bright side even in the sun. Maybe they'd even dated when she had left to study at the university, and she just didn't know about it. She had no dibs on him whatsoever.

"You brought Buttercup. I guess the talk didn't go that great." He waved at her.

Her heart did that little flutter it always did in his presence. If it reacted like that just standing beside him, what would it do if he kissed her? Several times on the roof, he'd looked like he might. Her heartbeat picked up at the thought. "She, um, she can help us look for ghost crabs." She started walking toward the beach.

"Or make them scurry away." He fell into step beside her.

"They'll scurry away anyway." She cringed. Was arguing her second nature now?

It wasn't his. "Good point. I'm happy to have Buttercup with us."

The puppy gave an approving bark.

Once at the beach, Marina stared at the ocean's mysterious dark waters, so different from the daytime. Then she put Buttercup onto the sand. "Behave. Don't run away and don't scare the ghost crabs."

Buttercup took the assignment so well that she just yawned and stretched on the sand. All her previous enthusiasm seemed to evaporate.

Far in the distance, flashlight beams indicated other people had the same idea.

"It's so different at night, isn't it? Like the ocean can whisper some secrets if you listen long enough," Kai said.

"I don't know. I hear many secrets revealed in court—none of them good. I like things clear-cut. Simple. Honest." Was she responding to his comments or to her pain over her ex-husband's secrets?

His expression turned pensive as he studied her. Then he demonstratively sighed. "That's it, then. I'm not going to take you with me when I go to look for pirate treasure."

Was it possible to be sad in his presence? Her lips tipped up, though she had to be the serious antidote to his fantasy-filled jokes. "It's only a legend. There's no pirate treasure here. At least, not on this coast. Someone probably made up that story to attract tourists." She fished out her flashlight and turned it on, then pointed the beam onto the sand.

"But there are ghost crabs! I see several getting out of their burrows in the sand. Look! Right there!"

Buttercup leaped to her paws, ready to dart after the tiny creatures. "Oh no, you don't. We're not supposed to disturb them." Marina lifted the puppy from the sand.

The pet squealed in protest as if to say, "Where's the fun in that?"

The three of them followed ghostly white—hence the name probably—crabs to the water, where the little animals wet their gills. Childish giddiness rose inside her. Consumed with trials and winning for so many years, she'd forgotten all the beautiful treats of nature.

"Maybe I buried myself in the sand like these crabs and refused to see the signs of my ex's infidelities." She cringed. Why did she keep returning to this?

Because she could trust Kai. Always. And considering her mother and sisters had never been fond of Travis, she didn't want them to say, "I told you so." Maybe they wouldn't say it, but they'd likely think it—and they'd be right. Plus, Marina couldn't risk her personal things being discussed in the town square. She'd reconnected with her cousin, but Skylar was far away now on her honeymoon. As for Marina's close friend at the firm... Apparently, Marina wasn't the only one from her family that friend was close to.

Her husband and her friend. Such a cliché.

Betrayal knifed her again. As if sensing her mood, Buttercup whined in Marina's arms. She tucked the puppy under her arm so she could turn off the flashlight with her free hand, and then slipped it into her purse.

Kai placed his hands on her shoulders and peered into her eyes. "Stop it. It was only *his* fault. Not yours. Never yours." His eyes darkened, becoming as dark as the velvet sky. "I wish I could exchange a few, um, kind words with him."

"Thanks." Tears prickled behind her eyes, but she didn't let them spill. She'd never let them spill. Her father had insisted big girls never cried. "I didn't mean to burden you with all this."

"It's no burden. At all. You know I'll always be there for you."

Would he, though? It was probably a miracle he was between conquests now. If she fell for him, would he trade her for someone else fast enough, too? She didn't want to think so, but then, she'd been unsuspecting about Travis's transgressions, as well.

Kai moved closer but not too much, probably because of the puppy between them. "Stop torturing yourself. Stop analyzing."

"But that's what I do best." She stumbled. "Well, not torture myself, though apparently, I'm also skilled at that. But analyze things."

"Sometimes one has to take a leap of faith." He spoke with such conviction. He shifted closer still, causing Buttercup to bark in warning as she must have no desire to get squished between two humans. Then a shadow passed over his face.

She tensed, sensing his mood change. "What is it?"

He stepped back and removed his hands from her shoulders, causing her to miss that proximity. On the contrary, Buttercup gave an approving bark this time.

"Barrett found out Blake had a lawsuit against him for a botched surgery. It was settled out of court." Kai stood there scowling at the sand like he wanted to burrow into it with the ghost crabs.

She processed that new information. "Blake kept his license. So most likely, he wasn't at fault."

"His ex-wife's comments on social media about him—well, they're far from favorable."

"We can look into their split, but I guess it wasn't amicable." She sighed again. "Look, while I'd never trash Travis publicly, I wouldn't give him a glowing recommendation, either. At least, not as a faithful husband."

"I'm sorry he hurt you." With such sincerity in his voice, he must mean it. "Have you ever danced in the moonlight?"

Huh. The question wasn't what she'd expected. But then, one always had to expect the unexpected from Kai. "No." Her chuckle was without mirth. "I haven't danced in forever, period. I, um, I never had time." No wonder Travis found his wife boring. Regret tasted bitter.

He extended his arm to her. "No time like now to start."

At first, she thought to refuse. Kai already created currents of emotions in her she shouldn't be feeling. She'd learned to suppress her emotions since she'd been a tween, always the responsible, sensible eldest daughter. But her entire being leaned toward him. She didn't want to miss this chance to dance with Kai in the moonlight. Most likely, she'd never get another one. "Fair warning, I might step on your feet a few times."

Twinkles danced in his eyes. "Step away."

"Well, my prom date had a different opinion." She cringed. "And he sure told others how clumsy I was."

His eyes narrowed. "Your prom date wasn't worth it. And maybe he was just covering the fact that he wasn't a good lead. Besides, what can be better than dancing with a beautiful girl?"

Maybe when you kiss that beautiful girl?

Her heartbeat became erratic, and she kept that thought to herself.

On the other hand, Kai was a great lead. And he always knew how to lift her spirits. How to make her head spin like now, though now he could also physically make her spin.

So the rational part of her told her to say no. But the irrational part made her place her hand in his. With her free hand, she settled Buttercup on the sand again far enough so the tide wouldn't reach her and gave the same instructions, hoping for the puppy to get sleepy.

"We'll watch her." Kai found a melody by a singer she liked on his phone and put it on low. "Is this one okay with you?"

"Perfect," she whispered. And it was. So perfect it must be a dream she'd soon awaken from. Since her divorce, she'd started dreaming of Kai, but this was even better than her dreams.

Because this was real.

She was far from a good dancer to start with, which her dad had pointed out when she'd wanted to go to a high school dance. The lack of practice didn't help. She'd avoided dancing ever since the disastrous prom date.

But Kai led her with such skill and confidence—*he* had had lots of practice—so she simply followed his lead.

As promised, he sent several glances at Buttercup, and so did Marina. Thankfully, Buttercup curled up and fell asleep, paying zero attention to the few ghost crabs that scurried toward the water.

A pleasant wave swept Marina up as Kai whirled her around, so close, so… dear. She'd learned to be tough, but she felt like putty in his arms, dissolving in the wonderful feeling like salt in the ocean.

The moments were magical, and yet she couldn't stop her analytical mind. "Are you having second thoughts about meeting Blake?" Or maybe she'd voiced the question because she was worried. Which she was. While she'd been pining about her past, his future was at stake. Finding someone related to him by blood could be a good thing—or a disaster. Family didn't always have your best interests in mind, as she knew all too well.

His jaw set tight. "I just have a weird feeling about all this."

"You want him to be a perfect brother, and he's going to be a human being with flaws."

He brightened somewhat. "True. So am I."

"So am I," she echoed.

"No, you're flawless."

Here we go again.

"Come on, I told you that you don't need to use all those compliments on me. Stay on topic, will you?" Guilt stung her though. It wasn't Kai's fault that Travis had given her compliments he hadn't meant. Or that Travis had used the same corny compliments on other women. Marina had overheard his conversation with *her* friend over the phone. Travis had refused to eat leftovers or consider used furniture, but he was all for recycling endearments.

Anger and embarrassment roiled her, but she pushed the churning down with a familiar effort. Her father regularly enumerated her flaws while she'd been growing up. He'd taken apart everything she did, from school assignments to home chores, and pointed out what she'd done wrong and why. He'd called it teaching her.

Her arm moved around Kai's neck as if needing support again.

Was she so eager to succumb to Travis's saccharine words because she'd been force-fed her father's criticism for so long? She made herself move away a little from Kai. She couldn't repeat the same mistake. She had to rely on herself, and only herself.

Even if just the intoxicating scent of his cologne and his understanding, compassionate eyes, combined with the supportive squeeze of his hand, nearly made her forget all her wise resolutions.

"I still can't see a single flaw in you." He shrugged. "But okay, let's stay on topic. Maybe I just don't want to have my hopes up if this thing with my alleged brother doesn't work out."

She stole a glance at Buttercup. Still peacefully asleep on the sand as if she didn't have a care in the world. Was it right to be envious of a puppy?

"It's natural to feel that way." And it was probably natural to feel all the things she was feeling now. But she had to fight them.

In the moonlight, with the glittering ocean backdrop, he looked even more like a dangerous pirate, the golden hoop earring glistening in his ear, the red bandanna covering his black hair. Only she wasn't a damsel in distress about to be conquered.

Though one wouldn't guess by her heartbeat thundering in her ears.

He dipped her, eliciting a delirious dizziness and a new whirlwind of emotions. But it wouldn't do her any good to succumb to them. And for some reason, tomorrow's meeting didn't sit well with her, either.

Chapter Six

Kai's rib cage tightened.

Talk about mixed feelings.

Being inside *that* cottage gave him an eerie feeling, but he was eager to meet his brother, who might also unlock some secrets to Kai's origin.

"Nice to meet you both." Dr. Blake Park shook Kai's hand, then Marina's. He did look a lot like Kai, but was it enough for them to be brothers?

"A pleasure to meet you, Dr. Park." Marina's smile was polite. She used to be uncomfortable with strangers before, but her posture was confident now. "I hope you don't mind me intruding on your meeting."

Blake had known about her joining them and had agreed to it. But it was still nice of her to ask.

She'd paired a cream pencil skirt with a wide cream belt decorated with a metal crystal-studded buckle, and her aquamarine long-sleeved blouse accentuated her eyes. Elegant and stunning, she brought out an appreciative gleam in Blake's eyes.

Jealousy stung Kai, but he dismissed it. He wasn't the jealous type. Yet he'd never forgotten his profound loss when Marina had slipped away from him to marry another guy.

"Not at all. And please call me Blake." Blake didn't add any compliments, and his gaze didn't linger on Marina despite that appreciative gleam, for which Kai was grateful. Blake gestured to the indigo-hued sofa. "Please take a seat, Ms. Helms and Mr. Lawrence."

"Thank you. Please call me Kai. And I'm glad to meet you, too."

The owner had replaced the beige sofa and love seat after blood and other things Kai didn't want to think about had splattered it all those years ago during Kai's adoptive father's suicide. Had she chosen the dark color so she wouldn't have to replace it the next time? Because sure enough, someone else died here last month.

Kai and Marina exchanged glances, his apologetic.

Then she bravely took a seat on the sofa. "Please do call me Marina, then." Kai followed her.

"You'd never believe how cheap the rent here was, especially considering it's tourist season already." Blake sat on the plush armchair that matched the sofa.

I wonder why.

No reason to voice that gloomy thought. Kai had already revealed the cottage's history, without mentioning one of the victims was Kai's adoptive father. But it didn't have much effect, and Blake preferred to stay in the air-conditioned space rather than stroll on the beach. Maybe Kai should've mentioned that significant detail.

Was he that used to avoiding the topic in the family? Or was some part of him curious about the place? The whole episode was still shrouded in mystery, partially because he didn't believe the man had committed suicide.

Well, Blake didn't look like one of the tourists who would stroll the shoreline, anyway. Overdressed in a tailored charcoal-gray suit, he tugged at his burgundy tie now, clearly nervous, and the gesture revealed a wristwatch, traditional and expensive, but not outrageously so.

His dark-brown hair had gone prematurely grayish on his temples, giving a contrast to his boyish face, and his smile was open and equally boyish. Overall, he gave off a positive vibe, but then Kai usually liked the people he met.

"Please help yourself." Blake moved the charcuterie board with meats and cheeses on the coffee table toward Kai and Marina. "Would you like something to drink?"

"I'm good. Thanks." Kai shook his head. No way he could eat or drink something in this place.

Marina didn't seem to have such qualms as she reached for a slice of Havarti. "I'm not thirsty, but I appreciate the offer."

Normally, Kai didn't have any issues chatting to people. But all thoughts flew out of his mind as he stared at the walls that had probably been repainted for reasons other than refreshing the interior. They were currently a warm cream color with white trim as if someone wanted to give the place a light and airy vibe. The same probably went for the ceiling.

He hadn't been at this place right after the fatal shot. Darius had, and his description had been too vivid. Should Kai have investigated it then? He'd been the only one in the family who hadn't been emotionally involved.

While he loved his mother and brothers, he'd never warmed to Mr. Lawrence because of the way the latter had treated his family. Yes, Kai had resented him for that. But he'd never suffered from his hand, so there was no profound hatred, either.

Or had he never questioned out loud what had happened here that night because he didn't want to know the answer?

And did he want to know the answer about his biological parents? Because one of them had abandoned Kai on the beach, where anything could've happened to the little boy, including drowning. The pause stretched too much, and so did his nerves.

"You were born and raised in Memphis, Tennessee, right?" Marina's question registered in the back of his mind. "I heard it has the best blues ever."

Blake's face lit up. "Oh, you should hear our jazz!"

"The city's music is amazing, period. Nearly twenty percent of the early inductees in the Rock and Roll Hall of Fame were from within one hundred miles of Memphis, correct?" She must've done her research. While Kai had done nothing. Most of the time, the same could be said about their lessons.

"That's right." For a while, Blake and Marina talked about their favorite singers and songs.

"We have great barbecue, as well," Blake said at last, looking more at ease. He'd slung an arm over the back of his chair and crossed an ankle over his knee, his posture relaxed, and he wasn't tugging at his tie any longer. He spread his hands now to include Kai, as well. "I'd love for both of you to come visit me."

Kai leaned forward. "I might take you up on that offer." Not to listen to the music or eat barbecue, though he appreciated a great song and a good meal, but rather, because his biological parents must've been from that place.

He'd love for Marina to join him, of course, but this was her first vacation in many years. And it wasn't a vacation, really, but to help her mother.

Had Kai been left so far from Tennessee to ensure they'd never meet in person by chance? Unless one of them ended up on TV or in a viral post on social media, which had likely happened. That also brought a question.

"Do you think our biological mother was from Memphis, or did she just give birth there?"

As if lightning and thunder struck in the room, the smile slipped from Blake, and the camaraderie Marina had created disappeared. Kai cringed over causing that, but then he sat up straighter. After all, what had Blake expected? That Kai wouldn't ask important-for-him questions?

He'd done a lot of pleasant chitchat in his life, and this wasn't it.

"From what little I know, she was from Memphis."

Kai's focus sharpened. That wasn't much, but it was something. "What else do you know about her?" Curiosity could run in the family, though Blake's attention span must be way better since he'd become a doctor. Hopefully, he'd asked his adoptive parents questions and maybe even gone digging on his own.

Marina took his hand as if to offer silent support. It brought back the memory of having her hand in his, holding her close as they danced in the moonlight with only the ocean and ghost crabs as witnesses, if not to count the other people in the distance searching for ghost crabs. Looking into her eyes while holding her in his arms and moving slowly... His heartbeat increased, but he couldn't let himself get distracted.

Couldn't let himself think that the dance wouldn't be repeated.

"I had some research done. Her name was Naree Jones. She was raised by a single mom who struggled. She never knew her father, not even his name. Maybe she wanted her child to have a better life than she had by giving me up for adoption. Maybe she wanted a better life for herself, as well. She got pregnant right out of high school, and she wanted to go to college to better herself. Considering she'd have to work while putting herself through college, she probably didn't think she could raise me." Blake paused. Was it because this was a difficult topic? Or because that was all he knew?

"Did she go to college?" Kai asked when Blake didn't continue.

"Yes. But she dropped out without getting a degree. She wanted to become a nurse, maybe even a doctor." His voice warmed, perhaps because of the similarities in their chosen paths.

"Where did she work?" Marina asked.

"As a maid at a local hotel."

Kai's mind whirled to process all this information. "You said there was no father's name on your birth certificate. Was it because she didn't know or because she didn't want to name him?"

"I can't say for sure. But I asked professors at the university she went to. They all described her as hardworking, diligent, and humble. It took a while to find people who studied with her. But once I did, they all said the same. She didn't attend any parties. Didn't even seem to date."

That could lead to two options, none of them great, and one significantly worse than the other. But Kai didn't want to go in that direction yet.

"Apparently, she died when I was six—you would have been three, I guess. Cancer. So if we're related through her, you have a medical history of cancer, too."

His PI brother already warned Kai that she'd died, so the thought didn't sting as much now. Instead, Kai tried to remain focused. He voiced the thoughts they all must be thinking. "The chances that we are full siblings—not half-siblings—are slim. So, if we're brothers, we must be related through either our mother or our unknown father."

If it was the mom, why hadn't she simply given Kai up for adoption in the hospital, too? Why risk severe punishment by abandoning her child at the beach two years later? Not to mention, risking her child's life?

Blake's lips thinned. "I've brought a DNA kit, but we can also do a second test later tomorrow in the hospital setting to make sure."

What would it show?

BY THE END OF THE NEXT day, Marina was falling off her feet again. Her extremities felt as if they were filled with lead. But it was a good day, and she was ready to close the restaurant. She'd already closed the cash register, and nearly everyone had left.

Jan finished mopping the floor. "Thank you so much for everything you've done for me."

"Please don't worry about it." Marina gave the waitress an encouraging smile. "I hope your daughter feels better soon."

Children got sick easily, and Marina knew it firsthand as she'd had to help tend to her siblings whenever they'd gotten ill. Her mother had taken care of them usually, but her father had expected Marina to assist—first because she'd been the eldest and second because she'd developed a good immune system so she rarely caught a bug from her siblings. She swallowed the bitter taste in her mouth as she checked last-minute adjustments to tomorrow's special and went over the inventory.

Growing up, she'd wished she'd get a cold so she could get some rest. Maybe it was selfish of her, but so was her father's decision to make her take on the role of the third parent to the others. Her mother had done her best, but she'd been so busy with Bay and Basin, Marina's siblings, and a demanding spouse that Marina hadn't complained to her.

But... shouldn't Mom have seen it herself?

Minutes later, Marina was on the way home, the takeout with her favorite shrimp scampi and biscuits on the passenger seat emanating a mouthwatering aroma. All she wanted was to inhale the shrimp scampi, cuddle Buttercup, fall into bed, and stay there for a week. Or two. Or three. Of course, morning would be here way too soon, but she wouldn't think about it now.

How did Kai's second meeting with Blake and their DNA test at the hospital go?

Throughout the day, her hands had itched to call him. But she'd barely had time to eat a sandwich for lunch. No, that wasn't it. She missed his voice so much she could've found the time to call. There was an inner barrier. Her fingers tightened around the steering wheel.

From an early age, she'd been expected to take care of people but not bother them, like not bothering her father or his friends when they'd come over. She'd been expected to bring dishes and drinks and stay out of the way.

She grimaced as she stopped at the red light. Was she the same way in her marriage? She'd brought what she'd thought was needed to the table and stayed out of the way?

Did Travis have a point, after all? She'd had no clue how to entertain, how to be fun.

The fish sandwich sank like a stone in her stomach. Was she the reason her ex-husband turned to other women as he'd claimed? Was it true that no man could survive being with her for long without cheating? That people needed spice and flavor, and she was too bland for anyone's palate to tolerate for long without getting that spice and flavor elsewhere?

She moved forward on the green light, and she should move forward in her life, as well.

But Travis's words still rang in her ears.

Hurt and heartbroken, she'd asked him why he'd married her, if he found her boring.

He'd met her eye then and said, "Because I knew you were hardworking, reliable, and trustworthy. And you had the smarts to become a good lawyer, especially considering I could teach you the ropes. So you'd double our income. You weren't the type to nag or complain. Plus, you practically raised your siblings so you'd make a great mom for our future children. But eventually, I realized that wasn't enough to keep my interest."

"Why haven't you told me, then?" she'd whispered, aching even more.

"Because no matter all your smarts, you still have principles. You'd have walked away. But the arrangement suited me at the time. It doesn't any longer because I met a special someone." He'd paused, meeting her gaze in the mirror as he'd adjusted his tie, clearly not a speck on his impeccable suit or unused conscience. "Don't look so hurt. You've gained lots of knowledge and some property in this marriage. You should be grateful."

She lifted her chin as she pulled up to her mother's house. She was grateful, but not for the reasons he'd mentioned. She could've wasted much more time on that guy. And while Kai was different, he clearly didn't want to settle with one woman, either. He was a great friend, though, and she should be happy with that and not ask for more. After all, she'd been conditioned to be happy with what she'd been given and not ask for more.

The moment she turned off the engine, her phone rang. Her heartbeat picked up when her hands-free phone announced Kai's name.

"Hello, Kai." She hurried to answer.

"Hello, Marina." Just the timbre of his voice sent tingles over her skin. So much for being happy with them being just friends. "I hope I'm not bothering you too late."

"You never bother me." And sometimes she wished he did. She faced the soft golden glow of lanterns around the azure house with white trim. "Like clouds in the sky," her mother used to say.

Marina never had her head in the clouds, so why did she now when it came to Kai? She considered going into the house but was afraid to wake up Buttercup and consequently Saylor. She'd expected Kai to make some joke.

But his voice was unusually serious. "I might need your help."

Her excitement dissipated.

Yup, that was her. The Helper. That was why people came to her. Not because she was fun to talk to or be with. But because she could help. Be it providing legal advice these days, or helping with homework while growing up, or making sure her husband's shirts were starched and ironed and the house sparkled for any unexpected guests he might want to entertain while she'd been married.

So she voiced her usual question. "What can I do?"

"I can't locate Blake."

She sat up straighter. "What do you mean, you can't locate him?"

"He didn't show up for our dinner meeting today. He's not answering his phone. I went by that cottage, and nobody answered the door. I did it several times."

"Is his rental car there?"

"No."

A shiver traveled down her spine despite the warm night, but she had to think logically. "He could've returned the rental car and flown home."

"Without saying anything to me?"

She considered the conversation in that cottage. "He could've changed his mind about the entire thing." Then she frowned. "Or... maybe me going with you was a mistake."

"Why?"

Did she have to spell out the painful truth? She sighed. "Well, though I seem to produce a better impression now than I did in high school, sometimes people don't warm to me. Hmm. Though if Blake didn't like me, that wouldn't be a reason for him to disappear without saying anything to you. After all, he went to all this trouble to find you and arrange the meeting."

"I believe he liked you just fine. You have a much bigger effect on people than you realize."

She nearly asked where those people were but stopped herself in time. It wasn't about her and the hit to her self-esteem. She didn't even know why she'd been rehashing memories of school bullies and her divorce.

Was it because she'd reconnected with Kai and wanted a chance with him? But he'd never pretended he wanted to settle, and her heart—and yes, self-esteem—hadn't even healed from the previous disaster.

Okay, okay. Back to the matter at hand.

Her mind whirled. "Wait a moment. Did you call the owner of *that* cottage? I believe Kennedy Crawford inherited it."

"I did—after I checked with the hospitals, which happily didn't have him or anyone unknown admitted." His voice turned gloomy. "She didn't pick up."

"Hmm. It would be a good idea to visit her, then. After everything that had happened at *that* cottage, they must've installed the cameras."

"I'd love to." His voice perked up. "But it's unlikely she'd let us in this late in the day. Besides, she has the reputation of a recluse...."

Marina searched her memory for an awkward, quiet teen dressed in designer clothes that cost more than Marina's parents earned in a month. "I used to tutor Kennedy in school. I might be able to pull that string. And I just happen to have her favorite food with me." She glanced longingly at the passenger seat and what was supposed to be her dinner tonight. Well, sometimes sacrifices needed to be made. And not only because of Kai. Blake's disappearance didn't sit well with her.

"Right!" Kai's voice brightened. "I forgot you tutored her. But then you tutored so many people."

Including not voluntarily. She thought of her brother. "Let me call Kennedy. I'll call you back. Oh, wait. Can you give me her phone number? She might've changed it since I had it last."

He rattled it off. "Do you think she'll pick up?"

"There's one way to find out."

He paused. "But you must be tired."

"It's okay. Really." Somehow, her tone sounded perkier than she felt.

"Thank you for doing this for me." His voice softened. And once again, just the timbre of it made the blood run faster in her veins.

"What are friends for?" She meant it, despite the words' bittersweet taste. "Talk to you soon."

She hoped. Because a large part of her was grateful for a reason to see him tonight. She winced. Of course, she also hoped nothing bad had happened to Blake.

Her lips pursed as she punched in Kennedy's phone number. How could she be glad to have an excuse to see Kai? Well, that was if Kennedy answered her call and was open to their visit. Was she getting pathetic or what?

"Hello." Kennedy didn't sound sleepy at all.

Good. At least, Marina didn't wake her up. And it was a miracle Kennedy had picked up seeing an unfamiliar number.

"Sorry to call so late. It's Marina Helms." She rushed into speech before Kennedy could disconnect. "I hope you remember me."

Taking a breath now, Marina tilted her face toward the starry sky, and the recent memories of stargazing on the roof with Kai made her heart squeeze. And then there was the best dance of her life, and not only because it was one of so few. Grrr... How could she concentrate when her mind kept wandering to him?

"Of course, I do. You're the only reason I passed the seventh grade. And don't worry. I wasn't asleep anyway. Insomnia. But I imagine you're not calling me to say hi."

Even better. Kennedy didn't expect any pleasantries. "My friend has been trying to reach Dr. Blake Park, the person who's staying at that cottage you own. Blake missed their dinner meeting and now isn't answering his phone calls or knocks on the door. Of course, he could be called away on an emergency, but I presume he'd have notified my friend. We just want to make sure he's okay."

The moonlight was basking everything in its mysterious glow.

Dance with me in the moonlight.

Kai's words and the soft music still seemed to caress something deep inside Marina.

Kennedy groaned. "Not again! If I could sell that place, I would! You know what? At this point, I'd even gift it." She paused. "You wouldn't be interested in a beachfront property, would you? Totally free. Seriously."

Despite the seriousness of the situation, Marina smiled. "Um, no thanks. And hopefully, I'm bothering you for nothing. But I do happen to have shrimp scampi takeout with me already." Her stomach protested at her suggestion as she breathed in the enticing scent before pushing out the final words. "Would you mind if my friend and I stopped by?"

Kennedy chuckled. "I imagine you want to see the camera recordings and the cottage itself."

"I wouldn't exactly say I *want* to see them." Marina fidgeted in the car seat. "I just think we have to."

"And your friend wouldn't be Kai Lawrence?"

Marina forgot to figure in the small town. "Yes."

"How soon can you get here?"

Yes! She calculated the driving time. No reason to change out of her vivid pink—and somewhat stained—Bay and Basin uniform. "Fifteen minutes or so okay?"

"I'll get the coffee going. I realize not everyone is an insomniac like me." Kennedy disconnected before Marina had a chance to thank her.

She called Kai back. "Kennedy will see us in fifteen minutes."

"Wow. You're amazing. You know that, right?"

His praise touched her, but he gave out compliments too easily. She started the engine. "No, I don't know that."

Maybe she shouldn't have said that, but too many times, she'd been taken for granted, though her siblings probably didn't know better while growing up.

Kai and his family had never taken her for granted, though. One of the many reasons she'd been drawn to them in whatever little spare time she'd had in those days—now too.

The motor revved up in his background, as well. "Don't hang up. Let's see what we know about Kennedy. And... I missed the sound of your voice all day."

Her heart fluttered, but once a flirt, always a flirt. She pulled up to the road.

Huh. While minutes ago her limbs felt like she could barely move them, she had a fresh energy surge now. Adrenaline must be pumping. Or was it her desire to see Kai soon, even if for a worrisome reason, even if they wouldn't be alone?

As she drove, she cataloged the things she knew about the reclusive woman. "Kennedy had the misfortune to receive that cottage and the fortune to receive two of the hotels in town as gifts from her uncle. She also helps her uncle with his remaining properties, two more hotels on the coast."

"I heard she's been doing a pretty good job with them. Well, she does have excellent managers."

She chuckled. Kai always had that effect on her. She continued, "She also had the fortune to nearly marry the prom king." While Marina had been told she should be grateful she'd been invited at all. "And the misfortune to call off the engagement for an unspecified reason. Until fourteen, she lived with her uncle, whose daughter disappeared when she was seven. Her father was a trust-fund child who spent his time playing golf and partying and so did her mother."

"Instead of raising their daughter."

Marina swallowed down a rush of compassion. "Yup. I remember Kennedy keeping to herself, sad most of the time. I thought it was because of her parents' attitude, but maybe there was more to it. She kept quiet a lot. But once she admitted she used to go to a private school and she missed her uncle a lot."

"Here's an interesting tidbit. Kennedy's late father and my late adoptive father used to be drinking buddies. Then they had a fallout after a bar fight."

Huh. She should've known that, and she most likely had. But her life had been so busy then that she'd forgotten. She slowed around the curb and opened the window to let the ocean breeze in. The traffic was minimal at night, and she liked it that way. "What was the fight about?"

"We still don't know. Dad said it was unimportant. But he didn't ever talk to his friend again."

Huh. Her fingers tapped the steering wheel. The unknowns shrouding Kennedy's life piqued Marina's curiosity.

Kai was already there when she parked before Kennedy's two-story residence, his white pirate shirt standing out in the dim light as he leaned against his car. She hurried out of her vehicle, and he met her with his bright smile and a hug far too quick for her liking.

Though what did she want from a *friendly* hug? Yet she felt her lips kick up as she mirrored his smile just as the ocean mirrored the moonlight. She breathed in cool fresh air that felt more humid and saltier. The ocean's nearby whisper was the perfect music, his signature exotic scent stirred the desire of her heart, and she wished for another moonlight dance. Despite her two left feet.

"You look gorgeous." His smile could brighten the night—it already had.

"Stop it." She waved off his words. She was exhausted and looked it. Besides, she was wearing a rumpled—*pink!*—uniform and more than a few food stains. When would he learn he could skip his compliments on her?

"No matter the reason, I'm glad I could see you tonight." He brushed aside a strand of hair the breeze had flicked into her face.

Her poor heart should've hardened after her experience. But one of his glances, one of his words, one of his little touches, and it melted like ice cream at the beach. "Me, too." She sensed movement behind a gigantic window. Most likely, they had an audience.

Besides, there was no time to waste. They had an important mission to complete. Her father, and her ex for that matter, only praised her when she'd been productive.

"Let's get this done." She moved away from Kai, even as disappointment stabbed her.

Some light dissipated from his eyes as if the moon disappeared behind a cloud. Yet he nodded. "Okay."

He'd rarely argued. As a person who constantly got into arguments with her siblings while growing up—and now was arguing professionally in court—she'd thought his easy acquiesce was because he didn't care deeply about things.

Was that the case here? While she cherished the extra minutes alone with him, he didn't care much? She marched forward stomping down on her disappointment. After all, that was what she'd done her entire life.

Chapter Seven

Marina managed a smile when Kennedy opened the front door before they reached it and could ring the bell. "Come on in."

"Thank you for agreeing to see us." Marina stepped inside. Kai followed as she handed Kennedy the take-out bag. "This is for you. A small expression of our thanks."

Kennedy smiled, but it didn't quite reach her eyes. "Thanks, but you didn't have to. I'll leave it for tomorrow's lunch. Please go ahead." She gestured to the living room.

In the daylight, the outside of this rectangular building looked like a block of ice with sunshine reflecting from the floor-to-ceiling windows, but having tutored Kennedy at the library, Marina had never been invited inside.

Marina's family and Kennedy's family had run in different social circles, especially while her mom had worked her way from a dishwasher to a waitress to a cook in the restaurant her mother-in-law owned. She'd been excellent in all those roles, working hard. Mom would've never been able to buy Bay and Basin, but to everyone's surprise—and Dad's shock—Grandma had left the restaurant to Mom in her will.

Well, not to everyone's surprise. Marina had expected it. Several times, Dad had told her he had no use for the place and would sell it as soon as he could. Marina made sure Grandma found out about that. She wasn't a lawyer in training for nothing.

Just like outside the place stood apart from the other homes, the inside was more modern and spacious than anywhere else in town. No nod to the coastal or nautical here, either.

Instead, glass and metal and geometric figures ruled. Tables with glass tops and long mirrors on the walls created the illusion of an even bigger space. Frameless oil paintings depicted spheres and squares, and geometric figures decorated rugs similar to the ones in Marina's apartment.

Now as she viewed them as an outsider, it made her wonder.

Had she chosen the ultramodern minimalist because she liked it? Or to contrast the multitude of children and knickknacks underfoot in her childhood home and the screaming opulence in her husband's? Had she needed the large unoccupied space and the illusion of more of it to put space between herself and her painful experiences? If so, the only thing she'd succeeded in had been creating emptiness inside.

She glanced sideways at Kai. What would he think about her apartment? He'd find things to praise, of course. That was his nature. Finding beauty in everything. But deep inside, he wouldn't like it. It shouldn't matter, and yet it did. A lot.

Everything here was from a black, white, and gray palette with the curtains and rugs adding an occasional addition of indigo and the succulents offering their salad greens.

Huh. Kennedy didn't have a family photo with her parents, though plenty with her uncle. Marina didn't have any family photos, despite her large family. But once she'd divorced and moved into her own apartment, she'd framed photos with Kai and put them up, one of the few splashes of color. What did that say about her?

The scent of freshly brewed coffee reached her, overpowering another subtle scent she couldn't quite place, maybe coming from the plants.

Round lights stood out on the walls like in a ship, but they weren't lit. Instead, dim light came from the candles on the table. Marina doubted it was to create an atmosphere. Then why? To keep something from being exposed? No, she read too much into it.

"Please take a seat." Kennedy waved at the white sofa and armchairs.

Thankfully, in contrast to the rest of the room, those looked comfortable and cozy. That sofa probably wouldn't stay such a pristine color for more than a few days in Marina's childhood house when she'd been growing up. But she already knew Kennedy didn't have children or pets. Curiously enough, Marina had a sofa just as pristinely white in her apartment. She'd rarely used it because she'd rarely been home. Something akin to regret unraveled deep inside her, but she ignored it almost out of habit.

Kai followed Marina to the sofa and sat with her while Kennedy moved toward the armchair.

"Would you like something to drink?" Kennedy gestured to the room the coffee aroma drifted from. Barefoot, she shifted her stance beside the chair, and her long silver-hued skirt shimmered around her ankles like moonlight while her white tube top floated above it like a life preserver on shimmery waters.

Marina considered the combination of a white sofa and possibly spilled coffee and shook her head.

"Thanks, but I'm good," Kai said.

Silver bracelets clanged as Kennedy settled in the armchair, and the sound put Marina oddly on guard. Kai took the lead by telling Kennedy about his alleged biological brother and how Dr. Park had contacted Kai and asked to meet, then their meeting in that cottage.

While he spoke, Marina studied Kennedy, who'd changed a lot since they used to meet in the library. If Marina had passed Kennedy on the street, she wouldn't have recognized her.

Kennedy was attractive with an innate elegance Marina didn't remember the awkward, chubby, and lonesome teen possessing, but the hollowness about her gray eyes put Marina on guard. Black circles rimming those eyes hinted this might not be the first night she couldn't sleep. Was it because Kennedy owned that troubling cottage, or was something else disturbing her?

In Marina's profession, she'd learned to sniff out people with dangerous secrets like Buttercup learned to sniff out dog biscuits. Kennedy just might be a person with a dangerous secret. Marina stifled her curiosity. They had a different secret to find out. "Could we please see the camera recordings? I mean, if you have the legal right to access and show them."

Kennedy's lips lifted in a half smile. "I do. I had it written into the contract. Dr. Park likely skipped reading that part when he signed it."

"Lots of people don't read contracts thoroughly. And thank you." Marina was getting more and more curious about this person, so different from the girl who'd been failing her grades.

Kennedy got up and returned with a laptop, which she placed on a glass-topped coffee table that displayed its sharp edges while hinting at a possible fragility. "Here we go." She tapped on a file and turned the screen toward them.

After the recording played, Marina agreed with the famous saying of Socates—she knew she knew nothing.

"Blake's suitcases are still there, as well as his clothes," she thought out loud. "Nobody visited him. He left the cottage at 11:14 a.m., then came back at 1:06 p.m. Then he left again at 2:36 p.m. He didn't return."

"So where is he?" Kai rubbed the creases forming where his brows pinched together.

"You'll need the key to the cottage." Kennedy moved her long blonde hair back, causing silver bracelets to clank again.

"That's probably too much to ask." Marina started slowly, inviting Kennedy to interrupt her anytime.

The clatter of those bracelets bothered her. Had she heard it before? If so, when and where?

"I'll give you a duplicate, but I'll deny it later if you get questioned. And I won't go in with you. As a landlord, I don't have the right to enter the cottage without the renter's permission." Kennedy grimaced. "And frankly, I have no desire to go there. Remember, the camera will record you entering it. How are you going to explain that?"

Kai and Marina exchanged glances. Marina was the more cautious one—by far. "Maybe we should wait until the morning and try reaching him again. Contact his parents, sister, and daughter."

"That would be a good idea." Kennedy got up, showing the meeting was over. She did bring the key while they walked in the hall.

"Thank you very much." Kai took the key.

Marina didn't mind. She was more fascinated with the bracelets, and not just because of their beauty. "That is some gorgeous jewelry." She used Kai's tactic.

"Thanks." Kennedy's gaze became melancholic. "They're my mom's. I also wear the same perfume she used to wear." Her gaze flicked from Marina to Kai and then back. Then she disappeared into the kitchen and came back with the take-out box and returned it to Marina.

Maybe Marina's memory failed her. "Oh. You don't like shrimp scampi anymore?"

Kennedy's lips tipped up a tad. "I still love it. But I saw you eye it longingly before handing it to me. Almost the same one as..." Her voice trailed off. "Never mind."

Despite the competing aromas—shrimp and biscuits coming from the box and coffee from the kitchen—Marina finally placed the mysterious scent that tugged at her memory. Kennedy was close enough now to recognize it was her perfume. Very subtle and vaguely familiar, though Marina felt sure Kennedy hadn't worn this perfume in school. No girls had.

Near the door, Marina studied Kennedy. Despite those warning bells, she had a strange feeling that in another time, had Marina been more attentive and less busy and Kennedy less reclusive, they could have become friends. Perhaps now, they could. "You didn't have to help us. Yet you did. Why?"

Maybe in Kai's world people helped each other with no questions asked. In Marina's world, things were quid pro quo, and people had their agenda.

"You were kind to me when few people were." Kennedy lifted a hand to cover her eyes, the sudden gesture causing the bracelets to clang again.

A few things clicked into place. Including where Marina might have heard those bracelets and smelled that perfume many years ago. A shiver traveled over her back.

She didn't like it. She didn't like it at all.

KAI FOLLOWED MARINA home, with her permission, to make sure she made it to her mother's place safely. Unlike Kennedy's large modern house, the cottage was located far from the ocean shore, in a way less affluent area. Marina's father had inherited it from his mother, and by then, the tiny bungalow her mother had inherited from her father, whom neither Kai nor Marina had ever met, had been bursting at the seams to accommodate all the children.

Now, Kai parked his sedan at the curb and hurried outside to open Marina's car door for her, but she'd slipped out already, frowning. It wasn't her frown from when she concentrated on something, but rather from when she was upset. Huh. Something had happened at Kennedy's place to lower her mood, but what?

She stared at the sky as if looking for distraction in constellations or thinking over a problem she didn't like.

"You're awfully quiet," he blurted out as he made it to her in a few wide strides. The cicada orchestra played somewhere nearby. Thankfully, Buttercup seemed to be deep asleep and didn't sense them outside yet. Good.

Marina's gaze moved to him, and the corners of her oh-so-kissable mouth tipped up a tad. "I'm *always* quiet."

Right. Unlike him.

She gestured to the porch swing. "Would you like to sit?"

They'd hung out on this swing more than a few times as children. As a teen, he'd once almost kissed her when she'd been looking at the stars. She still didn't have a clue.

She had her feet planted on the ground with all her responsibilities, but she'd also always looked at the stars, somewhere beyond him, beyond the horizon, beyond the earth even. By now, he should've accepted it. But a large, rebellious part of him didn't want to. Maybe the same part that sensed the dynamics between them started changing lately. Or was it his wishful thinking?

"Sure." He took a seat beside her, hoping this invitation meant she didn't want this evening to end, just like he didn't want it to. "But it's a different kind of quiet."

Her eyebrows rose as she placed the takeout nearby. "I have different kinds of quiet?"

He nodded. "Yes. Your eyes darkened, and your eyebrows moved together. This one is when something worries you. When you stick the tip of your tongue out, it's your trying-to-figure-out-something quiet. When you twist a tip of your hair around your finger, it's your curious quiet."

"You know me well." Using her toes, she rocked the swing, the slight scent of fried food lingering on her. She clasped her hands over her flamingo-pink uniform skirt, her shoulders tense. "And here I thought I worked hard on hiding my tells."

That still didn't answer his questions, but he didn't pressure her.

What kind of quiet would it be if he leaned to kiss her? His heartbeat kicked up, and he moved an inch closer. Would he ever know?

Wistfulness unraveled things inside him, but the takeout near her reminded him she probably hadn't had a decent dinner today. How hadn't he guessed it already? And she must be super tired by now.

He needed to let her go. Story of his life.

Huh. If he had to leave her, then maybe he could swing by *that* cottage.

"You're not going to *that* cottage on your own, are you?" She squinted at him.

"You know me well." He parroted her words to her.

"Promise me you won't. You could see it in the recording. There was no indication something violent happened there. Most likely, you won't find anything we didn't see on the screen already, but you'll be breaking and entering."

"I have a key. It could still be useful to poke around." He glanced away as she gave him a pointed look. Growing up, she'd kept him out of trouble many times. He'd have been in detention many more times if not for her, but she could dismantle his wildest ideas without even saying a word. "Okay, okay! I promise I won't. Not tonight at least. But I have to do *something*. What if Blake is in danger? What if he needs help?"

"Let's get some sleep and check on him again in the morning." She rubbed her temples. "If he still doesn't pick up his phone and there's nobody at *that* cottage, we'll call his family. In case he had to drop everything and return home, intending to pick up his things later."

"It does sound plausible." Ha! He used a big word again. Was he making a proverbial mountain out of a molehill, imagining things like in the pirate play for children he recreated every tourist season?

He nodded at the take-out box. Though he was reluctant to see her leave, her well-being came first. "Would you like to warm this up in the microwave? Or I could get you something fresh. Though I have to warn you, there's only one place open this late here."

She chuckled, the warm sound reverberated through him. "I remember." She opened the foam box. "It's okay. I don't mind it cold. And I'm willing to share if you'd like."

"I'm good." He was always good, or at least most of the time. On the other hand, she was outstanding way before she realized it. He hoped she did realize it.

She munched on the biscuits and shrimp scampi, the food disappearing fast to confirm his suspicion she'd skipped a decent dinner. "If we still can't locate Blake tomorrow, we'll go to the police."

He liked the sound of "we." A little too much. And he liked the sparkle of her eyes in the lanterns' golden glow when she decided on something. And the swell of her lips that he ached to kiss...

Stop it.

She'd been spreading herself thin again. And like so many people in her life—nearly all, frankly—he was taking advantage of her kindness and heightened sense of responsibility.

He shook his head, ready to get up. "I'd love your help. But you already have Bay and Basin on your hands. I can't add more to your plate. No pun intended."

Though hadn't he already added more to her plate? Yes, because he valued her input and her mind but even more because he craved her company. Simply craved her beside him. Guilt needled, mixed with longing. The breeze lifted her hair, and the air grew colder.

He took off his light jacket and snuggled it over her shoulders, rewarded with a smile.

"Gale is arriving tomorrow. Saylor and Gale should be able to handle the restaurant." She squared her shoulders as she forked the last remaining shrimp. "It's time for my sisters to step up more. Now age doesn't matter." Then she closed the empty foam box and set it aside.

"That's my girl." He placed his hands on her shoulders, then removed them, remembering something. "Not that you're my girl. But I'm proud of you for asserting your boundaries." Another big word! Thank you, internet search.

In his teen years, the load dumped on Marina bothered him. He'd tried to help her where he could. Well, he couldn't tutor other students or check her siblings' homework. But he could do the dishes or make sandwiches like nobody's business. He'd tried to tell her then that she'd been shouldering too much. But her father had run a tight ship, and with him at the helm, she'd been too entangled in obligation to start a mutiny.

Granted, the boys at the ranch had plenty of chores growing up, but the load was spread evenly.

Something flashed in her eyes but disappeared before he could decipher it. "Besides, clearly I'm not the sister best suited for cooking."

He spread his arms but jerked his hand back when he touched her arm. A blaze of awareness shot through him. "You have lots of other talents."

"Really?" She almost sounded... coy. Did she have any idea what that did to his senses?

Earth to Kai. He paused. As much as he needed Marina tomorrow, most likely, it wasn't what *she* needed. "Then you should take the day off tomorrow. Get some rest. You deserve it."

She hesitated as if considering it, then shook her head, sending those golden waves flying, mesmerizing him again. "I want to know what happened to Blake. And I do want to help you find him if I can."

Glad he'd see her tomorrow, he smiled. "Thank you." But she didn't say she wanted to spend time with him.

Then guilt needled again. He should be more worried about Blake. He was a bad brother. That was, if they were brothers indeed. He shouldn't let Marina become his entire world. And he did worry about Blake. Was it wrong that Marina so consumed his thoughts there wasn't much place for anything else?

How was he going to fill that gigantic void when she left?

Barks reached them from inside. Marina jumped to her feet. "I'd better go before Buttercup wakes up Saylor and the entire neighborhood."

The front door opened. "I believe it's too late for that." Saylor appeared on the porch holding a squirming dog against her pink pajamas and scuffling her feet in matching fluffy slippers. "At least, on my part."

She probably helped pick the pink Bay and Basin uniforms with their embroidered flamingo under the restaurant name. He suspected Marina hated those, though she looked so sweet and soft in the one she wore, and the color brought out the natural glow to her skin.

"Hi, Saylor!" He waved to her, and she returned the hand wave. Then he got up in case she wanted to sit on the swing.

"Oh hello, my darling! Did you miss me?" Marina opened her arms, and Buttercup practically leaped into them.

Kai knew the feeling.

"Well, hello to you, too, sis." Saylor ran her fingers through her already disheveled long hair, hair several shades darker than Marina's. "Thanks for waking me up in the middle of the night." Her tone lighthearted, she settled on the swing and rocked back and forth. Then she opened the empty container. "And add insult to injury—no food."

"Sorry. Thank you for taking care of Buttercup. I, um, I was just going inside."

"You sure were." Saylor smirked from Kai to Marina and back.

Marina visibly swallowed, then patted the puppy who happily licked her face. "I'll need the morning off from the restaurant tomorrow."

"You're not serious." Saylor grimaced, all teasing notes disappearing.

"I am." Marina pulled her shoulders back. "Gale will be here tomorrow and will help you. And I need a morning off."

You go, Marina! He mentally did a fist pump.

"I'm not so sure about Gale helping." Saylor sighed. "One has to push her in the behind most of the time to get anything done."

Kai searched his memory about Gale's likes and dislikes. "Or maybe you could lead her where you need her. You know, with food."

"Ha!" Saylor chuckled. "Good point. Works with Buttercup. I might be able to *bribe* Gale to work. And it's unfair you got stuck with doing most of the work by yourself again, sis. I'll cover for you. But you're taking Buttercup with you. I found a puddle during my lunch break today."

"Deal," Marina said fast. Buttercup rewarded her by snuggling in her hands.

"Thank you, Saylor." He rubbed the puppy's head, and if he accidentally touched Marina's arm, so be it. The simple touch sent something akin to an electrical current, but a pleasant one, through him. Marina looked up, her eyes wide.

"Huh." Saylor broke the moment. "I'd better head inside. *Some* of us have to work tomorrow morning. Good night, sis. 'Night, Kai."

"Me, too." Marina got up after her sister. "Good night, Kai." She disappeared inside the house, leaving a lot of unanswered questions.

How could he stop falling for her? What could've happened to Blake? How could they find him? And what had bothered her at Kennedy's place?

Chapter Eight

As Kai drove Marina home, the puppy stretched on her lap, taking a nap while lulled by the car's movement. Usually, Kai was the optimistic one in all circumstances, doing his best to make Marina smile. The roles were reversed this morning.

Since their visit to the police, Marina had told him several times that it would all work out somehow, and they'd find Blake. But, just as he knew all her facial expressions, he knew every tone of her voice. This was the way she'd sounded when she'd tried to persuade *herself* about something. For example, that it was her responsibility to take care of her siblings because she was the eldest or that her father had her best interests at heart by pushing her.

The news they'd received this morning was troubling, and even Kai was out of jokes. Blake still wasn't answering his phone, and that cottage seemed empty. Blake's relatives and friends hadn't heard from him. He hadn't returned to his home. He was missing. And it turned out, his sister was already in Port Sunshine, though she stayed at an inn where she'd miraculously found a room.

Kai slowed to take a turn. "We'll figure something out."

People often thought he was an eternal optimist. But he'd had to cultivate it from an early age. Granted, his mom and siblings had treated him as one of their own and never distinguished between bloodline or not. And while he'd never pretended to be like them—with an appearance like his he couldn't anyway—deep down he didn't want them to regret adopting him.

He'd also realized early enough that people liked someone with a smile way more than with a frown. Smiling so often had a negative side, though. Some people assumed him superficial for that reason and hinted he didn't care deeply enough. Marina couldn't be one of those people, could she?

Once again, guilt stabbed him. He should be thinking about how to find his supposed brother, not about Marina.

He was out of his league when searching for someone, but he knew someone who wasn't. Barrett. Well, missing people weren't his brother's specialty, either, but as a private investigator, he'd helped search for Skylar's grandmother's missing fiancé this spring.

"I'll ask Barrett to gather more information. And we're meeting with Blake's sister, Sue, today for lunch." He stopped at the red light, which caused Buttercup to lift her head and bark in protest. He glanced Marina's way while waiting for the light to change.

"I'll help. I mean, investigation isn't my forte, but I'm good with research. Blake couldn't have just disappeared into thin air." She rubbed the puppy's back with tenderness, but her expression was determined.

And while he loved seeing her smile, something about the combination of the soft sun-kissed waves of her hair and the gentle oval of her face with her mind at work—well, he found it irresistible. She was like a diamond, and not just because of her appearance but because her mind sparkled with ideas like diamonds and was just as sharp and clear.

"Thank you. Means a lot to me." And it did. His heart shifted, but so did the light to green. He took his foot off the brake and drove forward.

He'd called the police and the nearest hospitals yesterday. But he hadn't searched everywhere. There were plenty of other possible places. For instance... "Blake didn't look like the type, but do you think he could've gotten drunk and fallen asleep on the beach?" Optimistically, that would be the best scenario. Then he'd soon wake up and stumble back to *that* cottage. But too much time had passed for that, hadn't it?

"Or he could've drowned." As usual, Marina was the voice of reason. She must've noticed his wince because she added, "Sorry. It's most likely not the case. I'm just looking at different options. Force of habit."

He sent up a prayer for Blake.

Buttercup lifted herself on her paws and barked again as if not happy being confined to a car. Or it could be a different reason. Like...

Uh-oh.

He turned to the beach and pressed on the gas pedal. They'd better get there fast. "We can comb some territory. I'll call my brothers, and they'll pitch in searching the rest."

"I'm sure they will." Her voice was warm and wistful at the same time.

Was she thinking that her siblings had to be dragged kicking and screaming to help at the restaurant? And several couldn't be dragged at all?

Anger boiled under his skin like water in the pots they wouldn't oversee. He pushed it down. Some people called him impulsive, but they were wrong. Most of the time, he thought before he acted.

Buttercup's bark became more impatient.

"Yikes." Marina's voice became urgent. "I fed her, and she did her business in the morning. But it looks like she needs to do the latter again. We need a pet-friendly place."

He floored the gas pedal, then glanced at her lovely black blouse and latte-hued skirt. "That's a pretty skirt to ruin." Teasing notes coated his voice.

The moment he stopped the car, Marina shot out of it with Buttercup in her hands. She placed the puppy on the grass near the closest tree, and Buttercup marked her territory.

A chuckle escaped him. "Looks like we made it here just in time."

"Totally." One of those rare smiles brightened Marina's face. She crouched and petted the puppy. "Good girl."

Kai used the pause to call Darius and ask him to pass the information along. Then Kai, Marina, and Buttercup walked to the beach, the sun caressing their skin while the breeze played with her hair, making him a tad envious. Seagulls cried out in the distance. Several times, he nearly reached for her hand but stopped himself. There was a boundary he shouldn't be crossing, but oh how difficult that was!

The endless ocean stretched in front of them, sparkling under the bright sun as if mocking their sad reason for visiting. The waves' whisperings were quiet, soothing as if nothing bad could happen here.

Buttercup ran forward, sniffed the sand, ran back to Marina, barking about her findings, then ran forward again. She chased some gray bird, then wobbled back, whining that the bird didn't want to be friends and took off into the sky.

Oh, to be that young and curious!

Was he like that puppy, though? Running away from Marina, trying to forget her, and now coming back to her? All the while, she was clueless about his feelings.

He steered his thoughts toward his alleged brother as he surveyed the area. He'd purposefully chosen a more secluded, less touristy area since Blake would've been found in those already, most likely.

The puppy ran toward the water, and Marina scooped her up before a wave could get her. "Oh no, darling. You can't swim well yet."

Buttercup squealed, either from the water spray or from a protest over being restrained.

Marina carried the puppy away from the ocean.

Unlike Kai's mind, which often wandered, Marina's stayed on topic. "Why didn't Blake's sister call him sooner? Try to find him sooner?" She voiced the question he was asking himself. "If she'd already gotten here yesterday and had lunch with him?"

"Maybe they simply didn't talk in the evening." Kai had never had a sister—or a significant woman in his life other than his mother. He believed in marriage for life, but while he enjoyed dating, he hadn't met a woman yet he could imagine spending a lifetime with. Except Marina. Ironically, the one person who'd decided never to fall in love again.

She winced. "It's nice that his sister flew in to support him in meeting you. My siblings and I have often gone months without talking to one another. They probably wouldn't have done the same." Her hand flew to her mouth. "I shouldn't have said that. I shouldn't have made it about myself."

Anger surfaced again. Okay, maybe he *was* a bit impulsive. "It *should* be about you. You always help others. But it *should* be about you. You matter. A lot."

Especially to me.

"I didn't choose the way I grew up," she said. "And my life is different now."

Great. She was kind to him, and he blew up at her.

But he was right about some things.

His brothers did show up soon and divided the territory, Darius taking charge as he often had. While not the eldest brother, Darius was the embodiment of the responsible, silent type. Somehow, many years ago, he'd stepped into the fatherly role together with Dallas, the eldest. The rest of their siblings, no matter how rambunctious, had listened to them more than to their father. Never mind that Dad had acted with shouts, slaps, and beatings, while neither Darius nor Dallas had ever raised their voices. The siblings had respect for each other, but fear for their dad.

Sometimes Kai wondered if the combination of those feelings in one of them had led to what had happened to Dad in *that* cottage. In turn, Kai alternated between being a leader and a follower in the family, depending on the circumstances.

What kind of family had Blake grown up in? Besides his parents' professions, which Kai knew, he knew very little. And why hadn't he asked all those questions while he'd had a chance?

Well, because he'd thought he'd have plenty of chances. Wasn't life like that? Chances slipping away before one knew it. Like his chance with Marina had slipped away all those years ago.

Lord, please keep Blake safe wherever he is now. Please guide us in our search.

"I'll do some research to learn more about Blake's adoptive family. It's amazing how much people share on social media these days. Hopefully, I'll find something useful." Marina seemed to read his mind again—she did it outrageously easily, except for when it came to his feelings for her.

She worried about the case—*his* case—while his thoughts kept returning to her. She'd always been focused, which earned his admiration and irritation. Maybe because he'd never been the object of her focus.

"Thank you." He made sure he kept scanning the beach instead of looking at her. Then the memory of the way his father *allegedly*—he'd started to use Marina's words!—died made him frown. "You don't think Blake would commit suicide, do you?"

She stopped suddenly, and Buttercup bumped into her and growled, then wobbled around and ran forward. "You're thinking about your father, aren't you?"

"Yes." He kicked seaweed out of the way. Driftwood lodged along the tide line, but nothing a grown man could hide behind. Or his body.

Kai swallowed hard. No need to think like that. He'd just found someone who could be his brother, a connection to the identity that eluded him all his life. He wasn't going to lose him again.

If that made him selfish, so be it. Most people were selfish in some ways. He just hid it less than others. He stole a glance at Marina. Except her. She wasn't most people in many senses.

Buttercup pivoted toward a broken bottle.

"No, no, no!" Marina rushed after the puppy and scooped her up despite Buttercup's loud protests and enthusiastic squirming. "You don't want to cut your paw, do you?"

He picked up the bottle fragment to throw it away later. Children often ran barefoot here, and several families were at the beach already. But some people didn't care.

The puppy settled in Marina's hands by the time she joined him again. "Suicide could be a possibility, but I hope I'm wrong. No suicide note was left at *that* cottage from what we could see in the camera recording. Well, some people don't leave notes before attempting suicide, so there's that. Blake didn't look like a person feeling hopeless. He seemed excited to have found you. But from what I've heard and read, it's often difficult to say whether someone has suicidal thoughts. Maybe we can ask his sister today if he's ever made any attempts on his life, if he's been giving away prized possessions lately, or if there's a history of suicide in the family."

Like in his.

But in the Lawrence family, it was the opposite. If there was a feeling of hopelessness at the ranch before that tragic night, the entire family—minus one—could breathe easier afterward.

"I wouldn't say it in front of his sister," he cautioned.

"Right." She was quick to agree. "Neither would I."

As they walked further, he picked up another glass bottle, this one still intact. He stifled his irritation. Just as the Lawrences were his adopted family, this was his adopted hometown, and he felt protective of both. Some people left litter on the beautiful sandy beach where gentle cerulean waters had welcomed them. But then, some people went through life leaving a lot of trash in other people's hearts. It wasn't his business to judge, but it wasn't easy.

Lord, please forgive me.

"Sometimes I must ask painful questions in court. I don't have any other choice," she muttered as if trying to justify herself.

His eyes widened. "Do you... Don't you love your job?"

She paused before answering, and that was an answer in itself. "It's what I'm good at. It's what I worked hard for. It's what I trained for."

He kept his focus on his surroundings and the search. But something inside him ached, and he prayed for her. "All true, but does it make your heart sing?"

She sighed. "It's a job. A responsibility. I mean, does your job at the ranch make your heart sing?"

Good tactic, turning the question back on him. "Not always, but often, it does. I love knowing we're feeding the country. And I enjoy working with my brothers and our animals. Note how I said *and*, though some of my brothers can behave like animals from time to time. For example, Darius can be stubborn like a mule. Though I guess my brothers could say I chatter like my parrot."

"Oh, come on. Seriously, Kai?" Even without looking at her, he could tell she rolled her eyes. He was that attuned to her.

"And in other times... I'm a versatile cowboy. Work at the ranch is only part of what I do. I like making people smile as I run the stationery store. Or putting grins on children's faces as I pretend to be a pirate in the shipboard reenactment show." Was he scattering himself in different places because he still didn't know 100 percent where he belonged?

"You do great in all your roles," she whispered.

His heart warmed. But he had to give credit when it was due. "Remember how it all started with the pirate thing?"

"Yeah." She toed some kelp out of the way but didn't let Buttercup on the sand yet. "You got into a fight at school and had a black eye. Your mom made you wear an eye patch. They were looking for someone to play a pirate in the school play, and I said why don't you try out? You were the best pirate our school ever had, and not because of the eye patch."

"And you aced science fairs. But returning to your job." He wasn't letting her off the hook so easily. A large pile of driftwood tangled in a sun-bleached snarl, so he checked it before continuing. "Was it *your* dream or your father's?"

"Mine in the sense that it let me get away from my father. I was privileged. I got an opportunity not all of my siblings had, so I had to pay my dues. And then in a way, it became my ex-husband's dream. He liked having me as his protégée. Teaching me. Molding me."

"But what did *you* want?"

Another sigh left her lungs before the seagulls' screams carried it away. "It was easier not to ask myself that."

"Didn't you say sometimes we have to ask painful questions?" Was he pushing her too far?

"I did say that. Well, I don't have the answer yet. I'm too used to answering the question of what I *should* do. Not what I *want* to do."

"That's not right." He wanted to reach for her hand but stopped himself.

Then he made the mistake of glancing at her again. Buttercup, in the total reverse of mood, licked Marina's nose, and she chuckled before putting the puppy on the sand. Then she straightened out, and her blouse sleeves flapped in the wind like a sail on a pirate ship.

Maybe it was the way the sun lit her gorgeous hair or reflected in her blue eyes. Or maybe it was the way a soft beginning of a smile played on her delectable lips, like a budding spring flower with petals as gentle as her skin.

Or was it the pent-up longing he'd hidden over the years? Or his reckless impulse? But as she stared at the beach past him, he leaned toward her, desperate to brush his lips against hers.

Could he dare tell her how he felt about her? He might not get another chance. "I always wanted to tell you—"

"Look!" she screamed. "Look! Do you see it?"

"What?" He craned around to see what she was pointing at as his gut tightened. Maybe the missed opportunity was a sign he should keep his feelings to himself.

Barking loudly, Buttercup took off before Marina did. He followed them and caught up fast. They approached what appeared to be a folded pile of clothes on the sand. He scooped up Buttercup before the puppy could trample on it.

Marina leaned toward the clothes. "Doesn't that look like Blake's slacks and burgundy tie?" Her nostrils flared. "And they smell of whiskey."

Chapter Nine

The scent of freshly grilled steak teased Marina's nostrils as Gale glowered at her in Bay and Basin's kitchen hours later. "So you're going to dump all the work on me while you just enjoy lunch with Kai? Typical of you."

Marina cringed first from guilt, then from the unfairness of Gale's comment. But then, she'd partially created the dynamic herself, always feeling responsible for her younger siblings and picking up their slack. She could defend herself by arguing how she'd done most of the work growing up. Or how she and Saylor had been managing Bay and Basin since Mom left for the cruise.

Instead, Marina shrugged. "Yes."

Then she whirled around, picked up two glasses of iced tea, and strode out of the kitchen.

Saylor snickered behind her back. "Don't look so blustery. It's not like you have to live up to your name full time, Gale. Time to get to work. Lots of potatoes are calling your name, ready to be peeled."

Smiling, Marina looked over her shoulder. "And please send someone with shrimp skewers as appetizers when you have a chance, will you?"

Gale groaned before Marina swung through the door. Maybe Marina'd pushed things too far, but being kind and doing everyone else's work hadn't served her well all these years.

It was still early for lunch with Kai and Blake's sister, but Marina wanted a respite for herself. The place was buzzing already and would get worse with the lunch crowd.

She'd prefer to sit on the patio deck with its subtle marine watercolors where Skylar had long-ago painted the tables with pelicans and fish and the view offered a special portal into a dreamy world. But many other people preferred it, too. For this meeting they needed privacy, so Marina chose a booth at the end of the restaurant. She hurried there, nodding to several patrons, and placed the glasses on the table.

Then she sat on the bench as blue as the sea beneath netting strung across the ceiling and sipped sweet cold liquid to clear her mind. Usually, she kept her mind focused and everything in it organized into neat compartments. With her upbringing, she'd had to.

Lately, that mind was scattered, and Kai was the reason. Their relationship was changing, but how and how much, she wasn't sure. Did she want it to change? Her heart shifted. Okay, she *wanted* them to be more than friends. But she *shouldn't* want that.

Her fingers slid around the tall, smooth glass. She couldn't afford to have her heart broken again by a man who couldn't commit to one woman. And she was leaving soon anyway. Besides, she had other priorities right now, like finding Blake and keeping Bay and Basin afloat, the duty she skipped right now. She suppressed another sting of guilt.

Then all logical thinking flew out of the nearby window as Kai walked toward her, a slow grin spreading on his handsome face. Her heartbeat picked up at the mere sight of him. It took him longer to walk to the table than it had for her because people greeted him and he stopped for quick chats. They'd grown up in the same place, but he was extremely well-loved while she was... was just there.

Greedily, she wanted all his attention to herself. Her insides heated up, and she did her best to cool herself with more sweet tea.

Finally, he sat opposite her. "I'm so glad you're already here."

"Thanks." She basked in the glow of his smile, but then, so did many people here. She forced herself to think about the matters at hand. Practical matters, and not how he made her heart stutter. She slid the untouched glass along the table toward him. "I took the liberty of getting us drinks. And hopefully, shrimp skewer appetizers. But we'd better wait until Sue is here to order."

"Good idea on both." He scooped up a handful of sugar packets, lined them up, then ripped them open.

"Any news about Blake?"

His eyes turned sad as he poured the sugar granules into his drink. "No. I mean, not yet. The police said fibers on the carpet in that cottage matched the fibers in the slacks you found on the beach."

"But who'd go to the beach wearing dressy slacks and a dressy shirt?" Her mind whirled. "Plus, a tie?"

"Maybe if he'd been upset about something and not thinking?"

In her job, she'd learned things often weren't what they appeared. A lot of times, things were how someone *wanted* them to appear. She leaned forward, examining other options. "Maybe the answer can be found on his cell phone."

Kai's brows furrowed. "His phone is missing. And he didn't bring his laptop on this trip."

What about... "The whiskey scent? Did the police check the local bars?"

"If he got drunk, it wasn't there. Not at *that* cottage, either, it appears. There were no whiskey bottles there."

He stopped talking as Gale, who'd refused to wear the "childish" pink Bay and Basin uniform, stomped over to a nearby table with a tray, glaring at Marina, the aroma of biscuits and fried fish drifting to them.

Uh-oh. Marina tensed, ready to duck because she wouldn't put it past her sister to make her wear the food on the tray. Dear sis could claim she'd stumbled because hadn't Marina done the same her first day here? Made Kai wear the food?

Whew.

"He could've thrown the bottle away." Marina released a pent-up breath and drank more of her cold tea as Gale clomped away, thankfully with the tray intact. No appetizers for Marina yet, though.

"But most likely it was at someone else's place. Or it could be at the beach, and he threw the bottle in the ocean." She recalled Kai picking up several bottles lately, but they were beer bottles, not whiskey.

"Barrett is establishing the timeline and what Blake did the day he disappeared."

Marina nodded. "Good idea." A pleasant hum spread through her blood. She enjoyed this. Well, talking to Kai, being in his presence, his attentive gaze on her, of course. But also unfolding the mystery.

His free hand moved toward her. "I wanted to tell you something this morning. So, while we're still relatively alone..." Then his gaze flicked to someone she couldn't see behind her. "Or maybe we're not alone anymore."

What or who did he look at? And what did he want to tell her? Her breathing went shallow, and she did her best to ignore her disappointment over the interruption. She leaned outside the booth and glanced around.

Austin entered the restaurant, waved, then walked over. "I've got a lull between furry and feathery patients. Do you need help with the lunch crowd?" He jerked a thumb toward Kai. "Considering that my brother here is slacking off."

Wow. Kai's family was really something.

"Hey! I've got to eat. Besides, we're having an important meeting, bro." Kai tugged at his earring.

"And now I'm being dismissed." Austin feigned disappointment.

"No, it's not like that." Marina shot to her feet. "I do appreciate your offer. But we're better staffed today. And I roped Gale into helping."

"That must've taken a lot of rope," Austin muttered, then held up both hands in a stop gesture. "I mean, never mind."

Marina waved to the dining hall. "Why don't you have lunch since you're here? On the house."

"Thanks. But I'm good. I'll head back to the clinic." Then his eyes widened, and he stopped talking.

Marina shifted on the padded aquamarine booth to see who or what he was looking at. Thankfully, only one person was entering Bay and Basin then.

Kennedy.

She waved but didn't join them. The latter didn't surprise Marina. Kennedy had a reputation as a hermit and rarely visited local establishments, except for her properties, of course. Which made it surprising that she came here at all.

"On the other hand, as my brother put it, I've got to eat." Austin came out of his stupor.

Kai spread his hands. "It's about time you start listening to my wisdom."

"I won't intrude on your meeting, though." Austin walked away before Marina could protest. He didn't choose the same table as Kennedy who disappeared into another private booth, but he settled into a spot where he'd clearly see her.

Interesting.

Saylor strode to them, her cheeks flushed as bright a pink as her flamingo-hued uniform. She winked as she settled a tray of skewers with grilled shrimp and vegetables on the table. "Enjoy. I figured I'd better bring them here myself."

"You're awesome, sis." Marina breathed in the mouth watering aroma.

"Yeah, no kidding." Saylor laughed before she retreated to the kitchen.

Kai bowed his head and said grace. Marina's stomach clenched at yet another difference between them.

The appetizers were a feast for the eyes and the stomach, but once done with half of hers, she leaned forward and lowered her voice. "Do you know if your brother likes Kennedy? And if so, why doesn't he approach her?"

"Difference in social statuses." Kai shrugged over his skewer. "Plus, Kennedy isn't exactly the most approachable woman in the world. She could likely fill all the glasses here with ice with just one glance. And he probably doesn't want to appear a gold digger."

Marina shook her head. "Nobody who knows Austin would ever think that. Your brother is a great guy and deserves to be happy."

"I'll talk to him later. But I can't make him do what he's reluctant to do."

And Marina should back off. Had she behaved this way while growing up? She didn't think she'd bossed her siblings around. But sometimes, she'd felt she did know better than they did—felt nothing, she had known better than they did. But... Was that what Gale's irritated comment today was all about?

Kai checked his watch. "Blake's sister is running late. I hope she's okay."

Marina's gut tightened. "Me, too."

His gaze sharpened as he placed his glass on the table and studied her. "What did you get upset about when we were leaving Kennedy's place?"

Marina grimaced. But something about his comment tugged at her. Ice clattered in her glass as she took a sip, thinking. Yes, his acute attention to her, and it pleased her on a deep level. "Now you're going to tell me I have different kinds of upsets."

"You do. It was the *puzzled* kind of upset. But usually, when you're puzzled by something, you like figuring it out. Your brain likes a challenge. You didn't look like you wanted to figure out that one."

She tensed, but a part of her—a large part—was glad. "You know me well. Why?" And why did the answer matter so much?

"We've known each other since we were children. It's natural." He shrugged and wiggled a slice of red pepper from his skewer.

"Yes, but I've known your brothers and my siblings since we were children, too. They don't know me as well as you do." She munched on another shrimp. The cook deserved a raise, but it wasn't up to her to give it. Huh. Did this place start growing on her?

Growing up, she'd resented the restaurant because it seemed to have taken their mother away from them. Not only had Marina missed her mother's attention but she'd also had to shoulder the burden of looking after her siblings. And when she'd been called back here to do things she had no clue about, she hadn't been thrilled, either.

But now, relaxing at lunch with Kai, she saw the place differently and basked in its cozy, welcoming side.

A teen couple from a nearby table left with take-out boxes that smelled like french fries, and a couple of smiling retirees in sandy-toned flip-flops and Hawaiian shirts with bright magenta hibiscus print took their place.

But Sue was still a no-show. And while worry clenched Marina's stomach, deep inside, she harbored selfish gratitude for more stolen minutes with Kai. As long as the lady showed up alive and well.

"I paid attention to you." His gaze stayed unwavering on her as if to prove his point. He leaned toward her, his entire posture showing interest. His hand moved toward hers again and stopped only inches before touching her fingers.

Warmth spread through her, and her temperature kicked up a notch. She'd never met anyone who'd created such a whirlwind out of her feelings. Not even Travis, and she did love him. "Why?"

The buzz of voices increased, and more people passed by. But she could see only one person.

Emotions darkened his already dark eyes. "Because I cared. I still do. I always will."

She knew he meant every word, and her temperature kicked up another notch. Did she dare say it? "I care about you, too." Her fingers moved toward his and nearly covered the tiny distance between them.

But what if he meant it as a friend? She jerked her hand back and drained the rest of her iced tea. Then she nibbled at another crisp and juicy shrimp. She needed to keep her focus where it belonged. And she didn't answer his question. "I might be imagining things or remember it wrong about Kennedy."

Kai chuckled. "In all the time I've known you, which is nearly my entire lifetime, you've never imagined things or remembered them wrong."

Was that true? Or was she imagining attraction in his eyes now? "It's vague. It's the sound her bracelets make when she moves. And the scent of her perfume. I feel like I remember that sound and scent, but it's from so many years ago that I might be wrong."

"Remember from where?"

She hesitated, then plunged forward. "Your ranch when I was a teen. Your dad opened the door and said he was the only one home. I walked past him and said I'd wait. I think I heard that sound and smelled that scent then."

Marina rubbed her arms, her heart thudding over something else she needed to say as he sat there processing what she was insinuating. She shouldn't be sitting here alone with Kai, fantasizing that it was a date. He deserved to be keeping up his life, not catering to her. She took in a deep breath, then pushed the air and words out of her lungs. "I know you said you weren't seeing anyone. But if you want to ask someone out, please don't let us investigating this together stop you."

There. She was a good friend, right?

His eyes widened. "Why would you even say that?"

"Well, in high school, you were with a different girl every week, so…" She waved a hand as her voice trailed off. Great. She helped herself to more shrimp from her skewer to cover her embarrassment. Now her suggestion didn't sound so good. And she hadn't wanted to say it in the first place.

"People change. I haven't dated in half a year." His eyes darkened, and he now left his skewer untouched. "If we get a label in high school, it doesn't mean we have to carry it our entire lives. If someone is labeled a jock or a popular cheerleader or a mean girl or a player, in my case—"

"Or an awkward geek, in mine," she interrupted and, once again, put a foot in her mouth. Usually, she weighed her every word, but Kai had a strange effect on her. Yet a part of her—a significant part—was glad he hadn't dated in some time.

Marina didn't have a chance to say anything else because a tall, slender woman with stylishly curled chestnut-hued hair walked into the restaurant. She wasn't just attractive—she was movie-star gorgeous. No wonder, as she was an actress. Having looked her up online, Marina recognized the woman as Blake's sister, Sue Park.

Sue Park moved with the confidence of a woman who knew how stunning she was. At the entryway, she paused to tuck a designer purse against her designer lavender pantsuit, and dangling diamond earrings reflected the lamplight. Her plump cherry-red lips pouted, their luscious shape likely enhanced by injections to make them fuller, and one could sweep the floor with her eyelashes.

Then her expensive heels clicked against the floor before she stopped by their table, her smile beautiful but cold. "Good morning. Mr. Lawrence and Ms. Helms?"

Morning? It was lunchtime. Marina clamped down the comment. Apparently, Sue Park was *not* an early riser. While Marina was a morning person, she understood people worked different schedules or lived different lifestyles.

"Please call me Kai." Kai grinned and gestured to the seat. "A pleasure to meet you, Ms. Park."

She took her seat and slid her purse onto the table. Its oversized golden clasp clattered before a fish painted on the tabletop as if it were a lure trying to catch the thing. Like the same lure, her smile visibly warmed. "Call me Sue."

Riiight. Kai had that effect on women. Nothing unusual. Jealousy would be ridiculous. Especially after Marina had suggested he should ask someone out on a date—all while wishing to be that someone on a date with him just as she'd longed to when she was an awkward, gawky teen.

Marina resisted the urge to grind her teeth. Hopefully, the smile she foisted onto her lips didn't look like a scowl. Absolutely no need to assert her territory. Kai *wasn't*—never had been, never would be—her territory.

"And please feel free to call me Marina." She reached across the table to shake Sue's hand. "Great to meet you, though I wish it were under different circumstances."

As she slid her hand free, Sue's gorgeous smile dimmed as if she just remembered her brother was missing. "Yes. I wish that, too."

"I hope it's okay we took the liberty to order appetizers." Then Marina recalled a common allergy and suppressed a grimace at her oversight. "I hope you don't have a shellfish allergy."

Logically, Sue wouldn't have agreed to meet in a surf and turf restaurant, then. But extra caution wouldn't hurt.

"That's fine. But I doubt they have options I like here." Sue wrinkled her particularly petite nose at the laminate menu with its hand-drawn depictions of the scrumptious dishes. A reprinted version of the same menu Skylar had illustrated, and the dishes Marina's mother and now Marina had worked so hard providing. "This probably isn't the nicest place in town."

Marina tensed.

"It actually is," Kai said before Marina had a chance to. "They have excellent choices here. I'd recommend the Fisherman's Catch."

Jan came to take their order.

"I'll need more time." Sue pouted in Kai's direction instead of looking at the waitress.

"Well, I'm ready to order." Marina shouldn't be fuming so much that smoke might be coming out of her ears. But she wasn't going to starve on Sue's behalf, either. She smiled at Jan. "I'd like to have shrimp scampi, please. And extra biscuits."

Sue's eyes widened. "That's a lot of butter."

Marina beamed at Sue. "That's one of the best parts."

Kai opted for the lobster.

"Excellent choice." Marina sent an extra beam in his direction. Then she turned to Sue. "By the way, this is my mother's restaurant. I'm running it in her absence."

Sue shrugged as she rearranged her hair. "I don't know why anyone would work in a restaurant. So noisy and tiring."

Good thing that shrimp scampi hadn't arrived yet, or Marina would choke on it.

But Kai rushed to defend her honor again. Sort of. "That's like asking why some people work as ranchers. Backbreaking work and can be so... so dirty. But we love it, and we feed the country. I'm a rancher, by the way."

Instead of displaying any embarrassment, Sue batted her clearly false eyelashes. "Oooooh, you're an authentic cowboy. How fascinating!" Sue looked at Kai as if she were the cat and he the canary—or parrot. And no, Quiet wouldn't like the comparison.

It rubbed Marina the wrong way, but then again, she didn't have a right to feel territorial. The lingering taste of her shrimp skewer turned bitter, and she flushed it down with a drink.

This would be her life if she fell for Kai. She took another sip of the cold sweet liquid. It was high school all over again. Pretty, popular girls constantly flirted with Kai right in front of Marina. Everyone knew they were just friends, and besides, no female had considered a bespectacled geek with braces a threat.

Marina pulled her shoulders back. She was successful and beautiful now, and even if she wasn't, no need to feel insecure again.

Maybe Sue did feel Marina might be a threat because she waved a finger between them, her voice melodic. "Pardon my curiosity, but are you two...?"

"We're just friends." Uh-oh. Marina's growl wasn't melodic. She'd always had better control of her voice and expression. Usually, she was much more professional. And no need to antagonize someone who might have the information they needed.

But surprisingly, Blake's sister hadn't asked a single question so far about her missing brother. Marina filed away that important information. Often, the lack of something meant much more than the presence of it.

Barrett had done great research, and Marina could guess some dynamics in the Park family. But she shouldn't make any premature judgments, either. So she rearranged her features into a friendly expression and imagined herself slathering honey over her voice like she'd soon slather butter over her biscuits. "It must be heartbreaking not knowing what happened to your brother." She glanced at Kai, her heart going out to him. "Who might be Kai's brother, as well. I'm sure the police will do everything to find Blake."

Now of all times would be when Jan brought the tray with their food, giving Sue a respite to compose herself and even finally place an order. She went for a salad with dressing on the side and water with lots of ice and two extra lemon slices. No surprise there.

Marina savored her shrimp scampi, the shrimp sautéed to a perfect pink and expertly flavored—even considering she'd eaten in seriously posh restaurants with important clients in big cities. *So there.*

"Didn't the police find his clothes on the beach? And didn't it look like he was drunk? With his car abandoned off-road in the bushes nearby? Also, the police informed my parents earlier today that they found a handwritten suicide note. They're verifying whether it's authentic."

Marina winced at this new information. She didn't like to be unprepared. But worse, Kai frowned. Oh no.

Her insides squeezed painfully for the life taken so early and so tragically. She sent him a compassionate glance, wishing she could reach out to comfort him.

Their gazes met and held, the hurt and disbelief in his boring into her, and her hand moved toward him. She stopped herself and thrust her hand into her lap. When their gazes separated, she did her best to shut off her emotional part to think clearly.

She could relate to Kai's disbelief. The Blake she'd met didn't look like a man who'd given up. But then, lots of people who committed suicide didn't exhibit signs, often taking their loved ones and friends by surprise. Like in Kai's adoptive father's case.

She pursed her lips. That case didn't sit well with her, either, and Kai sometimes expressed his disbelief about it, too. But then there hadn't been a suicide note in his father's case.

Okay, okay. She'd best focus on *this* so-called suicide.

"That changes things a lot," she said carefully. "What did the note say?" She gave her shrimp scampi its due attention, though now she barely tasted it. Yet nutrition was important for the body and mind, and her mind couldn't live on coffee alone. Even though some days it felt as if it ran in her veins by now.

"Just that he couldn't take it any longer and he asked for forgiveness for the hurt his decision would cause." Sue poked her fork into the salad that arrived with her drink.

Marina did her best to work up some sympathy. This woman might've just lost her only sibling. How horrible that Marina had to make an effort for something that should've come naturally. Was it because of decades of hiding her emotions?

While she wasn't close to her siblings any longer, she'd be devastated if she lost one of them. And she shouldn't take it personally about the food. It must've been difficult to work in an industry that expected women to stay young and slim. Besides, Marina might be projecting her former insecurities from years of seeing Kai with pretty, outgoing girls who didn't have to hide their interest in him like she'd had to.

Maybe she should follow suit about proper nourishment. She looked at the biscuits with longing, breathed in their enticing scent, and assaulted her garden salad with a vengeance. "I'm so sorry for your loss."

"We truly are," Kai added, and something broke in his voice.

This time, Marina didn't fight it. She reached for his hand and squeezed his fingers, receiving a grateful glance in return. "For your loss, too." Then she withdrew her hand.

Sue's eyes narrowed. "That note was so typically my brother." She didn't say "our brother," maybe because they didn't have the DNA test results yet. Or maybe because that would add an icky factor to her flirting with Kai, even if they weren't related by blood.

"What do you mean?" he asked.

Sue moved toward him and smiled as if glad to have his undivided attention, and Marina had to work even harder to maintain an unbiased opinion while Sue coyly played with her hair. "So considerate, at least on the surface."

"He wasn't in reality?" Marina prompted when Sue didn't continue, then gave up on the rest of her salad and helped herself to the lonely biscuit. It melted in her mouth along with the butter.

"Listen, we weren't a happy little family. Blake was the perfect son. Always ready to follow orders. Like a puppy."

Huh. Marina's puppy never followed orders, and she had four pairs of shoes to prove it already. She swallowed around the lump in her throat because Buttercup wasn't really *her* puppy. Shoes were replaceable. Buttercup wasn't.

And she'd never be able to replace Kai in her heart.

"And of course, he just had to follow in Dad's career. How could it be any different?" Sue sneered and pushed her nearly full plate away.

Sometimes a direct approach was the best one. Marina took another bite from her biscuit and leaned forward. "I take it, you weren't a perfect daughter?"

Sue looked away. Those gigantic eyelashes hid the expression in her eyes and evoked memories of every large spider Marina had ever seen. "Yes, I acted out sometimes. But who wouldn't in my situation? My parents just threw money my way to shut me up."

Marina didn't act out growing up. Well, she didn't have a perfect brother but a bunch of unruly siblings she was somehow responsible for. "What are your parents like?"

Sue shrugged out of her jacket, and Marina scowled at the woman's revealing top. Well, this was just getting better and better. "Mom loves to play a prominent figure at charity functions. Dad used to be a workaholic who loved his career more than his family. Well, with the exception of Blake, but that was because my darling brother was going to continue Dad's important legacy. Dad tried to push me in that direction. I never had any interests in biology or chemistry and even less in working with human bodies." She shuddered. "How gross. I'll be a movie star one day and will show them all."

If Blake's suicide was staged, Sue had a strong motive to have a hand in his disappearance. Didn't she realize it? There could be another motive, as well. "Did Blake have a will?"

"Yes."

Marina thought so. Blake didn't look like a man who left things to chance. "Do you know who is named as his heirs?" Marina drained her tea. She glanced Kai's way again.

His face was stoic, and everything in her wanted to hug him. Even if she had to keep it a friendly hug.

"Sixty percent to his daughter and forty to me. Our parents are well off on their own." Then Sue's eyes narrowed again. "I should be grateful he left a suicide note. Or I could be under suspicion, right?"

No kidding.

"Was he under any distress that could've caused him to commit suicide?" Kai asked.

"I heard that some woman he dated dumped him recently. Makes sense. He wasn't popular with women. I'm sure his ex married him for money."

Ouch. But considering that Kai and Blake shared many facial features, didn't Sue realize that, by dissing Blake's appearance, she dissed Kai's, as well? And Marina—and many, many other women—found Kai extremely handsome.

"He seemed like a great guy," Marina cut in. "Besides being attractive. Lots of women would value a man like that."

Kai's gaze flickered to her and stayed longer than it should've. Her insides warmed under his attention.

"Well, apparently, whoever dumped him didn't." Sue waved off Marina's words.

"Where did you hear about that?" Kai munched on his fish.

Good question.

"I don't remember."

And a not so good answer. "What can you tell us about his daughter?" Marina had checked the posts online, but there, the girl just looked like a typical teenager.

Sue perked up. "She didn't take after Blake. I take her shopping sometimes. She *loves* shopping. Wants to be a fashion designer."

"Did Blake support that choice?" Kai's fingers wrapped around the tall glass.

"He said he did, but they still bickered from time to time."

And then there was an inheritance, which gave the young girl an extra motive. Was Marina so jaded after years on her job to think that about a girl who might be grieving her father right now?

Or maybe she'd simply learned the hard way that not everything was what it seemed.

Chapter Ten

Early the next morning, Marina settled behind her childhood desk where she knew every scratch. She opened a laptop in front of her and cuddled Buttercup on her lap. There was a purpose for both.

On the laptop, she arranged her mother's random lists into neat spreadsheets of restaurant supplies with the exact usage, cost, spikes, and changes amid other factors, then added formulas and conditional formatting. The same went for the budget. Mom most likely wouldn't continue using these, but an organizational bug in Marina prodded her to try.

The puppy in her lap had a different purpose. Marina scratched Buttercup's back, chuckling then as the little one turned to the side and exposed an unfairly unscratched tummy. Marina corrected the injustice as tenderness spread in her.

The first purpose was that Buttercup was a fantastic companion who never criticized Marina under the guise of encouraging her to do better.

I'm looking at you, Dad and Travis.

The second purpose was to prevent Buttercup from doing what she did at night—chew on Marina's shoes. So far Buttercup only chewed the right shoes, efficiently making both shoes unwearable.

"You should be grateful I didn't like those shoes much." Marina wiggled her fingers at the puppy.

Buttercup stretched, then tried to chew on Marina's finger as if to show she knew Marina wouldn't get angry anyway. She was right.

"Or are you saying I should change what shoes I buy? You see, those boring navy-blue loafers fit the image I needed to portray. You don't have to wear shoes or have an image to portray. You wouldn't understand."

Buttercup scratched behind her ear with her paw, which Marina took as yes on all counts. Marina reached for a new toy and placed it near Buttercup's nose because lots of shoes were still left unchewed, including Saylor's. And Saylor was way more attached to her fashionable shoes than Marina to her sensible ones. Buttercup latched onto the toy, and her little tail wagged fiercely.

"Good to be prepared, right?" Marina returned to her numbers.

The third purpose was to distract herself from thinking about Kai. Somehow, even in the middle of working with a multitude of numbers, her thoughts kept returning to Kai. Still, she managed to complete most of the spreadsheets, then scoop up Buttercup, and tiptoe into the kitchen.

"Let's refresh your water. And you deserve a treat for helping me with the spreadsheets." Marina refilled the water bowl. She'd already fed Buttercup and taken her outside first thing in the morning. But Marina loved spoiling the puppy, maybe because nobody had spoiled her while she'd been growing up. Except for Kai. He'd brought her candies first, books later, and then her favorite combo of books and chocolates.

Her rib cage constricted as Buttercup splashed water everywhere. The mischievous puppy already tugged at Marina's heartstrings. She'd never want to lose Buttercup.

And she didn't want to lose Kai. Which didn't make sense as she didn't have either of them to start with.

"Here's a treat for you." She handed Buttercup a biscuit, then soaked up the water on the floor with a paper towel. Buttercup would learn eventually. But would Marina's heart ever learn Kai was off-limits?

She washed her hands, the scent of orange liquid soap spreading in the kitchen, then filled the coffee pot, and turned it on. Buttercup chased her tail, then tired of it, and stretched in a sunspot on the tile to rest after all her hard work.

Marina's phone buzzed in her pocket as she settled with her coffee cup and a croissant at the table. She'd put it on low, mindful not to wake Saylor and Gale before work. Gale was grumpy as it was. Okay, fine, Marina just didn't want to deal with Gale this early in the morning. Or ever.

Marina fished the phone out of her pocket and smiled at Skylar's name on the screen. "Hello. How's the honeymoon going?"

"I don't think I've ever been so happy in my life. How's Buttercup? Does she give you much trouble?"

Marina's heart wrenched a little as she looked at the puppy. "She's perfect."

Buttercup stretched as if to show off all her perfection.

"Great! Can't wait to see her. How's it going at Bay and Basin?"

"I haven't burned it to the ground yet." Marina sipped her flavorful coffee, needing the energy boost. She'd sacrificed sleep to get work done, but it was getting more and more difficult. When would she ever allow herself to sleep in?

Skylar chuckled. "I hope you're still in Port Sunshine when we return, cuz. I missed you. A lot."

Marina's heart shifted, and she clattered her porcelain cup back to the table. "I missed you, too. A lot. But I have to go back soon."

"Have to or want to?" Skylar softened the hard question with her tone.

A lump formed in Marina's throat, but she pushed a bit of the flaky croissant and a sip of coffee with creamer past it. Nutrition was important. "I have to."

A sigh traveled down the line. "You haven't taken a vacation in years. Can't you take more time off? And I'm not just begging for myself. Other people I know would love to spend more time with you."

Kai?

Marina stopped herself from asking. "It's not as easy as it sounds. And... my life revolves around my job. It's pretty much my entire identity."

"I underestimated love once. Don't repeat my mistake. Though I understand our hometown wasn't such a good place for you because of everything your father and siblings threw at you."

Marina bit into her croissant as the lump diminished. Then she flushed it down with hot coffee. "You know, it's different this time. I dreaded coming here. But... it's like I'm coming up for air after drowning. I haven't smiled or laughed in years as much as I've smiled and laughed here these last days. I never thought I'd say it, but I dread leaving."

"Would that feeling be connected to a certain man named Kai?" Skylar's voice turned coy. "The grapevine says you've been spending *loooooots* of time with him."

Marina's heart skipped a beat. Buttercup got up, trotted over, toenails clicking against the tile, and placed her front paws on Marina's pajama pants.

Marina scooped the wriggly puppy to her lap again. "The grapevine wouldn't be your husband?" Who was also Kai's brother.

"Yup. But, Miss Smarty Attorney, don't try to deflect my question." If she were standing nearby, Skylar would be wiggling her finger now as Marina had done with Buttercup.

Marina drained her coffee, then scratched behind Buttercup's ear. "I'm helping him search for his missing brother."

"Huh. No other reasons? Didn't you have a crush on him as a teen?"

Marina cringed at her cousin's teasing. "Yeah, and he dated a different girl every month then. Sure, we're both single now, but I don't want to ruin our friendship. And if things turned serious—and I'd want them to turn serious—I wouldn't force him to leave his ranch and hometown where he's happy."

"And you can't leave your job." Skylar's voice grew quiet.

"Exactly. Besides, after a disastrous marriage to a player, I wouldn't dare put my heart on the line with a serial dater." Her glance landed on the framed photo of her and her siblings as children. Everyone was laughing. Except her. Even as a child, she'd been serious. "We're just too different."

"You know what they say about opposites attract. You liked physics." Skylar must've grimaced when she said that. As an artsy type, she'd never liked physics, and the closest she'd gotten to enjoying chemistry was mixing her paints—unless you thought of the chemistry between her and Dallas.

Buttercup slid off Marina's pajamas to the floor, thankfully without taking Marina's pants with her, and chewed on the hem before realizing the fabric wasn't nearly as yummy as shoes. So she went to splatter whatever water didn't get splashed around the first time.

Marina got up and did a cleanup, then refilled the bowl but with less water this time. "There's too much between us. And I can't imagine him committing to one woman."

After a pause, Skylar sighed. "You might be surprised."

"Well, I want to know how you're doing, and I've spent all this time talking about myself." Marina grimaced.

"I love married life." Skylar's voice perked up nearly to a squeal. "I know we'll have disagreements and arguments and differences. But right now, it's amazing. Maybe because we waited for it for so long."

"I'm happy for you." Marina truly was. But a small part of her wondered if one day she could meet a great man who'd love her as much as Dallas loved Skylar.

Or if she already had and kept pushing him away.

After their conversation, she'd just finished her breakfast when a text buzzed on her phone and Kai's contact flashed on the screen, making her smile.

Then her eyes widened at the words.

"I know it's last minute. But my brother found a friend of my birth mother in Memphis. As well as some of Blake's friends and colleagues. I'd like to fly there to talk to them and Blake's adoptive parents. I'd love your company and your help. Would you go with me, please?"

Her fingers hovered over the screen.

KAI COULD GET USED to Marina sleeping on his shoulder. She hadn't noticed that she'd drifted to sleep during the flight. He breathed in the subtle scent of her exquisite perfume and kept sitting quietly, afraid to stir. He'd have stopped breathing if he could. The plane trip was going to be shorter than he'd like.

Tenderness melted him as she nestled so close. But then his gut tightened.

What was he going to find in Memphis? Was the search even a good idea? Maybe he should've stayed at home looking for Blake. Worry dug its claws deep, and as Kai sent up a heartfelt prayer for his brother, urgency pressed on his chest. *His brother.* Yes, the DNA test results proved Blake was his brother, as well as an interesting and unexpected fact. They were *full* brothers, not half brothers. Hopefully, he'd find new clues about his missing brother and their birth family in Memphis. Either way, he was out of his comfort zone, and he had no experience searching for people.

Marina's hair tickled his neck.

Well, she had no experience, either. Still, she'd plunged into the search headfirst, no questions asked. She'd always amazed him.

His hand was becoming numb, but he didn't move it. He loved being in a close bubble with her, and his heart swelled again with mixed emotions, worry for Blake fighting with overwhelming tenderness for Marina. But he knew better than to try to change the path of a star in the sky.

He should be grateful to bask in her light, however long that might be. All he needed was to hear her breathing. She snored softly from time to time, and it made him smile. But he'd never mention *that* to her.

When their imminent landing was announced, he was ready to spring into action. Still, he wanted more time with her.

He touched her shoulder gently. "We're almost there."

She sat up with a start and blinked. "Oh, already?" Then she must've realized she'd fallen asleep on his shoulder because her cheeks pinked. Her golden-hued hair was matted on one side of her head, and it was beyond adorable.

"Yes. They announced that we'll be landing soon." He nearly had to sit on his hands to stop himself from reaching out to her.

"Thanks for waking me up." Her lips curved up. "And thanks for letting me sleep. Naps are important in my life." She clicked her seat belt closed and pulled her seat straight.

He hadn't touched his drink, so he offered the apple juice can to her. "Would you like it?"

"Sure." She nodded. "I'm thirsty. And apple juice is one of my favorites."

He knew it. That's why he asked the flight attendant for it.

Her fingers covered his, and for a few blissful moments, they lingered there. Their gazes met and held, and his heartbeat skyrocketed. Then the pink on her cheeks deepened, and she pulled her hand away and took the can without touching him.

"Thank you." She drained the can fast, probably because all the trays were supposed to be up and the flight attendant was moving along the aisle, gathering trash. Or maybe she really was that thirsty.

While he was thirsty for her. Warmth rose inside him. But so did his concern for her. "You don't have to work around the clock, you know."

She sent him a mischievous glance as she disposed of the empty aluminum can. "Even when I'm helping you?"

"Even when you're helping me. Or especially when you're helping me." The light to fasten seatbelts lit up, and he braced for increased atmospheric pressure in several senses. Including in the arguments with Marina.

"Now you're going to tell me there's more to life than work." She turned away and stared out the window.

He studied her beautiful profile. "There is."

When she faced him again, he winced at the pain in her cerulean eyes. Those eyes glistened as if she tried to hold in unshed tears, breaking his heart. "I'm not like you. It's difficult for me to make friendships. You're well-liked for *you*. I'm accepted for my contributions."

Did she believe that?

Everything inside him protested. "Not true. Okay, I'm indeed well-liked." Was it immodest of him to say that? But as an outsider, he'd put a tremendous effort into being well-liked. "But lots of people like you a lot." Him, for example.

Her eyes brightened, but her smile remained sad. "You're being generous, and I appreciate it. But I'm sure my siblings' opinions would be different. Except Saylor."

"Maybe that could change now," he said carefully. Usually, she bestowed words of wisdom on him, not the other way around. "Unlike in childhood, age doesn't matter now. You don't have to be a strict elder sister responsible for your siblings and stopping them from their shenanigans."

Her brows furrowed. "Is that the way people see me? As someone stopping them from having fun?"

He coughed as the pressure increased in his ears—and on his chest. Had he put a proverbial foot in his mouth? "No! Not at all. I'm saying that sometimes reaching out is difficult but worth trying. And in the interim, I'm happy to share my family." He smiled.

"Thanks. You all were always amazing to me. Especially you. But it's *your* family. And everyone loves you in town. Or at the ranch, animals included. As for me, work is all I have. It's all I am."

No! He leaned to her as much as the seat belt allowed. "Don't you know it? You're so much more than that. You're incredible, and you deserve to be where you're happy. Doing what makes you happy. Not just making others happy."

"I don't know where that place is any longer. And I don't like not knowing. The way I'm used to surviving is by structuring and organizing things. At least, in my mind."

"It's okay not to know sometimes. To take a leap of faith." He dared to place his hand on hers.

Her fingers fluttered, but she didn't remove her hand, which sent a jolt to his heart. "I don't know if I'm capable of that."

"You're capable of everything."

"Thank you." Her gaze lingered on him, and she shifted his way fully, sending his heartbeat into overdrive.

For a few seconds, her lips were so close to his that he had a wild hope she might kiss him. She removed her hand, but apparently, it was to touch his jaw with her fingertips.

Oh yes!

Emotion darkened her baby blues, and while he'd never drowned in the ocean, he was drowning in her eyes. The plane shook as it reached the ground, but it barely registered in the back of his mind. His pulse became even more erratic, reacting to her fleeting touch, to the anticipation of her kiss.

Then she leaned back in her seat as the plane landed and everyone started clicking their seat belts open. "You were always a great friend to me."

As she unlatched her seat belt, her words had the effect of a cold shower.

"You, too. To me," he said when he could find his voice, raspy as it was. On autopilot, he opened his seat belt. "I'll get our bags."

The announcement came to be careful with the bags in the overboard compartments as bags might've shifted during flight, but it was something inside him that had shifted.

"Let's wait until other people disembark." She stayed in her seat.

He'd wanted them to be more than friends so badly that he must've imagined his attraction was reciprocated. As people passed them, a teen boy chewing peanuts, then a tall, bearded man with a huge backpack that nearly knocked over a short bald guy behind him, Kai registered a weird feeling. As if... as if he were being watched.

No, that would be ridiculous.

"Now the clouds are above us again instead of under us," Marina said over the buzz of voices and footfalls. Despite her fascination with the stars and sky, she'd never had her head in the clouds to start with.

Did he, hoping for a future with her? His rib cage constricted.

Then she got up and slipped from her seat into the now nearly empty aisle. "Let's go find out more about your birth family."

Chapter Eleven

Was she afraid to fall in love with Kai because she was afraid to disturb the status quo? To plunge into the unknown, unplanned, and therefore so scary?

Or had she indeed been so heartbroken because of one player that she couldn't risk the same heartbreak from another one? And was the risk of losing her best friend even worth it?

For a minute on the plane, she'd forgotten all those questions and nearly kissed him. Her cheeks burned as he pulled out a chair for her at a cozy Memphis restaurant. She breathed in deeply, needing to ground herself in reality as dim lighting and a jazz band lent the atmosphere an intoxicatingly dreamy feel.

"Thanks." He obviously had no clue he could play with her heart as skillfully as the man on stage played his saxophone.

Barrett had found Kai's birth mother's closest friend and scheduled a meeting in an hour, so they had time. Marina took her seat, thanked the waitress for the menus, and then asked for a coffee and lemonade.

"Iced tea for me. Thank you," Kai said.

"Coming right up." The young girl with hazelnut-hued braids and dimpled cheeks smiled, then walked off, her heels clicking on the tiled floor, her braids jumping with each eager step. Oh, to be as carefree as that teen appeared!

"I hope you like it here." Kai gestured around.

He must've chosen this place because she'd mentioned she liked jazz. He'd always been attentive to her. Always encouraged her, be it to follow her childhood dreams or follow her happiness now.

Her insides warmed. "I love it. But I like the company even more."

While LED candles flickered on their table and glowed in wall sconces, the coffee aroma from a neighboring table reached her. Good thing she'd ordered one of her own. She needed an energy boost. At her age, she couldn't continue on pure willpower. Still, she couldn't believe she'd slept on the plane. Warmth uncoiled and stretched inside as she remembered waking up snuggled against his shoulder.

Focus, girl! She glanced over the menu, but she'd already looked it up when he'd told her where they were going and asked her opinion. She'd come prepared.

If only choosing her path in life was as easy as choosing a meal.

Hold on.

Did she think about choosing her path again?

Grinning, he set aside his menu and reached across the table as if to take her hand. Instead, he picked up the candle in its frosty red glass. "Yes, the company is the best. I could have a tuna sandwich on your porch with you, and it would be the best meal in the world and the best place for me."

How could she not smile in his presence, with such words? The corners of her lips curled up. "You don't even like tuna."

"Precisely." He turned the candle in his hands, its glow reflecting in his eyes. Or was that glow more? She could so easily imagine...

Marina nearly jumped when the young waitress then returned with their drinks and took their orders, breaking the interlude.

"I'll take barbecue ribs with arugula and roasted potatoes." Good, Marina managed to speak in her normal voice. All business, she returned her menu. "Thank you."

"That sounds great. Same for me." Kai handed over his menu, as well.

"Thank you," Kai and Marina said in unison.

Then he chatted with the waitress about the weather, the best ribs in town, and even the girl's favorite boy band.

Hmm. Interestingly, before walking off, the waitress smiled back only at Kai as if Marina didn't exist. Story of Marina's life. Whenever she went anywhere with him, people stopped to talk to the sociable Kai while the tense and awkward Marina waited on the side.

She picked up her lemonade, and her fingers tightened around her cold, smooth glass. She shouldn't begrudge him his popularity. And maybe it wouldn't hurt her to smile more and not look like she'd just swallowed a rod.

As soft, expressive jazz flowed, she sipped her cold, tangy liquid and studied him from behind the glass. He looked great in a dressy white shirt she'd never seen him wear, and his black hair was combed back and even styled with gel, another thing she'd never seen with him. A part of her missed his more relaxed, disheveled look. At least, he'd kept the earring that now glistened in the dim light from nearby sconces.

He'd been a great friend, but maybe she wasn't such a great friend in return. Yes, she'd joined him on this search, but when it came to emotional support, she wasn't the warm and friendly type. At least, not outwardly. No wonder she'd been called stuck-up in school.

She put the glass down. "How are you holding up? This place could be the one you came from." She stumbled. "I mean, the city, not the restaurant."

His grin didn't waver. "Well, you never know. Your mother once had to call the ambulance for mine when her contractions started early. But, yes, I know what you mean."

Was she poking into a wound she shouldn't be? For all her family's faults, they hadn't abandoned her as his birth family had. Her hand moved toward his. But touching him wasn't the right thing to do, so her fingers wrapped around the cold glass again instead. "If you don't want to talk about it..."

"I always want to talk." He chuckled, then took a sip of his drink. "I'm nervous, I admit. You're the only person I can talk to about this. Guys don't talk about emotions with each other."

What about one of your many girlfriends? Thankfully, she managed to stop the words before they slipped out. Was he on friendly terms with his exes? She only had one ex, and if she never saw him again, it would be too soon.

This time, she muted herself with coffee, its taste saccharine sweet with all the sugar packets she'd emptied into it. "It's okay to be nervous. Totally understandable."

"Well, you already know I have a marshmallow for a heart." He placed his palm on his chest in a dramatic gesture.

She smiled again. "I happen to love marshmallows."

Something changed in his eyes, but she couldn't decipher what it was because the waitress brought their food. When she stepped aside, Kai's strange expression was gone.

Marina's mouth watered at the sight of barbecue ribs smothered in sauce. He bowed his head and, based on the movement of his lips, silently said grace. Her heart shifted. She didn't need this reminder of how different they were. How different their lives were.

The food didn't look so mouthwatering now, but she picked up her fork with determination. Maybe partly because, in her childhood, you stayed hungry if you skipped a meal.

Then she did what she did best—worked with her mind instead of succumbing to her emotions. She munched on the roasted potatoes with purpose. Nutrition was important for brainwork. "Okay, let's go over the information Barrett sent about this friend." She paused because the saxophonist went over an exceptionally marvelous fragment. But she didn't come here to listen to jazz.

"Christine West was a maid at the hotel where my, um, alleged mother worked. They met there and became friends, probably because they were the same age, liked the same kind of music and movies, and both had college dreams. They went to college together. Christine did get a degree in nursing and now works at a hospital."

Marina filed that information in her brain as she munched on her barbecue ribs. They were delicious, proving the place's fame was well deserved.

Then something undecipherable put her on guard, and fine hairs at her nape stood on end. Almost as if... as if she were being watched. No, she must be imagining things. She'd been stalked once because of a case at her job. But she wasn't working on a dangerous case now. She swallowed hard.

Could this search be dangerous? Was there something in Blake's life—or in Kai and Blake's biological mother's life—a culprit wouldn't want anyone to find out?

Her insides went cold. But she was used to operating on the facts, not on her imagination. Nobody had stalked her or Kai yet, much less threatened them. What-ifs were never productive. She forked a potato and turned her thoughts where they belonged. "Is Christine married now? Any children?"

"Yes, on both counts. Two children. Girls, one a year younger than the other." He lifted his glass to his lips, and a wistful smile played on his lips. "Now studying in college on a scholarship for a music degree. The elder one wants to be a music teacher, and the other one is undecided. The elder one plays piano, and the younger one is a flute player."

She munched on the juicy rib and scanned the dining room again. Nobody seemed to pay extra attention to them. She must be paranoid.

"How fitting for a music city." Her heart warmed. Two of her sisters played musical instruments, and she'd been the one to chauffeur them to lessons and back as soon as she'd gotten her driver's license. They didn't choose it as their profession, but still, there was that. She hadn't thought there'd be a time she'd start missing her sisters deeply, but maybe it came. And time spent with Saylor now was a lot of fun.

But her thoughts should be directed to important matters, so she rerouted them to the next steps as she devoured the rest of her ribs, smothered in a rich sauce. "Hopefully, Christine might have an idea who your mother could've dated. And after that meeting, we'll be talking to Blake's friends, correct?"

"Yup, but we're going to his adoptive parents' place directly after Christine's." Kai gave due to his food, but something in his expression bothered her.

"We'll find your brother. And by 'we,' I mean the police, Barrett, and the two of us." Her stomach clenched. She had a few doubts, but he didn't need to know that. A friend's job was to be supportive. Though it wasn't just a job to her.

"Thank you for doing this for me." His voice softened as he pushed his empty plate away and studied her. "And it's probably selfish to say it under the circumstances, but I enjoy our time together again."

"Me, too. And... your brother will be all right. We have to believe that." While she was a realist, she'd spent time growing up encouraging her siblings, be it in studies or dating. She reached out and stroked his hand, but her heart reacted so strongly that she jerked her hand back.

With his gaze so unnerving, she ducked her head and concentrated on finishing her arugula. When she peeked up, her insides heated because he still looked at her as if she were the most important thing in the world.

He'd often made her feel like the center of the universe, and her heartbeat increased at the heat in his eyes. But then he'd done that with many people.

She rubbed her forehead and scanned the room again. A man in a felt hat at the farthest table seemed to look at her. He looked away once their eyes met, but it might be a coincidence. "Do you feel like we're being watched?" She kept watching the guy, but he seemed occupied with his dinner now, so she refocused on Kai.

His expression tensed. "I had that feeling on the plane. Why? Do you?"

She fidgeted in her seat. "Maybe. Or I'm just imagining things."

"Do you want to leave?"

"No," she said before she could think it over. "I like it here."

With you.

His wistful expression as he talked about Christine's children sat like a splinter under her skin, and she tugged at that instead of analyzing how he made her feel. "Do you want to settle down one day? Have children?"

"Yes." He didn't even hesitate.

She drank some more to give herself time before her next question. "I thought you enjoyed dating."

"I do. I love company, including female company." He chuckled. "Or often, *especially* female company. That doesn't mean I don't want to have my own family."

As such deep emotion coated his voice, she stared at him, trying to process it all. "I have difficulty imagining you as a family man."

"Then maybe you don't know me so well, after all."

That hurt. She'd always been close to him, and she needed that. But he'd just underscored one more difference between them.

He held her gaze. "Years ago, you told me that, after raising your siblings, you didn't want children. Did that change?"

"I... I don't think so." Which would be a deal-breaker, even if things were possible between them. Clenching her fingers around her lemonade glass as if she could hold onto something that had never been hers to start with, she ground her teeth against the pain crawling up her throat. Then to douse the question she was burning to ask, she downed the cool liquid. Once she placed the empty glass on the table, the words flashed free anyway. "But if you wanted to settle down and wanted children, then why didn't you?"

"Because the girl of my dreams was, well, unavailable."

So much sadness glossed his brown eyes that intense jealousy toward that unknown girl sent a shock wave through her. Good thing she was done with her food because her appetite evaporated. She wanted to ask whether the mysterious girl was someone she knew, but why prolong the torture? She threw the napkin on the table. "Oh. Okay. Well, sorry to hear that. I guess we're done here." At least when it came to romance between her and Kai. It was done without even beginning.

He gestured for the bill and paid it once the waitress brought it. Then he leaned forward. "Before we leave, would you like to have one dance?"

She should say no. Learning he'd been in love with someone else—actually in love, not just joyously drifting from date to date as she'd imagined him—stabbed her deeply already. Plus, he'd added one more obstacle between them. But besides that dance in the moonlight, this might be her only chance to dance with him.

"I'd love to."

"Great." His face lit up, and he led her to the small open space near the stage where two other couples were slow dancing.

The saxophone's soft notes tugged at her, but even more so dancing in his arms overwhelmed her as she swayed to the music that wove pensive enchantment through the dusky air. She did have to be fair, though. "Remember, I have two left feet."

"No. Everything about you is just right. And beautiful. And perfect. And—"

"I get the point." Her lips curved up despite her disappointment, and she floated along, dancing among the stars—well, soft LED candles that flickered on nearby tables and from the walls as if she'd ascended into the starry sky.

That unknown woman he had feelings for must be a fool to let a man like him go. Okay, Marina might be projecting her own feelings.

She glanced at the table where the man she'd caught staring at them used to be, and he was gone. Yup, she was imagining things.

She switched her gaze to the man of her dreams, and her hands slipped closer around his neck. Once, she'd thought she could look at the stars endlessly. Now she knew she could look endlessly in his eyes. "Maybe one day that girl will become available again and fall in love with you."

His eyes bore into hers while jazz underplayed the melody of her heartbreak. "I can only dream of that."

Right. Regrets and longing orchestrated their heartache inside her like a song of broken intentions. Shutting them out, she hid her face on his shoulder and breathed in his exotic cologne. She shouldn't have asked that question about him wanting a family. Then there would still be hope. Why did knowing he'd fallen for someone else hurt so badly? She didn't even have the right to be upset because he wanted children she couldn't give him.

Simple. Because she was falling for him. Maybe already had.

Had he fallen in love while she was away? Really, what did she want? She didn't have the right to ask intrusive questions.

He held her close while beautiful notes caressed her ears, and she took solace in the precious moments. She wanted him to be happy. She really did. So, if one day the woman of his dreams came back to him, Marina would squeeze her teeth, muster up her smile, and help plan the wedding. She'd even stand in as a bridesmaid if asked.

She'd be the good friend she claimed to be. Never mind her broken heart.

ON THE WAY TO CHRISTINE West's place, Kai frowned as he glanced in the rental car's rear-view mirror. "I hope I'm wrong, but I think a dark van with tinted windows is following us."

It was three vehicles back, but it had been there for a while. And when he changed lanes, the van had done the same.

"I see it. But why? Is it because we're poking into your mother's history? Or into Blake's disappearance?" Marina sat up stiffly. "If it were connected to my job, the following part would've started much earlier."

He winced as his gut twisted. He checked for an opening to change lanes again. "Has this happened before? With your job, I mean?"

"I received threats a couple of times, and a guy followed me home once. But they didn't 'follow' through, pun intended." She spoke as if it were no big deal. Then she craned her neck. "I can't get their license plate. Should we try to fake exit?"

"Good idea." He turned on the blinker and moved to the exit lane. The GPS protested, telling him to stay in his lane.

No thanks.

The van followed, and a shiver ran down his spine. This was more serious than a vague feeling of being watched on the plane or someone's gaze landing on them for too long at the restaurant.

For the third time, the GPS told him to move to the left, sounding much like Quiet when the parrot got a word—particularly his favorite word, *quiet*—stuck in his head.

Then, instead of exiting, Kai moved back to the left lane, though the spot was tight, which earned him some loud honking from the driver who had to slam on the brakes.

The mouthy GPS finally relaxed.

He couldn't see the van any longer, but it could be because the moving truck two vehicles behind him now obscured the view. "Do you mind if we exit early? Then I could make some extra turns to ensure we don't lead them to Christine West."

"Great idea. Let me look up the route."

This time, he didn't turn the blinker on when he moved to the exit lane at the last moment, earning another protest from GPS and much louder ones from a truck he cut off. He hated when people did that to him. He mentally apologized to the truck driver, hoping it wouldn't result in road rage.

Then he guided the rental through the exit and concentrated on making careful turns without getting lost in the unfamiliar city. He'd still have gotten lost if not for Marina. But she guided him almost too expertly.

"Have you been here before?" he asked.

"No. You can turn right on the red light here. Nothing is coming."

He eased up on the gas, and yet the turn was too sharp, making the tires squeal. Argh. "Did you study the map online?"

"Yes. I like to be prepared." Her voice pitched into her defensive tones. Maybe because he'd often teased her in their teens for thinking ahead. He shouldn't have and hadn't after realizing she used the technique to survive while dealing with many tasks thrown at her by breaking them into manageable chunks, organizing them, and planning.

"It came in handy. Thank you." He reached for her hand to express his gratitude.

Her fingers fluttered in his like a bird with broken wings, causing his heart to flutter in turn. Was it his imagination, or was that her sharp breath intake over the growl of the motor?

"We make a great team." He turned again at a lower speed this time, so the car movement was much more fluid. So far, the van hadn't reappeared in the rear-view mirror, and that eased some pressure on his diaphragm.

"Of course." Her voice was taut. Cautious. "We're best friends."

Best friends.

Right.

Disappointment cut deep, though it shouldn't have. Her friendship was important to him. While he valued the fragile connection with her, he forced himself to remove his hand from hers. His feelings for her ran way beyond friendly by now.

When he was sure the van wasn't following them, he pulled up to a quiet neighborhood with mature trees and a basketball stand in each front yard. Birds sang to them from those trees, and it made him miss his parrot.

He scanned his surroundings. "Hold on a second. Let's make sure it's safe."

While the white stone and stucco houses weren't opulent, they were more than decent, and their lush lawns were neatly trimmed. It wasn't necessarily an indication, but Christine seemed to be doing well for herself. Children shot hoops in a neighboring front yard, and one of them whooped as he made the basket. In another front yard, a lanky teen boy with shaggy surf-blond hair was teaching a little girl with blonde pigtails to ride a pink tricycle. The girl squealed in delight.

Marina's expression as she watched the children was gentle and slightly confused. She had such an expression sometimes when she had a thought she couldn't assign to its designated slot.

"It's weird how sometimes we might start wanting things we never thought we would." She clicked her seat belt open but didn't move out of the car.

Did she mean children? No, that must be his wishful thinking.

He opened his mouth to ask, but her lips tightened and she slipped out of the rental car. He hurried to follow and stayed close, shielding her, as they strode to a white stone two-storied home with an attached garage.

The area smelled of freshly cut grass with a faint scent of mesquite wood smoke. Someone was gearing up for a family barbecue. He wasn't up for idyllic suburbia but rather for ranch living. Still, the family scene called to him on a new level. The little girl squealed again while her brother cheered her on.

With one dad unknown and another one abusive, Kai didn't have a role model for how to be a father. He'd stifled the longing to be one for a long time. But their conversation made him realize how much he wanted to be a parent.

As they waited for Christine to answer the door, he looked at the woman in whose lovely face he could see the features of their future children. And he didn't want to stifle it any longer.

He'd meant it at the restaurant. He wanted a family. And he wanted his children to know their father. Too bad the woman he could see a future with didn't see one with him—and there were no children in hers.

The forest-green front door opened.

"Hello. You must be Kai Lawrence and Marina Helms. I'm Christine West, but call me Chris. Come on in." The woman with a salt-and-pepper bob and youthful gray eyes framed with smiling crow's-feet waved them inside, so he followed her fluffy bunny-eared slippers to the living room. As she sat in a brown recliner, apparently well-loved, judging by the wear and tear on the leather, she laced her fingers over her white slacks. Then she opened them to fidget with her short-sleeved blouse, making its blue-flowered print dance like wildflowers in a breeze.

Settling next to Marina on the tan sofa, Kai smiled, softened his voice, and gestured to the photos occupying most of the bookshelves behind her. "Are those your daughters?"

Christine brightened, and her posture relaxed. "Yes, my pride and joy."

"It looks like they are talented musicians." Marina nodded at the row of diplomas.

Good move, Marina.

"They are!" Christine beamed even more, then slipped into what seemed to be her favorite topic in the world as she talked about her daughters.

Kai nodded with enthusiasm, making confirming noises from time to time and inciting questions. But his mind drifted off. It was clear Christine loved her children, and longing unraveled in him again.

For years, he'd pushed aside his desire to become a dad. He'd told himself he'd been content playing a pirate for the children during the tourist season. Or volunteering to organize pony rides at the town's fair. And he was more than ready to be a doting uncle for Dallas's future children.

So why was that longing coming back in full force? Probably because his gaze kept sliding to Marina, though he did bring it back to Christine every time. In Marina, he saw the mother of his children. And she'd make a great mother, sweet and caring. His heart twisted. How tragic and unfair that she'd already been forced to become a third—and seemingly, the busiest—parent when she'd been a child herself.

He tuned into another accomplishment of Christine's daughters, hoping soon she'd be comfortable enough to talk about his bio mother. He should be more focused on this, and he was for Blake's sake. But to Kai, his mom was Amelia Lawrence. The woman who gave birth to him wasn't even a memory, but something ephemeral.

Meanwhile, the woman of his dreams was sitting nearby in flesh and blood, and his heart stirred. Throughout nearly all his memories, they'd had an invisible bond. Now, he needed a lot of willpower not to reach for her, not to take her hand to cement that connection.

Christine drained her coffee, the bluish ceramic mug giant enough for a bird to take a bath in. Well, if birds bathed in coffee. "Are you sure you don't want some? I just made a fresh pot."

Did she need to feel useful?

He nodded. "That would be great."

"I'd love a cup. Thank you," Marina said.

"Sure." Christine disappeared down the hall.

Leaving strangers in the room wasn't a great idea. Christine seemed to be too trusting. Something needled his memory, but he couldn't identify what.

She returned, carrying a tray with two large steaming ceramic coffee mugs and a pitcher of cream. "Would you like some sugar?"

"Creamer is more than enough. Thank you so much." Marina reached for her cup. The sun filtered through the window, highlighting her golden hair and lovely features and playing off the diamond studs in her ears. He had difficulty looking away. With the ocean or a worn-out sofa in the background, she was the most beautiful woman in the world—no, in the *universe*—to him.

She met his gaze and raised an eyebrow.

Christine almost hid a smile.

Heat simmered inside him and tingled up his neck, and he covered his embarrassment by snatching a warm coffee mug. "Would it be okay to ask what Naree was like?"

"Of course." Christine's features clouded, but she nodded. "You have the right to know. She was a bit shy, but once you got to know her, she showered you with kindness. Her life was difficult, but I never heard her complain. On the contrary, if I whined about something, she'd listen and find a way to encourage me. Very hard working. Even with all her workload, she'd help me out if I asked her." Tears clouded Christine's eyes, and her voice broke.

Marina handed over the tissue box from the coffee table, her eyes compassionate.

Kai's eyes stayed dry. Was that wrong? He mentally accepted Naree as his birth mother, but starting to love her, to be heartbroken because she was no longer here, was something different. Did that make him as callous and superficial as some people thought he was?

Okay, that character was different from Kai, but he liked the picture of her Christine was painting. He took a careful sip of his hot flavorful coffee, preferring his black.

Hmm, this didn't look like a person who would abandon her child at the beach. What was he missing? But then, she didn't look like a person who'd abandon her child at the hospital, either, and she had abandoned Blake.

Christine wiped her eyes. "Pardon me, please."

"We're sorry for your loss." Compassion glossed Marina's voice.

"Do you happen to have photos with her?" Kai asked.

"Of course." Christine got up and retrieved a photo album from one of the bookshelves. Now almost all photos were digital, but something was nostalgic about printed ones.

He leafed through smooth cellophane pages and peered at the photos.

A young slim girl with long straight hair so light blonde it had to be dyed and large doe-like eyes looked exactly like Christine had described her. A shy glance, slightly slumped shoulders, and a sincere, kind smile. She didn't seem to wear any makeup, and her clothing style consisted of simple, somewhat-faded T-shirts and jeans and sneakers. In her college photos, she often carried a stack of books, and it looked like she tried to hide behind them.

His fingers lingered over one of the photos, the smooth cellophane protecting them from smudges. He expected, even hoped for, a deep emotional reaction.

After all, Naree was his birth mother, and he'd give up his life for his adoptive one. But his heart didn't move. He still looked at a stranger. A stranger he hadn't forgiven yet and one he couldn't even confront, robbing him of closure.

Well, emotion did tighten his stomach and put acid in it, but it was an emotion he didn't want.

Resentment.

Why had she abandoned him at the beach, essentially putting her toddler's life in danger? Then a profound sadness twisted things up inside him. Naree was gone—her life cut short. He'd never get to ask her those questions, never get a chance to know her and his ancestors.

As if sensing he needed support, Marina reached over and laced her fingers through his. Her eyes held compassion. She didn't say a word, but he didn't need her to.

Her gesture gave him strength to go on. He tried to look at the photos from an investigative perspective, but nothing jumped out at him. But then, he didn't even know what he was looking for.

Hopefully, Marina did. She studied the photos as he did, and a slight crease lined her forehead.

"Do you have any possible explanation why she'd leave me at the beach as a child?" he asked the burning question. It might be too direct, but he needed to ask.

Christine looked down. "Sorry," she whispered, her expression miserable as if she'd shared her secrets with her best friend, but apparently, that best friend had kept huge secrets from her.

"But you knew about both pregnancies, right?" Marina asked.

Clearly, it would be difficult to hide.

Christine nodded and fidgeted with the yarn. "Yes. Of course, I knew. She wanted to keep Blake—she really did. But she thought it would be selfish." Her voice turned defensive. Her lips trembled. "I had no clue she left you like that at the beach. She loved you very much. I helped babysit you, and I saw her with you. You were everything to her."

Apparently, not everything. A lump clogged in his throat, and he flushed it down with hot coffee, even if it burned his tongue. "What did she say happened to me?"

"She said she gave you up for adoption. That it was better for you. But this time, she reacted differently. When she gave up Blake, she was sad for a while, yes, but with you... She was heartbroken. Totally. She cried all the time. And... and she seemed to be angry. I'd never seen her slam a table before then. She said she'd made a huge mistake. Then she just became a shadow of herself. Only ate when I begged her to. It was like life slipped out of her. A year later, I found out she got sick. I believe she'd have survived, but she didn't have it in her to struggle any longer." Christine sobbed into tissues. "When she lost you, she seemed to lose the will to live."

At last, some compassion loosened the tightness in his chest, his stomach. But he had to press on. "She didn't date anyone at the time?"

"No. She was extremely shy. And when boys asked her out, she said she wanted to concentrate on studies. But she was secretly in love with someone—I'm sure of that. She canceled our meetings from time to time, and she'd get that absent look on her face and a quiet smile as if she thought about someone dear to her."

Things didn't add up. Was it a forbidden romance?

Marina brought the giant mug to her lips. "Was she friendly with any professors?"

"There was this one, Professor Tucker." Christine hesitated. "She called him her favorite professor, but I don't know why. I didn't notice much interaction between them. Personally, I found him a bit... dry. I'm fairly sure nothing happened between them."

"Could something have happened at a party? Maybe too much alcohol?" Marina's voice softened the directness of the questions.

Once again, he was grateful for her presence, in more senses than one. She was used to doing cross-examination while he'd be lost. And he didn't want to ask questions that clearly made Christine uncomfortable in the first place.

Christine's gaze hardened. "She didn't go to parties. And she didn't drink alcohol."

"What about the hotels she worked at? Could one of the guests...?"

"I... I don't know." Christine responded when Marina's voice trailed off. "I don't think so."

Marina leaned forward. "Naree hid the baby's father's identity in both cases. Was it because she didn't know, like if a stranger had assaulted her? Or because she protected the man?"

Christine wrung her hands. "I just don't know."

"I'm sorry to ask these difficult questions, Chris." Marina's expression softened.

"I understand you have to do this, but I wish I was more helpful." Christine got up. "My daughters are going to be here soon."

Kai and Marina glanced at each other and got up. They were dismissed. But one thing he had to know before he left. He peered at Christine, his heart thudding. One thing he'd always wondered. "Can you tell me... what she named me?"

"Kwan." Christine held his gaze. "It means one who is strong, and it's obvious to me that you've lived up to it."

Kwan. His birth name. He'd read once that parrots were given a name at birth that they carried their whole lives. He'd had to rename Quiet, not knowing what name his parrot parents gave him, just as his adopted mother had to rename him, also not knowing what name his parents had given him. Knowing that had given him a connection with his pet. But now he knew his name. Maybe his adopted mom had named him Kai because she'd thought that's what he'd tried to say his name was as an abandoned toddler.

One who is strong? No. He preferred his real name, meaning sea. Something that defined so much about his life and his world—and his Marina.

Chapter Twelve

The drive from Christine West's house to Blake's adoptive parents' place was quiet at first. Kai glanced in the rearview mirror several times, but the van with tinted windows didn't show up.

His heart was heavy and yet somehow not heavy enough. He couldn't even form it into thoughts.

Marina placed her elegant fingers on his arm and squeezed slightly. "I'm sorry that wasn't more productive."

He frowned as he stopped at a red light and checked the rearview mirror again. "It's not just that. I should feel more emotion. More sadness."

"You feel guilty for not feeling sad or guilty." She always knew how to put things into words, to make complex things more understandable. No wonder he admired her mind so much.

He moved forward on the green light, feeling his frown deepen. "Instead, I feel resentment for her leaving me. For depriving me of knowing my family. Of knowing anything about them." His fingers tightened around the steering wheel as if he tried to tighten the lid on his resentment. "I should stop the self-pity party. I was blessed with a great, close-knit adoptive family."

While Marina's family had mostly taken advantage of her. And she didn't know much about her ancestors on her maternal side, either. Her grandfather—who had died before Marina was born—had never talked about their grandmother, and her mother remembered little about her. Marina had told him once that, for some reason, the topic was not mentioned in their family.

"Your feelings are valid." She stroked his fingers, her fleeting touch sending a wave of apprehension through him. "Please don't try to dismiss them. It'll take time for resentment to subside like a tide ebbing away. As for feeling guilty, sometimes I'm resentful toward my family, even toward Mom from time to time. You don't think I should feel guilty for feeling that way, do you?"

"Of course not!" The pressure on his chest didn't disappear, but it eased up, making breathing easier.

She'd always helped him put things into perspective. She was the only one he'd talked to about his adoption. He didn't want his mother or siblings to think he didn't appreciate what they'd done for him. Did Blake feel the same way, based on Sue's words? Kai was far from the perfect son Sue had described, but he'd made an effort to show his gratitude to the Lawrence family.

"I'm here to talk, whenever you need me. Including when I..." Marina paused before continuing. "Including when I return to my regular job."

His heart shifted. As much as he appreciated the offer, he wanted more than her ear and sage advice. "Thank you."

"I'd love for you to visit me in Charleston. And I'll visit Port Sunshine more often, as well. I don't mind doing some logistical work for the restaurant, helping with the spreadsheets. And Saylor said she's considering coming back to Port Sunshine. Reconnecting with her has been fun."

"I'll visit you in Charleston. And I'd be thrilled to see you in town again." While gratitude warmed him that she suggested it, it couldn't thaw the resentment.

Following GPS prompts, he made another turn and entered an affluent neighborhood where sprawling trees sheltered large homes. They had to go through the gate into the community, but the guard had been notified about their arrival. Then they passed an endless golf course and a sparkling swimming pool so large it felt endless, as well. No doubt, every yard had a swimming pool, too.

His heart shifted. Maybe he was greedy, but seeing Marina from time to time wasn't enough. And while he'd been fine not knowing anything about his birth family before, getting crumbs of information wasn't enough now.

He wasn't ready to let them go, to let this be goodbye to something he'd never even had. Plus, this felt too much like goodbye with Marina already, and his insides clenched painfully.

"I'd love that…" Her voice trailed off as if she wanted to say more, but she fell silent because he pulled up to the curb of the house the GPS determined as their destination.

However, the destination for his journey so far seemed unreachable. He scanned the neighborhood, but based on cameras on every house, even a leaf wouldn't fall here unnoticed. A few yards further, dogs barked, an efficient addition to cameras. One never knew, though, so he stayed on guard.

He turned off the engine and clicked the seat belt open. Then he hurried outside because Marina slipped out of the car fast, determined as always. She'd always been goal-oriented while he went with the flow. Now he had a goal—a dream, really—of life with Marina and their children. But it was impossible, and that tore him apart.

He shielded her as they strode to the front door that, of course, had a camera on it. He admired the security and was extra grateful for it, considering the circumstances, but he didn't know if he'd want everything in his life recorded.

A maid in a tidy uniform opened the door nearly immediately after they rang the bell. Middle-aged, she'd pulled her shoulders back in a posture as strict as her tight bun, and her smile looked as trained as the rest of her persona.

"Good evening. We're here to see Dr. and Mrs. Park." He hoped he didn't sound sexist by using the man's title.

"Good evening. They are waiting for you. Follow me, please." She walked inside where everything seemed to be marble or cherrywood.

The slight derision in her voice made Kai glance at his watch. They were one minute late, which must be unforgivable here. The patriarch's time was clearly worth a lot.

They passed a hall where oil portraits of distinguished ancestors scowled from the wall. Unfairly, only the male ones had been depicted. Then they were seated in a large room. Huh. People in this gated community seemed to believe in having everything large. Bright chandeliers reflected on hardwood floors, floor-to-ceiling windows overlooked sparkling-in-sunlight fountains in the backyard, and the nearly floor-to-ceiling oil paintings in gilded frames must be originals.

Everything seemed to be sparkling. Shiny. Polished?

Of course, he didn't expect a worn-out sofa like in the previous house or yarn on the coffee table. But the opulence slightly blinded him, the lifestyle so contrasting from the place where he'd grown up. Being biological brothers, they'd ended up in such different homes and families.

He wasn't envious. Instead, compassion squeezed his heart when Blake's adoptive parents entered the room. Most likely, they'd give up all their wealth for Blake to return home safely. Kai and Marina got up from the sofa to greet the hosts.

The patriarch was as large a version of a man as everything else here was oversized. Not overweight but stocky and tall, he made his imposing presence felt immediately. Even at home, he wore a tailored black suit paired with diamond cufflinks, a golden ring, and an expensive rose-gold watch. His hair and mustache were gray, his shoulders were slumped as if from a heavy burden, but his gaze was still astute.

His petite pearl-blonde wife approached with her shoulder-length hair beautifully styled and matching her platinum belted ankle-length dress. Her face was impressively smooth for her age, and Kai barely ventured to wonder whether it was from lotions or a scalpel. Rays of sunshine caught the prisms from her diamond bracelets and anklet. Yes, everything seemed to sparkle here, but her eyes did so from a sad reason and what he suspected were unshed tears. Compassion squeezed his heart further.

"Thank you so much for seeing us. This is my... my friend, Marina Helms. She's helping me search for Blake and investigate my birth mother's history." He shook hands with Dr. Park, then his wife. The man's handshake was firm, but his wife's was limp, fast, and somewhat reluctant.

After brief greetings, they sat down. Mrs. Park chose the furthest chair from the group.

Hmm. Maybe it was because of their differences in sizes or because of Dr. Park's aquiline nose, but a comparison to a vulture and a canary came to mind.

"It's great to meet you. I just wish it were under different circumstances." Sadness coated Marina's voice.

Did she think, like he did, how awful it would be to lose someone close? He didn't even want to imagine what he'd do if she disappeared. Yes, he'd lost his adoptive father, but to his shame, he'd mostly felt relief at the time. Not for himself. But for his family.

He pushed away thoughts about the man's possible affair with Kennedy's mother. The sound of bracelets and the scent of perfume didn't mean much, right? Because if they did, it added to the list of people to wish his father harm.

Dr. Park raked his fingers through the gray hair that matched his mustache. "I wish *many things* were different. I wish I paid more attention to the signs."

"What signs?" Marina's gaze sharpened.

"That Blake was going to commit suicide." Dr. Park's voice sounded bitter.

Kai's heart went out to the couple. "Please don't blame yourself. And until the body is found, there's hope."

Mrs. Park covered her eyes. "Do you really think so?" Her voice trembled. She must be suffering a lot. To lose a child was devastating. Kai shuddered at the thought. And he didn't even have children.

Sadly.

"I pray so." Even as he spoke, he sent up another prayer for Blake. He'd asked his family to pray for Blake, as well, and he knew they all would.

"How was Blake growing up?" Marina leaned forward, her hands clasped in her lap, her gaze acute.

Mrs. Park brightened. "He was wonderful," she gushed, sitting up straighter, and her diamond-clad wrist sparkled as she waved a hand as if to encompass the whole world. "We couldn't ask for a better son. Studious. He loved bringing me gifts, be it tiny pebbles when he was little or flowers when he grew up."

Then a tear slipped out of her eye. She reached for the tissues on the cherrywood table and wiped the tear away.

Dr. Park got up and hugged her, then returned to his seat. His expression was stoic. Maybe Kai got the family dynamics wrong.

Mrs. Park's description fit with what Sue had said. Did it also fit with her claim that her brother was the favorite?

If there was foul play and the suicide was staged, Blake's sister and daughter benefited from his death by inheriting his fortune. They had a motive and an opportunity. Sue had claimed there was no resentment between them, but was it so in reality?

"He turned into a fine young man. Every father expects their children to go far, but I was right in expecting great things from my son." Pride in Dr. Park's expression shattered when he seemed to remember he might've lost his son.

Kai exchanged glances with Marina.

"What about Sue? What was she like when she was growing up?" Marina's voice flowed like honey now. Her posture and the timbre of her voice mimicked Mrs. Park, but not in an obvious way.

Dr. Park's brows rose. "I don't understand how that's relevant here."

Mrs. Park sniffled and waved him off. "It's okay. Sue was, well, opposite from Blake. She was a rambunctious child. Very disobedient. Always wanted to do everything her way. Whatever she could break, she would. Then she became a rebellious teen. Whatever rules we tried to establish, she made it her job to break. We hired the best tutors, enrolled her in the best schools. She didn't want to study. She wanted to be an actress—but again, she didn't want to study or do the work to become one. She gets roles from time to time, but it's not much. I worry about her." The words tumbled down as if she had a need to talk about this to someone. "She has an inheritance from my mother, but she's going through it way too fast."

Uh-oh. "What happens when she's spent her inheritance?" Kai asked. The motive might get bigger.

Mrs. Park sighed. "She'll be on her own."

"That's enough," Dr. Park interrupted his wife. "She's our daughter. I won't support her financially any more, but we love her regardless."

"Was there any sibling rivalry?" Marina turned to him. Her fingers drummed the sofa's cream-colored fabric.

"And that's relevant to my son's disappearance how?" Dr. Park's eyes narrowed.

Kai tensed. Their host was getting aggravated, and they didn't need that. Usually, Kai could liven up a conversation, but this was a different matter.

"Well, it might be far-fetched, but maybe there were disagreements between them that might have affected him deeply and influenced his decision to take his life?" Marina said quietly, her body moving back a little, deferring.

Seeming to consider that, Dr. Park rubbed his temples. Mrs. Park kept quiet this time as if deferring, too. Finally, Dr. Park released a sigh. "I don't want to say anything bad about my daughter, but... With personalities so different, what do you expect? Sue resents her brother's success and isn't shy to voice it. But it's her own fault she hasn't succeeded. She had all the opportunities Blake had. She's the one to blame for not using them."

But Sue clearly didn't think they'd given her the same opportunities. Of course, Kai didn't say it aloud, and neither did Marina.

Huh. He leaned against the sofa back that seemed to arrive from a magazine about great homes. For a man who didn't want to badmouth his daughter, Dr. Park seemed to have done just that. Was there some gender bias here? Or was this a father who regretted what he considered his daughter's unrealized potential? But did he realize the disobedient daughter could now be all he had left in the sense of children?

Mrs. Park seemed to because she sniffled again. Then she straightened her back. "Pardon me. I'm not being a gracious hostess. Would you like something to drink?"

"I'm good," he started to say.

"Oh, I'd love some coffee." Marina perked up in her seat. "That would be marvelous."

He sent her a surprised glance. Didn't she just have a gigantic mug of coffee at Christine's place?

"Of course." Mrs. Park called for the maid the old-fashioned way, with a tiny silver bell.

Huh. Shouldn't that be done with the help of technology these days?

Once the maid disappeared with the request, Marina squirmed in her seat. Then she smiled sheepishly. "May I use your restroom, please? I drank too much liquid before getting here. Those iced tea glasses in the restaurants here sure are large."

Mrs. Park started getting up. "I'll show you the way."

"No need. I'm sure I'll find it." Marina sprinted down the hall.

Kai tensed, feeling the need to continue the conversation. But he wasn't great in grief counseling or cross-examination. Besides, if the couple provided any useful information, he wanted Marina to be here because he wouldn't know what was useful about it. But he lived worlds apart from the Parks, so he doubted they watched the same movies or listened to the same music.

His gaze moved along the wall, skimming all the awards Dr. Park had received and then the rows of expensive rum bottles behind the bar. Then it fell on the football paraphernalia, including a football signed by famous players and Dr. Park's photo with one of them. Football could unite people of different social statuses, right?

He nearly slapped his hands in joy. He could talk football, and now he knew Dr. Park's favorite team. It turned out to be a conversational gold mine because both Dr. and Mrs. Park were huge fans and had even met at a football game.

The atmosphere was still sad but more relaxed when Marina returned. By then, an elegant gilded tray with tiny golden-trimmed porcelain cups was on the table. Yes, it was all about traditional shiny elegance here, though those cups likely fit no more than three sips of coffee, and not thirsty sips at that.

A generous smile blossomed on Marina's face as if she hadn't seen coffee in forever instead of twice in the afternoon. "Thank you so much! And the set looks so beautiful! Like a work of art."

"That's because it is." Mrs. Park preened but didn't elaborate further.

"As is everything about your place, it's extremely impressive." Marina clearly added flattering notes in her voice.

"Would you like creamer in your coffee?" the maid asked.

"Yes, please." Once the maid left, following a gesture from Mrs. Park, Marina turned to their hosts. "If it's not too painful to answer, do you have an idea what could've caused Blake to commit suicide? As far as I understand, he's doing fantastically well professionally."

Kai suppressed a frown. Why was she so concentrated on this version? Just like in his adoptive father's case, he wasn't sure it was suicide in Blake's case, either.

"He was." Dr. Park's bushy gray eyebrows furrowed. "We believe it's because of the new woman he was seeing."

His wife reached for a cup and lifted it in a sophisticated gesture. No doubt, Mrs. Park even sneezed in a sophisticated way.

"What new woman? Do you have a name?" Kai felt like a hound dog who picked up a needed scent. He tried his black coffee and nearly spat it out. It tasted bitter. Now he was grateful for the miniature cup.

Marina stoically drank hers.

Mrs. Park released another sigh as she took a delicate sip. "Sadly, we don't know. Usually, Blake isn't secretive. But he didn't tell us who she is and refused our invitation to meet her."

"He must've been very taken with her. He was extremely focused on his work, which didn't leave much time for dating. So she must've been important to him."

At the disapproval in the doctor's voice, Kai recalled the row of ancestral oil portraits in the hall, each name having *Dr.* in front of it. Was Blake so focused on his career because it was what he wanted or because it was expected from him? The latter was the way Marina had felt for years, and the unfairness of it still boiled Kai's blood.

He glanced at her beautiful profile, drawn to her more and more. She'd done great in her career, but that didn't mean she was happy. And with everything in him, he wanted her to be happy. Even if it was on a path different from his.

Gratitude for his family stirred him. His family hadn't hung high expectations on him. Had never clipped his wings like was done with his pet. Kai could be what he wanted to be.

Mrs. Park sniffled again and put down her empty cup. She must have a stomach made of steel. "Then he told me she broke up with him. I've never seen him so heartbroken. He was *crying.*"

"He seemed okay when I met him." Kai placed his cup with its bitter contents on the shiny tray. Life was too short to be bitter or drink bitter things.

"Blake knew how to put up a cheerful front." Dr. Park spoke with approval.

One probably had to in this family. Thankfully, Kai didn't blurt that out.

"Is there any way to find this mysterious woman?" She placed her cup on the tray. Empty. Huh.

"If there is"—Dr. Park growled with a low menace—"we'd love to know about it."

Marina's eyes narrowed, then sympathy reclaimed her expression. "Could someone else wish Blake harm... ahem, affect him in a way that he'd commit suicide?"

"His colleagues envied him. But I doubt it would reflect on him." The good doctor checked his expensive designer watch.

Though no words were said, Kai sensed the meeting was over. He got up. "Thank you very much for seeing us."

"We appreciate it." Marina rose to her feet again, her expression slightly puzzled, but that bewilderment disappeared so fast he could've imagined it.

"It's the least we could do for our Blake's brother." Dr. Park's eyes glistened, but he shed no tears. Perhaps he never did.

"If you could keep us updated on any developments about Blake, it would mean a lot to us." Marina handed the couple her business card.

Dr. Park likely ran background checks on them both before letting them inside the house and had their contact information already. But he probably wouldn't admit to it, so the gesture was useful.

Kai didn't have a business card. What would he put there? Cowboy? Rancher? Pirate impersonator? Stationery salesman?

The maid showed them to the door, and the patter of drops hitting the roof outside made him tense. It was pouring, and he didn't want Marina to get soaked.

But the moment she stepped onto the porch, she pulled an umbrella out of that giant purse of hers. Always prepared.

"Is it okay if I hold it?" he asked.

"Sure." She handed him the black umbrella and huddled close as they rushed to the rental car.

A part of him wished the distance to the car was longer as he liked having her close, but he corrected himself. If there was any danger, it wasn't a good idea to be out in the open. He opened the door for her.

Once in the driver's seat, he took off, wipers swishing fast, more than a dripping umbrella between them.

She handed him a pack of gum. "To remove the taste of that coffee. Though creamer really helped me tolerate it. I have over-the-counter pills for stomach pain if you need them."

As she leaned to him, her breath smelled of peppermint already. The desire to kiss her wasn't just unreasonable under the circumstances—it was reckless. Yet his blood stirred.

"Thanks." He popped the gum in his mouth, enjoying the fresh minty taste. "It probably would've tasted better if I just bit off the porcelain."

"Yup. I'm still not sure if they gave us that coffee to make us leave or if it's the coffee they offer others, as well."

"You sure have a lot of things in your purse."

"I'm used to it after the times I had to look after my siblings. As for the over-the-counter pills for stomach pain, you'd be surprised how whimsical little tummies can be." Often, there'd been some resentment in her voice when she'd talked about taking care of her siblings. But now... now nostalgia lingered there, too.

He glanced at her, and her expression was surprised as if she realized it, as well. He didn't have the luxury to look at her for long. He had to concentrate on the road, especially once they left the gated community and made it to the freeway.

About ten minutes later, Marina said, "I believe we have a tail again."

Everything in him went on high alert. With the roads wet and slippery and the visibility low, the risk of an accident was higher.

His fingers tightened so much around the steering wheel that his knuckles became white. Adrenaline surged in his veins as he pressed on the gas. He deemed himself a good driver, but then statistically most people considered themselves above-average drivers.

Then she said, her voice surprisingly even, "I have an idea."

Chapter Thirteen

The next day after breakfast at the hotel, Marina and Kai drove to the park to meet with Professor Tucker. This time, Marina was behind the wheel of the white rental sedan. She checked several times. So far, there didn't seem to be a tail, and she relaxed her grip on the steering wheel. The vehicle had that new-car smell, but it came from the air freshener.

"Driving to the police station yesterday was a good idea," Kai said from the passenger seat.

Secretly pleased, she shrugged nonchalantly. "It's just common sense. Besides, I remembered it was nearby. GPS or not, memorizing the map was useful." She changed lanes, then did that again, paying attention if someone behind her did the same. Nobody did. "Wish all the knowledge in my head was this useful. I'm still waiting to apply all those chemical reactions and math equations I learned."

Kai chuckled, the sound reflecting inside her in a strange way. "Me, too. Though one of the guys in our town who moved to New York applied his lessons in chemistry well."

Her curiosity piqued. With an opening in the left lane, she put on a blinker and changed lanes again. So far, so good. Nobody followed. "What did he do?"

"Explosives."

It wasn't a laughing matter, but she laughed. Kai always knew how to make her laugh. He'd been unusually pensive yesterday, which was understandable under the circumstances. Her insides warmed to have his merry self back.

And maybe she wouldn't have to fake an exit today. Or should she? She zoomed in on the exit to the park, far ahead. "Do you see anyone following us? Should I miss the exit and then take the next one and come back?"

"Nope. You're good." He paused. "You're great, actually."

"Oh please!" She waved him off as she turned on the blinker, then moved to the right lane, then another one.

But deep inside, she basked in his admiration. She'd worked so hard to earn praise in childhood, but Dad had given it to her sparingly. And then her ex had seemed to have an agenda when he'd praised her.

Kai's praise was always sincere and generous like the man himself. She steered her car into the exit and stole a glance at his handsome profile. Could they have a chance if she risked it, no matter their differences and his player reputation and different locations?

But she'd just discovered that he'd been in love with someone else. And he wanted children. It was a deal-breaker because, if one person wanted children and the other one didn't, it would never work. Her heart grew heavy even as he started talking about shenanigans the puppies—Buttercup's brothers and sisters—got into at the ranch.

She'd gotten deeply attached to the man who'd never be hers. And she'd gotten attached to the puppy who'd never be hers, either.

After practically raising a large family, she'd thought she'd been content on her own. And she was. But it turned out, she was much more content when Kai was nearby. She'd created her own bubble of happiness. But Kai had made that bubble much bigger and, well, bubblier. When she left, that bubble was about to blow up in her face.

They made it to the park safely, and she looked around before sliding out of the rental. Neither one of them liked the idea of meeting in a park, and they'd cancel it if the van followed them again. They also arrived with time to spare to make sure the area didn't look suspicious.

"We can go back." Kai seemed to read her mind.

"The professor seemed to be skittish already. Besides, he needs to leave for his vacation. And my vacation will soon be over." Regret clenched her stomach as she said the latter. "Let's be on guard."

She was goal-oriented, but she hoped she wouldn't regret that decision now.

Everything flourished after the rain yesterday, the grass and foliage lusciously green as they walked to the designated bench. So far, nobody had seemed to follow them.

Two twin boys with backward baseball caps practiced on skateboards, and further away, a dad was helping a little girl in bubble-gum pink overalls fly a marmalade-hued kite. The girl squealed and jumped up and down, and so did her cute pigtails.

Kai's gaze followed in the same direction, and longing twisted his expression.

Her heart stuttered.

Lord, whoever the woman he loves is, please help her return to his life and answer his feelings.

A lump formed in her throat. Ironic that, the first time she prayed, it was for something she wanted and didn't want at the same time.

"I want you to be happy," she said. Even if it wasn't with her. She meant it, but the lump increased in her throat.

"Ditto."

When he took her hand, she didn't move away.

She paid attention to their surroundings and noticed him scanning it, as well.

His jaw set tight. "Meeting here wasn't a good idea. Nobody seems to have followed us, but it's too out in the open."

She grimaced as she sat on the bench. "I agree. But the professor didn't want to meet anywhere else, and beggars can't be choosers." She stumbled. "Not that we're beggars." She wanted him to know more about his bio mom. Of course, still a lot would be missing. But she didn't want him to be in danger, either.

"Do you think it could be a trap?" His eyes narrowed. "We should leave."

A shiver ran down her spine, and she moved her purse closer. Due to aspects of her job, she'd bought a gun, had learned to shoot, and even gotten a license to carry. But not in this state. Besides, using those skills fast was a different matter. "Okay."

But a man in glasses and a hat was rushing toward them already, waving at them. "Sorry I'm late! Sorry I'm late!"

"It *is* late. Too late to leave," she whispered to Kai. "We'll have to be extra vigilant." She opened her purse zipper for faster access to the gun.

"Thank you for waiting for me." The professor huffed, slightly out of breath. "I'm Professor Tucker. I presume you're Kai Lawrence and Marina Helms?"

"You presume right. Great to meet you, and thank you for agreeing to talk to us." She extended her hand while keeping the surroundings in her peripheral vision. Just because someone had seemed to follow them yesterday didn't mean they'd be shot at, but one never knew.

His palm was dry and narrow, and so seemed to be the man himself. Maybe because he wore a brown suit and a narrow beard and was thin and tall with long limbs, but he reminded her of a branch without any leaves. He looked to be in his sixties based on his wrinkles and stooped back, though his hair, mustache, and beard were still hazelnut brown. He kind of fit the stereotype of a university professor.

His university website bio stated he'd done a lot of scientific research and published it in prestigious scientific journals. He'd written three textbooks and often participated in conferences and seemed to be accomplished in the academic world. He'd worked at the same university his whole life. He could've retired by now but preferred to continue working.

According to Barrett's research, Professor Tucker had a group of friends he met for billiards from time to time and another group who traveled to different places for bird watching. His colleagues referred to him with respect, and his students did, as well, but there was no enthusiastic admiration on either side. His neighbors said he was quiet and his lawn was always neatly trimmed, and that was all they cared about, so a good neighbor overall. He never got married and didn't have any known children.

Her heart shifted. Did *she* want to be a branch without any leaves, as well? She was fine with it, preferred it that way. There were plenty of other branches to carry on the family name. But that was before she'd reconnected with Kai.

Knowing the man was Naree's favorite professor made Marina look at him closer. Kai did, as well, probably searching for his own features on the man's face. She couldn't see a clear resemblance. Maybe something in the nose. But then not all her siblings were the spitting image of their parents, either.

The professor's and Kai's personalities, of course, seemed totally different.

She fished out a small water bottle from her purse. "Would you like some water?"

The professor took the bottle. Good. "Don't mind if I do. Thank you."

She offered one to Kai, as well, who accepted with thanks. The bottles were identical, but she'd already marked the one she'd given to the professor.

"What can you tell us about Naree Jones?" Kai asked.

Barrett already prepared the soil for this conversation and why Kai had needed to know, but the professor didn't have to agree to talk to them. Yet he had. Why?

She looked around again as goose bumps erupted over her skin. But so far, there was nothing suspicious. Yet.

The man brightened. "She was a great student. Intelligent. Studious. Lots of students want to party. She wasn't like that. She clearly worked hard. I was saddened when she dropped out years later."

"Do you know why she dropped out?" Marina asked softly. So far, what he'd described fit the picture. But she felt he wasn't saying something.

He looked away, then found a loose thread on his jacket. "I didn't ask."

"Did you know you were her favorite teacher?" Kai leaned forward.

The man's nostrils flared, and he sat up straighter. "Look, before you insinuate something, we didn't have any kind of inappropriate relationship."

Kai lifted his arms, palms up, in a gesture of surrender. "We're not in–*sin*–u–ating anything. Honest."

Professor Tucker seemed to relax and took another swig from his bottle. "Frankly, I was surprised. I'm not a fun professor. I don't tell jokes at my lectures. And sometimes those lectures can be rather... rather dry. And it can be difficult for me to connect to people. Especially ones who are decades younger than I am. Maybe the reason she said it is..."

When his voice trailed off, Kai and Marina waited patiently, both keeping their surroundings in their peripheral vision.

Finally, Professor Tucker rubbed his eyes and exhaled wearily. "She was sick and missed a few lectures. I let her take the exam anyway. I didn't gift her the grade, mind you. She passed the tests on her own. But I had this... this feeling not many people were nice to her."

Something moved inside Marina. She'd done her best not to like Naree because of what the woman had done to Kai. But the more Marina learned about that woman, the more sympathy she felt.

"Do you have any idea if she dated someone?" Kai asked. "Maybe you saw her with someone at lectures or between them?"

The man's eyes narrowed behind thick glasses, and he placed the half-empty bottle on the bench. "The only person I saw her with was—What was that girl's name? Christine West. I hope you're not insinuating—"

"No!" Kai's arms went up. "Not at all."

"And you didn't hear any kind of rumors about her, did you?" The question was probably useless, but Marina had to try.

"No." Professor Tucker shook his head for emphasis.

He was withdrawing, and she could feel it. To get an answer out of him, she'd need to have him relax and think it was over. Then she'd strike. The tactic had worked well for her in court, but she winced from a stab of guilt to use it on this man.

"Thank you for your time." She rose to her feet.

"We appreciate it." Kai followed suit.

Professor Tucker sighed out his relief. "You're very welcome."

Then Marina said fast, "You didn't say no when I asked if you knew why she dropped out. You heard she got pregnant again after giving up the first baby for adoption and she kept the baby. She dropped out to raise it. You felt... maybe a little disappointed?"

"I felt sorry for her, okay? I had nothing to do with any of her children, but I wanted to help," the man said through squeezed teeth.

"What did she say?"

"She thanked me and said she had no right to accept it. That she didn't want people to think what you're thinking now." He glared at them. "To harm my reputation in academia. That was the kind of person she was."

"I didn't make those kinds of assumptions." Marina softened her voice. "Your interest in her wasn't as a woman. It was as a daughter you never had, and she felt it."

Professor Tucker closed his eyes as if he didn't want them to see his expression. Or maybe he tried to hold in tears. Then he drew his head into his shoulders, got up, and left, walking much slower than when he'd arrived.

Marina picked up the water bottle he'd left on the bench because evidence was always more important than her conclusions. Then she glanced at the sky where clouds gathered. The air grew heavier. "Let's get back to the car."

They hurried back.

"You were spectacular." Admiration rang in his voice.

"I'm afraid I was cruel."

A large tricolor ball dropped near her. The same girl she'd seen flying the kite earlier ran to her.

Marina scooped up the ball and handed it to the girl.

The child tilted her head as she accepted it. "You're pwetty."

"Thanks." Marina couldn't help smiling. She had a weird urge to straighten up the girl's askew left pigtail. "So are you."

Kai chuckled. "You're both right."

The little girl in bubble-gum pink overalls grinned. "Are you someone's mom?"

"No." The word emerged from somewhere hollow in Marina.

"Why?" The child blinked. Then the child's father called for her, and she ran away.

Kai and Marina fell into step again.

"Are you okay?" His fingers squeezed hers in silent support.

"Yes." She was. But something was missing, and as she contemplated it, Kai didn't interrupt her. For all his chattiness, he always knew when to stay quiet. But he looked around, so he stayed vigilant. She tried to do the same.

Marina couldn't rewrite her history, but she could choose what she did from now on. Raising her siblings while somehow still excelling academically had been forced on her. She'd thought she could never do anything like that again.

Children weren't an experiment. It wasn't something one tried to do. They were a lot of work, and she knew it firsthand. One had to be sure one wanted children. Like Kai did.

She barely noticed how she moved closer to him on the narrow path. She could imagine the future with him, then going together in life like they did now. But could he, even if he forgot about the woman who'd stolen his heart? Or would he get tired of Marina soon?

Then there was the question of children. Like she did sometimes, she tried to visualize the solution before finding the path to it.

They reached the playground area. She imagined herself near a swing with a little girl who'd squeal from joy if Marina pushed it harder. Who'd hug Marina with little hands and whisper, "I love you, Mommy." Imagined running around with Kai and the girl and a little boy who'd have Kai's brown eyes and infectious laugh and would be the life and soul of every gathering from his birth onward.

She took a lungful of fresh air filled with the scent of grass. It wasn't difficult to imagine at all. Of course, life was much more than fun and games at the children's playground. And two children would be her limit.

"How many children would you like to have?" she blurted out. She usually measured her words, but this time they escaped before she could stop them.

"Two." He didn't hesitate.

She stopped from surprise, but then resumed her pace. "Really? You grew up in a large family, so I thought..."

"You grew up in a large family, too."

"Right." She nodded. "Point taken."

"Squiiiiilel!" The child's voice shrieked from the playground.

Kai chuckled. "The little girl must've seen a squirrel." He pointed to the foliage of a nearby tree. "I can spot a squirrel, as well."

"Me, too," she whispered.

"Can you see the squirrel?"

"No. I mean, yes, I can see it. But I wanted to say, two probably would be it for me, too."

This time, he stopped. "Have you changed your mind about possibly having children?"

She searched for the right answer and didn't find it. The budding realization was too fresh, too fragile. "I'm not sure yet."

"And one has to be sure." His eyes darkened, but his demeanor changed to more open, maybe.

"Yes."

"Thank You, Lord," he whispered. Then he frowned. "I forgot we shouldn't be out in the open like this. I didn't see anyone following us, but it's still not a good idea."

"True. But we're close to the place we parked now." She reluctantly increased her pace. She wanted to spend more time with him in such a peaceful environment, but he was right.

They needed to be careful.

She glanced at the sky. "And clouds are gathering in the sky. It might begin raining again."

He kept up with her easily. "You memorized the park layout."

"Yes. But I also have excellent topographic skills and a high level of spatial intelligence."

Kai snorted. "And I don't even know what topographic skills and spatial intelligence are."

She smiled. "It's okay. You have lots of other great qualities."

He did. Sure, she knew what path to take in this park. But what good were her topographic skills if they couldn't tell her what path to take in life?

"Like what?" Kai grinned at her. "Not that I'm fishing for compliments."

He never had, and she'd been sparse in her praise for him while he'd always lavished her with it. "You're fun, kind, supportive. You genuinely care about people and animals and make them laugh, especially me. I mean, you make people laugh, not animals."

"I've heard horses neigh at my jokes," Kai said modestly.

She chuckled, proving her point. The air grew heavier and more humid. "You're a joy to be around. You're already a great friend, brother, and son, and you'll make a great dad one day. And you're an awesome driver while I'm best as a navigator. So you'll drive us back, okay?" She fished out the car keys from her purse and placed them in his hand as they reached the car. Her fingers touched his skin, and a wave of awareness crashed through her.

Kai walked taller, and he was tall enough already. "Thank you very much." His eyes widened at her touch.

"Let's get inside the car. It's about to rain again."

"Right." He clicked on the fob.

The moment they settled inside the rental, the rain started hitting the hood and windshield. She made sure to lock the doors. Then she scanned their surroundings to ensure nobody was outside. "Maybe it's best to wait a few minutes until the rain subsides." She checked the weather app on her phone, and the rain was supposed to stop soon. "We still have plenty of time before our flight."

When she looked up at him, his gaze was intense.

He moved closer, giving her a whiff of his exotic cologne that wreaked havoc on her senses. "You're leaving soon, and you're my best friend. I value your friendship very much, so it doesn't make sense to do this."

Her heartbeat became erratic. "To do what?"

"Kiss you." Emotion filled his eyes.

Heat pooled in the pit of her stomach, and she tilted her face to give him easier access to her lips. "It makes no sense whatsoever."

He cupped her face, sending a delicious shiver through her, making her impatient. "Right."

There was a question in his eyes. But everything in her already responded to his touch, and she didn't think, didn't analyze, didn't plan anything any longer. She wrapped her arms around his neck and brought him closer as she leaned in enough for their lips to meet.

Maybe because she'd yearned for this for so long, the effect was electrifying. Everything in her seemed to come alive and fill with so much delight she could hardly hold it within. She knew the meaning of the word *euphoria*, but she hadn't felt it before.

Until now.

Chapter Fourteen

Kai was going home with more questions than answers. And based on the line creasing her forehead, so was Marina.

She'd clicked her seat belt closed in her airplane seat and was typing furiously on her phone. He had a feeling it wasn't for entertainment.

He settled in his seat to let people pass and clicked his seat belt, then watched people walk in the aisle. Concern tightened his gut. Whoever followed them in Memphis wouldn't get onto the plane, as well, would they?

Not knowing what that person looked like made things more difficult. He guessed it wouldn't be a stooped woman who looked about ninety years old and leaned on a young man whom Kai presumed was her grandson. But one could wear a disguise.

Or this tired mom who smelled of vanilla ice cream and urged her triplets forward. One of the boys wore some of that ice cream on his white T-shirt where a dinosaur caricature prowled as if sniffing out the treat—or maybe trying to play with the green rubber dinosaur in his hand. Freckles generously peppered the boys' round faces, especially their upturned noses, and their eyelashes and eyebrows were ginger like their tousled hair.

Longing for children unraveled in Kai's heart again. Then the second boy hit the first one with the toy dinosaur as they ran through the aisle, and the first one hit back but got the third boy. That one wore a toy saber, and screams and fights ensued.

"He did it first!"

"No, he did it first!"

"That's because you ate my ice cream!"

"I had to!"

"Why?"

"Because it was melting!"

"Give me my ice cream back!"

"You are not gonna like it if I give it back!"

The mom groaned and tried to calm the triplets down. Kai's longing for children decreased significantly, but he clicked his seat belt open and hurried to the boys.

He asked the woman's permission, then played one of the word games he used at the pirate ship reenactments if the children became unruly. He didn't have the helpful pirate disguise this time, but the distraction still worked.

"Thank you so much!" The woman wiped sweat from her forehead and wrangled her boys into the seats where she had the seat belts hold them in place. The boys protested and tried to wiggle out.

"You're a lifesaver." Then she sighed miserably. "It won't last long, though. Our second iPad broke, and soon we probably won't hear ourselves think from their screams."

The female flight attendant flinched and paled. Across the aisle, so did the young couple with wedding rings on their fingers and newlywed love in their eyes. That couple was probably rethinking having children anytime soon.

The mom rubbed her temples, and the dad was nowhere to be seen. "I'll give them my phone and our other iPad in airplane mode, but that would only calm down two out of three. I feel so bad for the other passengers." Guilt twisted her tired features indeed.

He returned to his seat to pick up his phone to give it to the boys' mom. He'd grown up without any gadgets at the ranch, but he'd never judge parents who used them to distract children, especially in this situation.

Marina handed him an iPad. "It's clean. I mean, I don't have any personal information on it. Brand new, actually. I know they look young, but you wouldn't believe what kind of things children can dig up on your phone. Tell the mom it's my gift."

"That's sweet of you." He took it, and her fingers brushed against his skin, causing pleasant tingles. "You happened to have a brand-new iPad in your purse?"

"Yup. As for being sweet, it's also in our interest to have a quiet flight." She returned to her phone. Clearly, the touch didn't affect her nearly as it had affected him. That awareness shouldn't send a jolt of disappointment, but it still did.

The pilot announced a delay in takeoff due to a missing part. A shiver went down Kai's spine. He didn't mind the delay, but how important was that part? And why was it missing in the first place?

Well, nothing he could do about it.

Angry and worried voices erupted around him from passengers, especially the ones who had a connection. A tall man with a five-o'clock shadow dressed in camouflage pants and T-shirt snatched his forest-green backpack from the nearby overhead, wafting the scent of cigarettes before he asked the flight attendant to be let out.

Kai moved along the aisle and gave the iPad to the busy mom. "Here we go. It's yours."

Tears welled in her eyes. "Seriously?"

He nodded, hoping this iPad lasted longer than the previous one in those little hands. "Yes. It's from my friend."

The relief on the woman's freckled face was priceless as she handed the thing to the gadget-less child. "You must have an amazing friend."

His heart expanded. "I do." But oh, how he wanted to be more than friends!

He returned to his seat.

Marina met him with an admiring smile, making him feel like a hero even though she'd saved the day and passengers' ears with a spare gadget. "You're great with children."

"You are, too." He wasn't pushing the issue, was he?

The blonde flight attendant walked through the aisle, making sure everyone was buckled up. The color returned to her face now.

Marina looked out the window. "I don't know. If I could have a do-over, I wouldn't be so strict with my siblings." Then she reached into her purse and handed him a stick of chewing gum. "So your ears don't get clogged up due to changes in atmospheric pressure."

"Right. Thanks." He made sure not to touch her fingers this time as he accepted the gum, then popped it in his mouth, filling it with a minty taste. He leaned to her, and the scent of peppermint drifted to him.

As he was about to dispose of the wrapper, he noticed his finger was bleeding. He'd heard of paper cuts, but to cut a finger with a gum wrapper?

"Oh, I have antiseptic pads and a disinfectant cream. And a Band-Aid." She produced just that out of her purse. Then she wiped his fingers with a tiny square that smelled of alcohol and squeezed the disinfectant on his finger and... and blew on it.

It felt... pleasant. "Um, what was that?"

"Force of habit." She smiled sheepishly up at him. "I used to do it for my siblings when they'd cut themselves. I said it helped it heal better. And they'd stop crying." Then she placed the Band-Aid on his finger, her touch gentle. "All good."

"Thank you." He nearly regretted he'd only cut one finger. "How many things do you have in that purse?"

She chuckled, the sound reverberating through him. "It's a big list. I do have some water if you need it. It's important to stay hydrated."

Her laughter was the most beautiful sound in the world. Well, the cry of their newborn baby would be the most beautiful. His heart stuttered. As it didn't look like they'd ever get married and have children, he'd never know that one.

"Thanks," he said again. He and Quiet needed to expand their vocabulary. "You don't have to work all the time, you know."

"I have a lot I need to finish on this vacation."

"Which wasn't a real vacation thanks to your mother's request and later mine." Guilt stung him.

"The restaurant kind of grew on me. And I loved spending time with you. I just wish I could help resolve what happened to your brother."

Tenderness for her and worry for Blake warred in his heart. "You will." Or did his faith in her abilities put too much pressure on her? Was Marina's intelligence her downfall? People always expected too much from her, and he fell into that category. "But if you don't, you already did a fantastic job."

The pilot announced they were still searching for the missing part, resulting in an angry hum from the passengers.

"That's one of the many things I love about horses. They don't miss parts," he muttered. "But sadly, they can't fly."

Marina deflated. "You don't think someone messed with the plane because of us? I mean, there are these other people here, including children."

His teeth set on edge. "Maybe we should get off this flight." They could rent a car. It would be a very long trip, but... "We should tell the authorities, so the flight is canceled."

At that moment, the pilot announced the takeoff. The missing part was found.

Marina waved for him to sit. "I believe I let my imagination get the best of me. Let's think logically. What do we have so far? The van seemed to follow us, but it could've been mere coincidence. And even if someone followed us, it wouldn't suddenly escalate to messing with a plane. Besides, it's not easy to do. Everything is checked and scanned thoroughly. I reported the possible stalker to the local police and told them about taking this flight. They didn't advise us against taking it. I also talked to the airport authorities already."

Of course, she had.

He sat down again and started praying. A lot.

The blonde flight attendant in her navy-blue uniform walked along the aisle again, making sure everyone was buckled up.

The plane shook and moved forward. Kai tensed. But the flight didn't seem to bother Marina as her expression didn't change. She started typing something on her phone. While he probably would kiss the grass once they landed.

Riding horses on their ranch had never sounded so appealing.

The plane shook again, more violently this time as it lifted off the ground, and he squeezed the armrests. He prayed with renewed enthusiasm.

Marina placed her hand on his. "It's going to be all right."

The sound of her voice and the warmth of her gesture, rather than the words themselves, released tension from his chest. But then yearning for her filled the vacated space.

She leaned to him, giving a fresh whiff of that peppermint gum, then lowered her voice. "I'm going to send samples for DNA tests as soon as we land."

He planned to do a happy dance as soon as they landed. And send prayers of gratitude. Then it registered. "What samples? What DNA tests?"

"I bought several DNA tests to spare." She patted her purse. "As for samples, why do you think I went to the bathroom at the Parks' place? Okay, don't answer that question."

Heat rose up his neck. "I wasn't going to."

Her lips curved up at his embarrassment. "I didn't dare to steal Dr. Park's toothbrush—good thing his wife's was pink, making his obvious. Hopefully, what I got from it will be enough."

"Ooooh, and then the water bottle you picked up after the professor drank from it…" He peered at the water bottle she'd placed on the tray in front of him. "You're not trying to get my DNA sample, are you?"

Her smile widened, making his heart flutter. "No, I've got yours already. Remember the extra swabs?"

"Right. Do you always think several steps ahead?"

She shook her head, sending that gorgeous hair flying. "No. I can't even figure out one step ahead with Buttercup. Except that, she's *definitely* going to chew more of my shoes. Just the right one from each pair." Her smile turned wistful. "Yet I miss her a lot."

And he missed Marina a lot already, even though she was near him.

"I have some ideas, but I need more information. I sent several texts to Kennedy and will see if she can help." Marina glanced at her phone screen.

"Help with what?"

"With visitors who stayed in our town during the time you were left at the beach. I prefer to rely on evidence. But sometimes I have these nudges, and I learned not to ignore them. And I have this feeling it's all connected to that event."

He ached to tell her what kind of feelings he had for her but stopped himself.

Clueless about the struggle inside him, she continued. "I know people do things out of character. But what we learned about your bio mom so far doesn't fit with someone who'd abandon her child in danger."

He wanted to believe that.

Her eyes grew sad. "I'll need to help at the restaurant tomorrow the entire day. Or Gale will have a conniption—and hers are worthy of her name. So I won't be able to meet with you."

His rib cage tightened, but he nodded. "I understand. I'll need to make up for missing time at the ranch as well."

"But I'll work on this case as much as I can."

"You don't have to." His gaze lingered on her lovely face. He couldn't look away, and he didn't want to. "Where does all this leave us?" His question had several meanings.

Her eyes grew sad as if she understood both of those meanings. "I don't know. But I hope to figure it out eventually."

After they'd landed and he made it to the ranch, he didn't just send up prayers of gratitude and do a happy dance at the stable. He sang a happy song, as well, with horses as an audience.

And he couldn't wait to hear what kind of ideas Marina would come up with.

LATE THE NEXT EVENING, Marina rocked herself in the porch swing with Buttercup on her lap as if it could quiet her sadness. It didn't. Maybe because she remembered sitting on this very swing with Kai.

Buttercup yawned, then stretched, and Marina scratched the puppy's head. Usually, the little one filled Marina with joy and tenderness, but not today.

The swing's chains squeaked, grating on her nerves. Or was it the silence grating on her? She'd asked for time away from Kai because of her responsibilities. But with a void inside her, she missed him already. This was just the beginning, and the thought nearly made her wince.

Her fingers itched to call him despite the late hour. But he needed time to rest after a day of hard labor. And she needed to organize things in her head into neat compartments. She couldn't do that with his presence scrambling her thoughts.

She'd pulled strings to get the DNA test results faster than normal. Still, getting them by tomorrow would need a miracle.

Saylor and Gale had gone to sleep early after a tiring day at the restaurant. But after changing out of her uniform, Marina lingered on the porch of her mom's house. She hadn't done much neat organizing yet because her thoughts kept returning to Kai.

The light faded to dusk, and lampposts turned on.

A growling motor made her look up. A sleek silver sports car, unusual for their neighborhood, pulled up to the curb near the modest house. Kennedy slipped out wearing a flowy dress with a metallic tint and her hair hidden under a wide silvery scarf long enough to reach her waist. Once again, she reminded Marina of the moonlight.

Kennedy moved just as quietly as she walked to the house as if she'd long learned to do her best to stay unnoticed. Buttercup lifted her head and gave a baby growl but fell silent when Marina told her it was a friend.

"Mind if I join you?" Kennedy stopped, uncertainty pinching the edges of her eyes.

"I'd love it." Marina gestured to a salad-green cushion beside her on the swing painted a chocolate color.

"Thanks." Kennedy sat, the chains creaking their protest. Salt-crusted, they'd need to be oiled.

Buttercup wobbled in their guest's direction and sniffed Kennedy's hand, the puppy's tail wagging already.

"Aren't you adorable?" Kennedy patted Buttercup. The tail started wagging with more force.

Satisfied that indeed it was a friend, Buttercup gave Kennedy's hand a thorough lick to express her own friendliness, then plopped back on her behind on Marina's lap, her duty done.

Marina smiled. "She likes you."

"She's a sweetheart," Kennedy said, and Buttercup preened. Then Kennedy drew a deep breath. "I hope I'm not intruding. I was just passing by and saw you."

Alone.

Kennedy didn't say the word, but she didn't have to. Marina had felt that way after her divorce. She'd felt that way for most of her marriage. She and her ex had worked a lot, so the loneliness wasn't as noticeable. But he'd withdrawn from her long before she'd found out about his infidelities, and she hadn't known how to reach him.

As Kai changed everything in her life again, she'd forgotten the feeling of loneliness. Now she was going back to that oppressive feeling. She patted Buttercup. She couldn't even take the puppy with her. Because it wasn't her pet. Just like her husband wasn't her man for years.

"I'm glad you joined me," Marina said carefully. They'd both been introverts, and she wasn't sure how to carry the conversation.

Buttercup had broken the ice, but what now?

"I often drive at night, without a direction in mind. Sometimes I just go along the coast and look at the ocean." In the dim light, Kennedy's expression was unreadable, but Marina suspected it would have been just as hard to decipher in blazing sunlight.

"Can't sleep?" Marina studied her unusual guest.

"Nope."

Was her insomnia because of Kennedy's parents' death? Or was there something else? Marina didn't have the right to ask.

Instead, only the buzz of the nearby cicadas and the whisper of the distant ocean interrupted their silence. But if Marina knew something about introverts—and she knew a lot—it was that they were great listeners.

Her mind couldn't find a solution so far, so maybe Kennedy could help. And while Marina could talk to Saylor or Gale, she already knew their opinions because they were part of their company and liked Kai. Marina needed a reasonable, unbiased person.

"How do you walk away from someone who means a lot to you?" she whispered, looking at the moon instead of Kennedy.

"With heartache."

Marina winced. That wasn't the answer she wanted. As if sensing the change in mood, Buttercup whined, and Marina scratched her back to calm the puppy—and to prevent her sisters from waking. Buttercup closed her eyes.

"Do... do you have to walk away?"

At Kennedy's softly voiced question, Marina hugged the puppy. "We're too different and live in different places."

Darkness fell, cloaking them in a starry velvet blanket. The air grew colder. Yet Marina didn't move from her place.

"Geographic distance doesn't matter nearly as much as the distance in one's mind." Kennedy's scarf slid back a little, and she corrected it. Then she rubbed her wrist, covered by many bracelets, and frowned. She wore the same sophisticated, expensive scent, but it sent an unpleasant reminder through Marina.

"True. But I also don't want to have my heart broken by a player again."

Kennedy's pale lips moved up a little. "I believe you're very wrong about Kai."

"You know?" Marina sat up straighter so fast the motion shifted Buttercup on her lap.

The pup opened one eye, closed it again, and curled up, not a care in the world. Who couldn't envy the puppy? But then, didn't Kai make her feel that way sometimes? As if she didn't have a care in the world?

Kennedy's lips quirked. "I wouldn't be good at my job if I didn't know what was happening in the town. But it doesn't take much to notice that Kai loves you."

The words struck a chord, but Marina must think rationally, not romantically. "Loves me? That's an exaggeration. He must fall in love with every woman he dates—and we've never even dated."

"I don't think even you believe any of those statements are true except for the question. But then, I've never been an expert on love. I just know it's easy to lose things and..." Kennedy visibly swallowed. "And people. So, once you have a person who makes you happy, you should hold onto that person with everything in you."

Her guest's unexpected passion made Marina look closer at her. But once again, it was difficult to read her eyes.

What, or rather who, did Kennedy talk about? And how could Marina help? If this tentative friendship survived her leaving town, maybe she'd get a chance to.

"What is the place where you're happy?"

Kai's question rang in her ears. At that time, she didn't know how to answer.

But after Kennedy's words, she had clarity. And not only because she'd started healing in her hometown, the experience so different from when she'd been growing up.

She was happy with Kai. Plain and simple.

Even if it didn't fit into neat compartments.

The wind sent hair into Marina's face, and she pushed it back. "Do you love your job?"

"I am... I'm fine with it. Do you love yours?" Kennedy's eyes probed her.

Marina lifted her chin in defiance of her doubts. "I achieved a lot in my field. I've proved myself in it."

"What are you proving now?"

Marina's eyes widened. "Good question." She loved talking to a fellow intellectual, especially one who didn't look down on her like her ex had. "But can I turn my world upside down? Can I throw my organized life into chaos?"

Kennedy tapped on the swing's wooden planks. "When I started working in the hospitality business, my uncle explained there's no logic when it comes to most people. You wouldn't believe the requests we get sometimes or what people do in the rooms. I used to panic sometimes or get flabbergasted or upset. It helped me a lot once I understood that life is, in essence, chaos."

Kennedy stared at the starry sky for some time. Did she search for constellations, as well? Finally, she said, "Regarding the research you asked me to do—"

"I'm sorry I put that impossible task on you." Marina waved it off. "It happened over thirty years ago. And those people might've rented a house instead of staying at a hotel. Most likely under false names."

"They did. They rented *that* cottage."

Marina froze. "What?"

"Like you said, under false names, of course." Kennedy sighed. "Somehow, *that* cottage always gets mixed up in weird things, so I figured I'd check. My uncle helped." Her usually even voice warmed unexpectedly at the words *my uncle*. "At that time, *that* cottage looked way better than it does now. But the best part for them must've been its remote location."

Marina's head was spinning. "How did you figure it out if they used false names?"

"The photos you provided, of course. Thankfully for us and not so thankfully for the couple, there was a minor leak in the kitchen sink, and

Uncle's manager had to call our company plumber. He's retired now and mostly does fishing, but he still has an excellent memory. As well as three adorable little granddaughters."

Marina stared at Kennedy. "You know his granddaughters?"

Kennedy's expression softened. "You have no idea how important plumbing is to hotels and rental properties. Besides, every person who works for or worked at our company is important to me."

Marina nodded. "I believe that." She didn't have high respect for many people in her life and held admiration for even fewer. She already had high respect and admiration for Kennedy. This woman was also more complicated than she showed at first glance. Marina would like a friend like that. With mutual respect, including respecting personal boundaries.

"Anyway, he recognized Dr. Park and Naree Jones when I showed him the photos. He couldn't repair the problem the first time because he needed to get a necessary part. And here's another interesting tidbit. The plumber heard a little boy laughing and chattering the first time he visited and a female voice quieting the rambunctious child."

"What about the second time?"

"The plumber didn't even make it inside. Dr. Park looked disheveled and upset, and a guilty look flashed in his eyes as he ran after a blonde woman who was hurrying away from the cottage carrying a suitcase. Her eyes were red as if from crying. The plumber felt he was intruding on a family drama, so he hid behind a tree, ready to step in if the man hit the woman. At least, that's what he told me. Here's the approximate conversation."

Kennedy handed over a typed-up transcript as if she'd recorded a court session. She shrugged. "I wanted to write the scenario down verbatim as the plumber told me."

Nodding, Marina took the paper and read it.

The man screamed, trying to catch the woman's elbow, and pleaded, "Please don't go!"

The woman whirled around. "Leave me alone! How could you? Because of you, I lost our son. You tricked me! You said you'd take him to the beach while I felt unwell. Instead, you *left* him there. What if he drowned?"

The man's hand dropped. "I wasn't going to let that happen. I just went to get him ice cream, and he wandered off."

"I don't believe you." The woman spat.

"Believe what you want." The man's posture stiffened. "But it all turned out for the best. He's getting adopted into a great family. The Lawrences. I checked it."

Tears streamed down the woman's face, and the hand free from the suitcase fisted. "I'm going to the police. I'm getting my son back."

"First, try to prove you didn't abandon him." The man stepped back from her. "Then, let's say you throw me under the bus and get the boy back. You don't have long to live. You don't have any relatives. I can't risk taking him without jeopardizing my reputation. What's going to happen to him? He'll go into the foster system. And here's a ready-made family preparing to adopt him. You're thinking about yourself. Think about our son."

The woman's eyes widened, but her hand was no longer fisted. "I can't believe I once loved you."

FOR A FEW MOMENTS, Marina digested the information. "Why didn't the plumber go to the police?"

Kennedy shrugged. "He had no explanation for that. But I checked, and around the same time, he received a large payment that helped put his daughter through college."

"Then it wasn't in his interests to reveal this story to you now." Marina raised an eyebrow. It was getting colder, and she wrapped the jacket tighter.

"Maybe he needed to relieve his guilty conscience. Besides, I can be very persuasive sometimes."

Marina smiled. "I have no doubt." She needed to tell Kai this.

"I've got to go." Kennedy rose, sending the swing swaying. "Hope this was useful."

"Tremendously." Marina rose, as well. Some things still didn't add up, but she had a much better picture now. "Thank you so much. I owe you."

"You owe me nothing. Good night." Kennedy started walking toward her car.

"Um, I'd like us to be friends. Maybe we could meet for tea or something when I'm back in town?" Marina called after Kennedy, her stomach clenching. It was the first time she offered friendship to someone. How awkward and liberating! Usually, people befriended her, like Kai or Dallas had, and Marina hadn't resisted too much.

Well, it was going to feel much more awkward and way less liberating if the richest woman in town said no.

Kennedy glanced back, and her lips lifted up, just a little. "I'd like that."

After Kennedy left, Marina hurried inside her childhood house while carrying Buttercup, slipped into her room, and settled on a chair. Then she called Kai while stroking the puppy. Just the sound of his voice made her heart swell.

"Sorry to call this late." She kept her voice low to avoid waking her sisters.

"Are you kidding me? I'm happy to hear from you at any time."

Her heart swelled some more. But she had things to tell him, so she plunged ahead and repeated all Kennedy had told her. Once done, she chose her words carefully. "Your mother didn't abandon you. She loved you very much."

In the pause, she wished she'd told him all this in person. Then she could take his hand or hug him to support him. Even if all that did weird things to her heart. Well, just talking to him did weird things to her heart.

At last, a rush of his breath vibrated the speaker. "I needed this. I needed it more than I realized. But how does Blake's disappearance fit into all this?"

"It looks like he found out what his father did. I'm still trying to decipher the rest."

"So... Dr. Blake Park Sr. is my father, as well."

The bitterness in Kai's voice made her ache. She nodded though, of course, he couldn't see it. "It appears so. I hope to receive the results of DNA tests tomorrow."

"It was a great idea to sneak into his bathroom to get a swab from his toothbrush."

"It was no big deal." Her cheeks warmed. No matter her words, she loved him praising her. Of course, that was only one of many things she loved about him. Did she... did she love him?

She froze.

He misinterpreted the pause. "You must be tired. Can't wait to see you tomorrow."

"Me, too."

After their conversation, she lay awake for a long time, resisting falling asleep just as she'd resisted falling for Kai. But it was no use. She couldn't resist her feelings for him any longer and didn't want to.

In the morning, she received the DNA test results. The professor wasn't Kai's father, but she didn't expect him to be. Dr. Blake Park Sr. was. And he wasn't just Blake's adoptive father. He was Blake's biological father, as well. He had a lot of things to cover up. She texted Kai the results.

She frowned as she carried a steaming coffee cup to the breakfast nook. Things still didn't add up. Unless...

Unless she'd missed something. She breathed in the enticing scent of freshly brewed decent coffee. Saylor had already left for the restaurant, but Gale was still in her room, most likely stewing over another day of work. Marina added hazelnut creamer, took a few sips, and nearly purred with pleasure.

Buttercup plopped down on a sunny spot on the tile, full after kibble and tired after chewing another shoe at night.

Marina wiggled a finger at her. "This has got to be the last straw. The last shoe, I mean. No more chewing. Or we're going to puppy obedience school."

In response, Buttercup turned around and showed her tummy to the sun.

Marina rolled her eyes. Kai was her sunny spot. He made her happy. Kennedy had a point. Why wouldn't Marina want to be with the person who made her happy? Why was she running away from him?

But could *she* make Kai happy? Could she be the loving mother for the children he wanted so badly? Could she be the only one for him, forever and ever? Or would he get bored? He wouldn't cheat on her, wouldn't leave her, but if he emotionally checked out, it would destroy her.

There was only one way to find out.

Kai wasn't like her ex. There was a difference between people who felt a deep emotional connection and people who by the end just lived together, finding their emotional connection elsewhere.

Waaaaait a moment.

Then things started to fit. She snatched her phone and texted questions to Barrett and included Kai in the group chat. Then she texted Kennedy a question along with another photo.

She had to wait for the answer. Then it would be the time to go to the police. And she needed to talk to Kai. Would she dare to tell him about her feelings? Premonition squeezed her rib cage.

Gale wandered toward the breakfast nook. "Don't even try to tell me you're going to ditch the restaurant today. You won't get away with pulling that again." She walked back to the hall without waiting for an answer.

So Marina just whispered to herself. "Watch me."

When the doorbell rang, she tensed. Oh no. "Gale, don't answer." Usually, she had to ask Gale to do things. It had been years since she'd told her not to do anything instead.

But this time, Gale yelled from the hall. "Someone's here asking for you."

Marina's heart fell. She texted Kai, "Send the police to Mom's place." Then she snatched Buttercup, opened the window into the backyard, and let her slide onto the grass.

"I'll be right there!" She slipped the steak knife into the fold of her pajamas and rushed to the front door. She could've escaped through the window, but she couldn't let her sister deal with the mess she'd created. At the same time, she hoped she was wrong.

She met the barrel of a gun.

"I didn't expect two people instead of one, but I guess it doesn't matter at this point."

Chapter Fifteen

An hour earlier...

A rancher's day started early, often with the sun, especially in the summer.

Kai rose at dawn, queasy over the time he'd taken away from the ranch during their busy season. And yet he couldn't wait to have more time away again to see Marina. Just thinking about her stirred his blood.

He placed biscuits in the oven for breakfast, then had a gust of cold from the fridge as he got bacon.

Though his reason to see her wouldn't be a joyous one. His insides grew heavy, and even the sizzle of bacon in the skillet and the yummy scent spreading in the kitchen didn't cheer him up. She'd sent him new information this morning, and they'd be meeting up to go to the police station at lunchtime. He'd prefer they went first thing, but she said she needed more information from Kennedy first.

He frowned as he decreased the gas under the bacon skillet, then broke eggs into a large bowl and started to beat them using a hand whisk instead of letting the electric beater make its clamor. He didn't want to wake anyone yet.

Why did she need to wait? She'd texted him the DNA test results. His hand stilled, the metal whisk clattering to the edge of the porcelain bowl. So Dr. Blake Park Sr. was his father. Blake's biological father, as well. Things were clear now—or mostly clear. But Marina still wanted to have them neatly organized in her head. So did Kai.

Like knowing where Blake was. Was he still alive? Did he really commit suicide, or did someone make him disappear because he'd found out the truth about their father?

Faced with way more questions than he could answer, Kai resumed beating the poor eggs. Where did he stand with Marina now? They'd kissed, but did that mean as much to her as it did to him? To him, she was way more than a friend.

Okay, all those questions made his thoughts more scrambled than eggs.

"Someone is up early."

"Good morning." Kai whirled toward Austin. "Just a little something to make up for my absence lately."

Austin rolled his eyes. "You don't need to make up anything. And what can I do to help?"

"Quiet has a different opinion about me not making up for my absence. He's been sulking and uncharacteristically *quiet* since I returned." Some might think the name odd for such a noisy pet, but quiet was the bird's favorite word. He often shouted out into the silence after having had it said to him too much and too loudly when he squawked in his early days. Thus, with his attention-grabbing antics, he'd earned the name. "I tried to explain that taking him on a plane wasn't a good idea. But Quiet probably thinks he could fly to Tennessee on his own. Which reminds me, he's getting a bit too good at flying. He needs his wings clipped again." Kai added another dash of milk, then poured the egg mix into a preheated nonstick pan. "You could get coffee going, please. And turn over the bacon."

"Sure." Austin started with the bacon, which was the right call before it could get overly crisped. "And you can bring Quiet into my office anytime for his wing clip. Wanna tell me about your trip and what's bothering you?"

"We'd need more than the few minutes we have here. Are you leaving for the vet clinic after breakfast?" Kai checked on the biscuits, turning away from the heat wave pouring from the oven. A few more minutes, and they'd be ready. The scent was mouthwatering already. He closed the oven door and eyed his brother.

"I cleared my morning to do vaccinations for our herd." Austin placed a filter into the coffee pot, then measured coffee in, spreading the bean aroma around.

Usually, Austin had a smile ready in the morning. Today, he was more thoughtful. Maybe it was because his favorite horse had an infection in his leg or because of a heavy load at the clinic due to the tourist season. Yet Austin had found time to help out at the ranch.

Unlike Kai for the last few days. "I'll help." He grimaced. "But I'll need to leave before lunch."

Austin poured the water in and turned the coffee on. "It's fine. You work hard at the ranch. You don't have to spend every minute on it. We love you because of you, you know. Not the work you put in here."

Kai's heart shifted as he scrambled up the eggs in the skillet with a spatula. "Sometimes, I feel like I owe you all the hard work at the ranch. For taking me in."

"Nonsense!" Mom entered the kitchen, then tied an apron around her waist, its tangerine hue as bright as her sunny smile. "You're a huge blessing to us."

Grateful tears prickled behind his eyes. "It might be a horrible thing for me to say, but I'm sorta glad my father left me at the beach that day. I don't think I'd have thrived in the Park family. But I got adopted into the best family in the world."

"Oh, you'll make me cry." Mom scooped him into a bear hug, and Austin joined in, then Darius, probably drawn by the scent of bacon, joined, as well.

Kai would've stayed in that hug forever, but then he remembered. "The biscuits!" He eased out of the embrace and whirled to the oven. He got them out just in time.

The fresh-baked-biscuit aroma joined the promising one of coffee and bacon as Mom leaned over the tray and breathed in deeply, her smile approving. "Made like a true Lawrence. I couldn't have made them better myself." Then she touched his arm. "Sounds like you've got new information to share? You said your father left you? And you mentioned growing up with the Parks. So your blood connection to Blake is through your father?"

"More than that, actually. We're full siblings. Plus..." While they finished making breakfast and set the table, Kai told his family a short version of what he'd learned about his biological father and about his feelings for Marina. While he received compassionate pats on the back and wows over the story about Dr. Blake Park Sr., nobody seemed to be surprised about Marina.

"You should tell Marina about your feelings," Austin said.

"Hmm, and yet you don't tell *your* crush about yours." Darius patted Austin on the shoulder as he passed him with the bread basket.

Kai lingered near Austin with a lemonade carafe that chilled his hands. "What's that about?" But then after how his brother had looked at Kennedy in the restaurant... "Right, I might have some idea."

Austin groaned and clattered the bacon platter to the counter. "My case is different. By the way, Darius, not a good idea to tease the person carrying bacon. I could drop the plate, you know."

"Don't you dare!" Darius yelled from the dining room.

"I don't want to lose Marina." Kai took control of the conversation again, rescuing his brothers from any awkwardness as he always tried. "But I don't want to tie her down, either. And now, the worst part is that my search might've put her in danger."

"If two people love each other, they'll find a way to make it work," Mom said with authority as she placed her favorite cow-shaped creamer and sugar bowl on the oak table. Kai remembered him and his brothers saving up to buy those for her one Mother's Day. "By the way," Mom continued, "if you *do* make it work, we'll need to find a way to invite Kennedy to the wedding and make her sit near Austin."

"Mom!" This time, it was Austin who yelled from the dining room. But thankfully, he was no longer carrying the bacon.

The rest of the brothers wisely filed in once the table was already set.

Once they all gathered at the table, Kai sent up a prayer of gratitude while Austin took his turn to say grace. Clasping hands with his mother and Darius, Kai did miss one person at the table.

Marina.

He missed her with his whole being already, and she hadn't even left yet. But she would, in only three days. Despite the idyllic—or almost idyllic situation with his family—a cold chill squeezed his heart. A premonition? Or just nerves? Might be because Blake was still missing—or most likely worse. Or because Marina was leaving soon.

The feeling of gloom pressed on his chest.

HER INSIDES TREMBLING, Marina moved to stand in front of Gale. "My sister has nothing to do with this. Please let her go."

"What's going on?" Gale shrieked.

Marina flinched, and a chill iced her blood. They hadn't been on the best terms lately, but she'd never want anything to happen to Gale. She was still her little sister who Marina loved deep inside. Well, veeeeery deep inside.

"Please," Marina said again. At the same time, her mind whirled, searching for a way out. Anything she could try to do without putting her sister in danger.

She should've called 911 in the few spare seconds she had instead of texting Kai. He might not see her text for a while. But she'd need more than a few seconds for that, and she'd been scared Gale could get shot in the interim.

Marina's heart stuttered at the thought of Kai, but she couldn't allow herself any distractions.

Lord, please keep Gale safe. Please let Kai see my text in time.

Would the Lord answer her prayers? In the hurt of her husband's infidelities, Marina had lost not only her trust in men but also the faith she'd been raised with. Now, she was desperate to get both back—and not just because she needed to believe God could help her but also because she needed to believe Kai could love her.

Her unwanted guest sighed. "You should've thought about this before you started poking into my life. It's your own fault. Now your sister is just collateral damage."

"What?" Gale shrieked again behind Marina's back.

Guilt slammed Marina, but she had to keep her mind clear. She had to figure this out. She soothed her voice as much as she could, despite everything shaking inside. "It doesn't have to be this way. If you leave right now, I won't press charges."

"*I* will!" Gale tried to move forward.

Not helping, sis.

"My sister will keep quiet, too." Marina raised her voice a little. "If she knows what's good for her."

Gale must've realized the gravity of the situation because she didn't say anything else. Buttercup started barking in the yard. Would she attract enough attention from neighbors? Probably not, but at least, the puppy was out of danger.

The armed and uninvited guest frowned. "It's too late for that. You've already destroyed everything I worked so hard for. You know what happened at the beach with Kwan that day."

"How did you find out that we knew?" Marina slapped herself on the forehead. "The plumber. He thought he'd found the way to pay for his granddaughters' college, too, right?" Her gaze scanned the room. She couldn't get to her gun in time. And whatever she did would leave Gale exposed. Now she knew how Skylar had felt in a similar situation.

Would Kai come through for her like Dallas had come through for Skylar? Or would this be it for Marina and her sister? A cold shiver traveled down her spine. She did have the knife, but a bullet was much faster than a knife.

All she could do now was to keep her cool and keep the perp talking like Skylar had.

"Yes. I made the mistake of leaving a loose end back then, and he just had to blab everything after all these years. Hoping for another payment, he called me and told me he'd been asked by a woman what happened that day. I guessed straight away who it would be. It seemed time to tie off all the loose ends, starting with you."

Phew. At least Kennedy was safe.

"If you kill us"—Marina did her best to ignore the gasp behind her back—"it'll be much worse for you. Double homicide compared with child abandonment, which you could claim to know nothing about. Or is that triple homicide?"

"You don't understand." Gray eyes narrowed.

"Explain it to me." It was a tactic to stall, but Marina couldn't understand this. Paying someone to follow them—that she understood. But showing up to shoot her and an innocent bystander to stop the truth from coming out? She didn't get it. Or maybe she didn't want to believe what was happening. "Is it because of your social status?"

"People like you don't get it." That part was true. "We're upstanding citizens. Our reputation has to be spotless. We matter a lot in society. This would destroy my husband's career."

Marina stopped herself from asking "why."

Kai, please, please read the text on your phone.

"But aren't you taking a huge risk now?" Marina measured the distance in her mind and whether it was a good chance to lunge, but she'd need a distraction first. And once again, it would leave Gale in the line of fire. Ice crystallized in Marina's veins.

"Not really." The guest smirked. "Nobody will know. The gun has a silencer. Your neighbors aren't at home. I checked. And I know how to wipe the cameras before I leave."

"You can't hope to get away with killing everyone who knows. Us. The plumber. And Kai knows the truth about his biological father, and has probably told his family." If only she'd called him the moment she'd realized everything!

"I doubt he figured out what you just did."

Marina might as well say it. "What? The part where you killed Blake, and why?"

Chapter Sixteen

Marina studied the woman's reaction and received the information she'd looked for. Widened eyes, a backward movement as if recoiling from a slap. Yes, she got it, but it was too late. And she wasn't in the safety of a courtroom. But it did buy her some time.

Gale sank down in a chair, sobbing now. Marina's heart went out to her sister, but she couldn't comfort her right now.

"Now why would I do that? Blake was the pride and joy of our family." The gun moved a little closer.

How much chance did Marina have to stab before that gun could be fired? Not much at all. And despite her hope, the gun hadn't lowered even a fraction yet.

Marina wasn't great in hand-to-hand combat, but she was good with presenting arguments, her kind of combat and the perfect battleground. "Your husband's pride and joy. Not yours. He was doing so much better than your own daughter. And I'm guessing you never wanted to raise a son who wasn't yours. And then he saw Kai on social media, and started getting closer to knowing the truth about how you talked your husband into abandoning his other son."

"I was patient!" Mrs. Park spat out. "I was very patient. But my husband wanted to cut our daughter off. And I had to pretend to support that decision. Imagine that? Do you know how it feels to raise a child who is the result of your husband's affair? Have you any idea?"

"It must've been very difficult for you," Marina said. Was that a motor's growl? Or just wishful thinking?

Mrs. Park waved the gun but didn't put it down. "He lied to me the first time. But I figured out that Blake was really his son. The second time, he wanted to adopt the child again. I put my foot down, and he eventually did what I wanted. No one guessed the truth. But then Blake started asking questions. I tried to talk him out of contacting his brother. Even sent Sue here to try to stop him from having the DNA tests done. I couldn't let him ruin our reputation. Have charges pressed against my husband for child abandonment."

"It would've been hard to prove that. The charges wouldn't stick." Marina lifted her arms in a placating gesture while meeting Mrs. Park's glare. "But yeah, I get it. It's all about reputation. What did you do with Blake's body? I'm guessing you put some sort of poison into something he used often. His water bottle maybe? Then made it look like suicide by drowning."

"Coffee. The bitterness covered the taste. I intended it to look like an overdose. But it seems he then went for a swim and drowned." Mrs. Park shrugged. "No problem. It still worked perfectly with the suicide note I'd faked. His own notepaper, with his fingerprints on it."

Smiling, she even seemed proud of what she'd done. Yet something still didn't add up. "But—"

"No more questions!" Mrs. Park steadied the gun with both hands, pointed right at Marina's chest.

Marina's heart dropped on the unforgiving tile. She wouldn't be able to stall any longer. She and Gale might have only minutes—or seconds!—to live.

Lord, please help us. Please help us survive. And if it's not in Your will, then... then help Kai and my family grieve. Buttercup, too.

In the next moment, she'd have to risk it all. Instead of finding a solution, her mind traveled to Kai. When her life was at stake, she had no doubt she loved him.

Her life didn't flash in front of her eyes. Instead, just moments with Kai. His infectious laugh. His tenderness when he looked at her. Their first kiss that probably arrived too late. And the incredible way he made her feel.

She didn't only want moments of all those things that would soon disappear with the gun smoke. She wanted a lifetime of them.

Gale didn't just cry by now, she howled. "It's all your fault, Marina! It's all your fault!"

Unshed tears prickled Marina's eyes. "Sorry, Gale. I'm so very sorry."

Now Marina wanted all the things that might never happen. This was her moment of truth, and it took a gun to her face to show her what mattered. Like loving Kai. Reconnecting with her family. Rediscovering her faith in God. And in her mind's eye, she saw Kai and herself playing with a little boy and girl in their yard. He'd be a hands-on dad. A great one. She could love those children with motherly love. Not a forced third-parent love.

But most likely, she'd never have a chance.

"I'm too young to die!" Gale wailed.

Marina slipped the knife closer to her palm. Due to the nature of her job, she knew it was a misconception that one could easily kill with a knife. Even multiple stabs might not accomplish that unless the person didn't get help in time and bled out. Of course, if she struck a carotid artery or another important artery, it was a different matter. But that was hard to do. Mrs. Park would be able to fire first.

But maybe... Marina recalled something Kai taught her when she'd been bullied in school "in case he wasn't around to help."

"We've talked too long already." Mrs. Park's eyes narrowed. "It's time to get this done." She sounded indifferent, as if she were about to mark off another item on her shopping list.

Lord, please send a distraction.

Then a noise sounded from the kitchen, and the next moment, Quiet flapped into the room in a blur of blue and green and yellow, probably arriving through the window she'd left open.

The bright bird screeched and flew right at Mrs. Park's face. She raised her arms to defend herself.

Yes!

"Gale, duck!" Marina threw herself at Mrs. Park's legs, plunging the knife into the woman's ankle.

Mrs. Park stumbled and howled in pain. The gun went off, the silencer reducing the sound, but the shot was still loud. Nearly immediately, another shot sounded.

At the same time, the front door flung open, and people rushed inside. Marina saw mostly boots from her vantage point as she didn't dare get up yet. One set of boots were different from the others—painfully familiar, scuffed cowboy boots.

Then a male voice read Mrs. Park her Miranda rights. Someone chastised Kai for getting inside through the window. Quiet screeched again.

Quiet was alive. Kai was alive. Marina was still alive by some miracle. Relief flushed over her. But she didn't hear Gale yelling, blaming her for everything, and for the first time, Marina missed that.

"Gale, are you okay? Please help her!" Marina would never forgive herself if her sister was wounded or dead. All because of her.

A MOUNTAIN OF GUILT weighed on Kai's shoulders as he and Marina walked on the beach the next day. How could he have drawn her into something that nearly killed her and her sister?

Maybe some people were right, and he didn't think through things. He was superficial. Marina was better off without him. The moment he'd learned what was happening was the moment he'd admitted to himself what he'd known all along.

He loved her.

His heart sank into the sand. No matter how difficult letting her go would be, he had to. "I'm sorry I dragged you into all this."

Even Quiet perched on his shoulder and Buttercup running back and forth, sniffing things and reporting back with a bark about her findings, didn't cheer Kai up. While usually just waking up cheered him up.

"Oh please!" Strolling alongside him in a flowing peach dress, Marina scoffed. "It wasn't your fault at all. Besides, you didn't drag me into it. I sort of volunteered. I... I enjoyed doing this search with you." Then she grimaced. "Minus the standoff and nearly getting Gale killed, of course."

"Is she okay?" Kai winced from another load of guilt and Quiet spread his newly clipped wings in protest.

Kai was grateful his brother had freshly clipped the exquisite creature's wings so he could bring Quiet outside again without fearing the bird might hurt himself.

On the other hand, he thanked God that Quiet's feathers grew back after clipping. If the bird hadn't been able to fly strongly yesterday, the scene with

Mrs. Park might have ended in a heartbreaking way. Why he'd even taken his parrot with him was a mystery. Purely God's prompting.

And Quiet's loud squawking when he'd tried to leave the bird behind.

Marina moved her blonde hair away from her face, then accepted with words of gratitude a twig Buttercup had brought. "Gale's a bit shaken up. And ready to strangle me. But otherwise, unharmed."

He shuddered that it could've ended so differently for Marina and Gale. He couldn't imagine his life without Marina.

"It wasn't your fault. If anything, it was mine," he said.

"Let's stop trying to place the blame. Well, no. It was Mrs. Park's fault. That's it." She leaned to pet the puppy, then turned to him. "I'm so sorry your biological father agreed to abandon you. Are you going to be all right? What can I do to help?"

His heart swelled with even more love for her. She'd just been through a horrible traumatic experience, and yet she worried about him.

The wind threw her golden hair into her face again, and he moved it back, enjoying touching her face in the process—yes, enjoying it way too much. He let his fingers linger. "Thank you. I still have difficulty grasping it all."

She nodded. "It'll take time. I'm here if you need me. Even if it's just by phone." Her forehead creased a little, the sign that something concerned her. "Would you mind if we go by *that* cottage?"

He stopped in his tracks so suddenly his parrot screeched and dug in with his talons in order not to fall off. Kai resisted the urge to grind his teeth from the pain. It wasn't the bird's fault. Besides, his bird was a hero for saving not only the day yesterday but also, more importantly, the woman Kai loved. He'd already bought what should be a lifetime supply of treats for his pet. "Why?"

"Why? Why? Why?" Quiet screeched.

Shading her eyes, Marina stared at the ocean. "I've been having some thoughts."

"You always have some thoughts."

"True." She chuckled. Then her expression grew serious again. "I know that place has sad memories for you, but please humor me. Come with me?"

He'd go to the other side of the earth for her, not just *that* cottage. "Sure."

Then he realized they were already walking in that direction. She'd clearly known his answer before she'd asked. She knew him well. Except she couldn't see how much he loved her.

Buttercup stopped running back and forth and stood on her hind paws, placing her front ones on Marina's long dress and barking her demand.

"Did you get tired, darling?" She picked up the puppy, not paying attention to the wet paws now stamping sandy imprints on her gorgeous dress.

That brought the puppy in closer proximity with the parrot, which caused another enthusiastic bark. Kai had worried how their pets would get along, but mostly, Buttercup was excited to see Quiet, and Quiet had ignored Buttercup based on the rights of being there first.

Kai took her hand, and warmth spread through him when she didn't remove it. "Why do you want to go to *that* cottage? Kennedy said Blake's belongings had been shipped to his daughter, and a new tenant's there now."

"I–I don't want to say anything yet in case I'm wrong." The straw hat protected her face from the sun, but it also hid most of her expression.

And he desperately wanted to see it.

Even if they remained just friends, her mere presence was a treasure. People had been searching for pirate treasure on the coast, believing the legend. But his real treasure was right in front of him.

Quiet chirruped as if agreeing.

Kai was heartbroken about his biological brother, but so far, he hadn't moved in his stages of grief. He was still in denial. No matter what the culprit had said, Kai couldn't believe the brother he'd just found was gone already.

So he avoided thinking about Blake.

Marina looked up now, her eyes luminous, as if she sensed his thoughts. Captured by that expectant look as if she wanted him to say something, he wanted to tell her many things, first of all how much he loved her. Usually, he was nearly as talkative as his parrot, More so because Kai knew more words.

But today, he had to hold it in. The breeze ruffled her gorgeous hair, but this time, he didn't even dare to reach for it, afraid he'd give himself away if he touched her again.

It had all come full circle, hadn't it? Once again, he'd have to remain her friend and cheer from the sidelines as she returned to her life and achieved all the heights she was clearly capable of soaring to. Yet he could only hold in so much. "I hope you know how much you mean to me."

She looked up again, and the longing in her eyes struck him. "You, too. To me." Buttercup licked her face, and Marina chuckled. "And you, of course. I didn't forget about you." Then sadness settled in her eyes. "Until you, Buttercup, return to your rightful owner."

He couldn't handle seeing her sad, so he reminded her of a few mischiefs from his childhood. By the time they reached that cottage, she was laughing. Well, until the moment she climbed to the porch.

Then she looked serious, her features determined. "I hope I'm not making a mistake." She touched his bare forearm, her warm palm sending a sweet current through his veins. "And if I do, huge apologies in advance."

His curiosity piqued, mixing in with apprehension over being in such a place. What was all this about?

She knocked on the door.

To no answer.

So she knocked again, this time louder and calling out. "Mr. Olson, we need to ask a few questions. The sooner you open, the sooner we leave."

Finally, footfalls sounded inside as if someone dragged their feet. The door flung open.

"You're intruding on private property." A stooped man, his weathered forehead deeply wrinkled, leaned on a cane and glared up at them from under white eyebrows, his eyes bleak. Behind the white beard and mustache covering most of his face, he appeared about eighty-years-old. His voice crackled again. "I don't have time for any questions."

A suspicion entered Kai's mind, but it was too... too preposterous? Yes, that was the word Marina would use.

"Just one question, then." Marina shifted closer to the man but slowly, carefully, lifted her arms in a placating gesture. "Please. Then we'll leave."

The man coughed profusely. Then he growled. "What's that?"

"The danger seems to have passed. Why are you keeping up the charade? Why wear the disguise, Blake?"

Chapter Seventeen

One could've knocked Kai over with his parrot's feather. Quiet bobbed from one foot to another on Kai's shoulder as if to remind him he shouldn't even think that, because Quiet wasn't sharing any of his feathers. Not even the soft short ones on his green forehead before they faded into that gorgeous teal blue on his nape, back, tail, and wings. And definitely not the stunning golden-yellow ones of his now-puffed up chest or hidden beneath his wings.

He had to focus on his parrot, because he couldn't believe what he just heard.

The man sighed and waved them inside. "Come on in." He didn't ask for introductions, but if Marina's statement was right, he knew who they were.

Kai and Marina stepped inside. The place looked tidy, as if unlived-in and awaiting a new tenant.

The man gestured for them to sit, and Kai and Marina took seats on the indigo-hued sofa. Kai kept quiet because he was speechless.

Quiet filled in the pause. "Quiet! Quiet!"

Well, at least he wasn't swearing.

The man sighed as he placed the cane near the wall and walked to the armchair without it. He didn't stoop any longer and didn't drag his feet on the floor. "I could pretend I don't know what you're talking about. But you'd find some way to leave this place with my fingerprints. You already have my DNA, or you'd make an excuse to go to the bathroom and get a new sample to compare." His voice sounded about four decades younger now.

Marina spread her arms. "Then you can save us all time."

Quiet spread his wings but didn't try to fly. Even with freshly clipped wings, he could still glide a little. "Quiet! Quiet!"

Kai couldn't let the parrot do all the talking. "You're alive. You tricked us. And everyone else. Did you meet with me for this..." He couldn't find the right word, so he might as well recycle Marina's. "This charade?"

Blake winced as he lowered himself in the indigo-hued armchair. "I'm sorry. Not for being alive, but for deceiving you and others. I genuinely wanted to meet you, Kai. But when I saw the video of you rescuing that boy, I made the mistake of sharing my theory that we might be related with my adoptive mother. She let her mask slip when she asked me to meet her near here. Turned out she'd resented me all my life. I suspected she'd poisoned the coffee she brought with her, but I pretended to drink it. Then after she left, I found a fake suicide note she must have left in my car. I knew I had to do something to stay alive. I decided to play along with her plan."

"So you faked your own suicide." Kai raked his fingers through his hair. Processing this would take some time.

"I hope you'll find it in your heart to forgive me." Something glossed Blake's eyes as his voice dipped. He leaned forward, reaching one hand out to Kai. "Yes, I wanted to survive. But I was also afraid to bring danger to people close to me. And that included you." He grimaced as his gaze moved from Kai to Marina. "I heard it happened anyway. It was not my intention. I hoped my disappearance would keep everyone else safe."

"I chose to get involved." She waved him off. "Though it would've been better if you'd gone to the police instead of pretending to drown."

"I had no proof. Only suspicions. But how did you figure it out?"

She shrugged nonchalantly. "I didn't believe in the existence of the mystery ex-girlfriend your stepmother and sister talked about. None of your neighbors or colleagues mentioned her. And while often signs of suicide are hidden, there were no factors that usually increase the risk. Like a history of suicide in the family or in the person's history, giving away prized possessions, hopelessness, and so on. Plus, you went to a deserted stretch of beach. Wearing slacks and a tie. To the beach."

Blake frowned. "Yeah, probably not my brightest idea. Sloppy work."

"The opposite. If it was a genuine suicide, wearing those things to the beach isn't completely unlikely. But the slacks and tie were so *neatly* folded. In a moment of severe emotional distress, a person probably wouldn't be as tidy. Then the scent of whiskey. People who knew you said you didn't drink. You were a doctor who followed his own orders."

He jutted out his chin. "But people drink in—how did you word it?—a moment of emotional distress."

"Sure." She folded her arms. "But I imagine you'd go to something familiar. Like the expensive rum I saw in your father's cabinet." Then the corners of her lips curved up. "But all that was only suspicions. I bluffed my way out there on the porch today."

Gawking at her, Blake chuckled. "And it worked." Then he waved at Kai. "Don't let this one get away."

Air whooshed from Kai's lungs. If only he could follow that advice! But he and Marina didn't belong together to start with.

Compassion for his brother tightened Kai's rib cage. That was how he knew he'd forgiven Blake. He'd received the gift of a brother, and he wasn't going to throw it away like some people threw empty bottles into the ocean. He met Blake's eye. "Maybe one day, when this is all over, we can meet for dinner and get to know each other better."

Blake brightened. "I'd love that."

"Maybe you could also tell me about my ancestors." Nostalgia stirred Kai. He'd finally be able to learn about his roots. "Well, besides the fact that most of them were doctors." Would those ancestors be disappointed in him?

Blake smiled. "Not most of them. That's just what Father chose to display in the hall. We have relatives who are artists and farmers and even one gymnast. Oh, and we have a relative from Korea who works as a chef and makes great barbecue..."

The atmosphere in the room warmed.

Then Marina's gaze sharpened again. "I feel bad bringing it up, but... Blake, you know we'll have to go to the police. While I understand the reasons for your actions, that doesn't make them legal."

"We'll do what we can to help," Kai hurried to add.

Blake's frown deepened, but he nodded. "I understand. Well, do you know a good lawyer?"

Kai smiled. "I know the best one."

Chapter Eighteen

Kai's heart squeezed as he and Marina strolled along the beach. Twilight had long since surrendered its dusky hues to velvety darkness. Now, stars twinkled in the sky, and the ocean lapped the sand. Quiet perched on Kai's shoulder while Buttercup wobbled near Marina, stopping from time to time to examine something. She sneezed adorably as a ghost crab skittered away, probably sending some sand into her nose. Marina was gorgeous in a long teal dress and dearer than ever.

The night was magical, but he had difficulty being cheerful, even with all his practice. Because she was leaving tomorrow.

He laced his fingers through hers, and his heart stuttered when she didn't move her hand away. How long would it be before she returned here? Many years again?

"Beautiful! Beautiful!" Quiet chirruped on Kai's shoulder.

And it was. *She* was. Everything about Marina was beautiful. Everything about the night was beautiful. Except for the fact that both would leave soon.

"Beautiful, it is," she whispered as she stared at the ocean. "How come I never fully appreciated the beauty here?"

"Maybe you didn't have many chances to be on the beach. With all your responsibilities growing up." His gut clenched, something in it turning hard and leaden. And now she had new responsibilities and new opportunities, and both would prevent her from being here.

Or with him.

He'd wanted to tell her about his feelings, but in the end, he hadn't. He couldn't be a stone on her neck, couldn't drag her down, burden her, suffocate her.

"But you always knew to appreciate our hometown, the ranch, the ocean." She moved a suspicious stick out of Buttercup's path.

He stroked Quiet's smooth feathers. "My childhood was different. I had a supportive family. And I never had your aspirations or your abilities, for that matter. I get to work with my brothers and our farm animals. I even have the variety of helping tourists at the stationery store and making children smile at the pirate ship reenactments. I only had two things missing. One, knowing about my birth family."

When he paused, she looked up at him. "What's the second one?"

You. Marrying you. Having a family with you.

He didn't have the right to say it. A legal eagle and, well, a parrot didn't fly in the same sky. She'd be flying free tomorrow, soaring off to a big city and a big job. Meanwhile, he'd be grounded, wings clipped, content to stay in his comfortable world. It still took all his willpower because he glimpsed longing and attraction in her eyes.

While he could never soar as high as her, maybe it was time to glide in her tailwind. His fingers tightened around hers as they stopped again, Buttercup investigating a pebble. "Would you be okay if I visited you in Charleston?"

"I'd love that, but..." She drew a deep breath. The wind threw her golden hair into her face.

He swept it away, letting his fingertips glide along her delicate skin, apprehension tightening his gut. There was a but, of course.

"I won't stay there long." Vulnerability flashed in her eyes.

Was this a worse goodbye than he'd expected?

"Oh no, you don't!" Marina leaned to her puppy as the latter tried to snack on the pebble she'd been playing with. "No! You can't eat that!"

His gut hardened further. "Did you accept a higher-level job somewhere else? If you're okay with it, I'd travel there, too. Unless it's on the moon." Then he waved to the sky and tried for a chuckle from her. "Never mind. I'd travel there for you, as well."

But her gaze was intense and serious. "I'll stay in Charleston as long as it'll take to wrap things up. My apartment lease term is coming up next month, and I'm giving my intent-to-vacate notice. I'll resign from my position."

He stared at her. "You know I'll support you whatever you do. But what's the plan from there?"

"I don't have a plan."

"What?" He goggled. Did he hear her right?

She'd always had a plan. Since she'd been seven years old and maybe even before that.

"Whaaaaaat?" Quiet screeched as if to emphasize the point.

She dipped her chin, her smile sheepishly endearing. "Well, there are some things I *want* to do. You were right. It's time to reconnect with my siblings. Not from the point of obligations and responsibilities, but from the point of affection. And I enjoyed solving puzzles with you way more than my current job. I might get a PI license. Barrett said he'd show me the ropes."

Hope flourished inside him. That changed everything. Or at least so many things. He could tell her he loved her now. He could risk it all. But first, he wanted her to be happy and not get disappointed later. "Are you sure it's what you want?"

Her gaze became pensive. "Not at all. But it might be what I *need*. Remember you told me to take a leap of faith?" Then she groaned and sprinted away. "Buttercup! Don't run into the water! You're still so little the waves can carry you away."

He was about to offer to supervise while her puppy swam, but then he had a different idea. He'd tried to tell Marina the difficult words to no avail several times already. Maybe it would be better just to write them.

He found a stick and wrote in the sand.

He didn't hear her any longer, so once done, he tossed the stick aside and turned around to make sure she and Buttercup were all right. If Buttercup had run into the water too far, the tide could wet Marina's long dress, making it heavy, and undercurrents could drag her down.

The pressure eased on his chest as she walked toward him, a sight to be seen in the moonlight.

Buttercup squirmed in her hands and barked in protest. Then, when Quiet barked back, imitating the puppy, Buttercup stopped mid bark as if in shock.

Marina's eyes widened as she read the words in the sand, and his heartbeat became erratic. What would her answer be?

The decision to confess his love had been simmering inside for so long it boiled over by now, but the decision to propose was a spontaneous one. Was he taking it too far?

"Could you please step aside? I can't read the entire thing." She placed the squirming puppy on the sand, and Buttercup ran to the inscription.

Right. That would've helped. "Sure." He stepped aside. Now his heartbeat was a staccato in his ears. His life was about to change forever.

Her expression became melancholic. "There must've been a young couple here before us. There's a touching romantic confession in the sand."

"What?" Great. He must sound like his parrot.

Quiet confirmed it by screeching, "Whaaaaat?"

Her oh-so-kissable lips stretched in a wistful smile. "Yeah. The girl's name must've been Mary."

To Kai's credit, he didn't say "what" again, but that was mostly because he was speechless. He whirled around to see what she was seeing. Then he read what he'd written while Buttercup ran in the sand, efficiently erasing the last word. "I wrote this!"

"You're in love with the girl Mary and want to marry her? Is that the mystery girl you told me you'd fallen for? Did she come back?" Her questions came fast and loud, striking him like bullets and unmasking her hurt.

"Marry! Marry!" Quiet screeched, spreading his wings, flapped off Kai's shoulder, and glided to the sand.

"Quiet, you're not helping." He took Marina's hands in his. "It's supposed to be 'marry' not 'Mary.' Buttercup trampled on the word *me*, and I missed one *R* in a hurry." He'd slap himself on the forehead if his hands weren't occupied already. Unlike her, he'd never participated in spelling bees, but how could one miss an *R* in the word *marry*?

"Oh. But there's supposed to be either a period or a semicolon between two sentences, i.e. before marry me, not a comma."

He groaned. Only Marina would get all legalistic over a proposal. "I'll never forget the importance of punctuation again," he said grimly.

Tears rushed to her eyes. "Do you mean it? That you love me with a forever kind of love? That you want to marry me?"

"Absolutely." How had a beach proposal worked so well for Dallas? Kai would now advise his brothers that, if they were ever going to propose in writing, they'd better do it on a banner and check the spelling a million times. "You're the only woman for me. Forever and beyond. In this universe and all other ones. But if you're not ready... If you need time to think it over, to weigh pros and cons—"

"No."

His heart dropped to the misspelled and mangled words in the sand. She didn't love him. Or didn't want to marry him. Probably neither.

"No! No!" Quiet parroted.

Thanks for the reminder, buddy.

She picked up Buttercup and hid her face in the puppy's fur. Was she trying to spare his feelings? When she raised her head, her eyes glistened. "I don't need to think things over this time. I know with everything in me how much I love you. I was jaded after my divorce, but you reawakened me to life. It's with you that I experience life. There are no cons, really. Yes! I'll marry you."

"Yes! Yes!" Quiet screeched.

Euphoria filled Kai to the brim, though he could barely believe this. His chest expanded. He removed the ring from the chain on his neck. "It's very modest. It's not an engagement ring but a promise ring. I'll be happy to take you to buy you an engagement ring."

"It's not about the ring." She offered her left hand, and he slid the ring onto her finger. She angled it into the moonlight, a soft smile caressing her lips. "When did you get this?"

"I bought it the day before you told me you met Travis."

"Oh..." Air rushed from her lungs, and her hand fell to her side. She tilted her head, her gaze quizzical as she peered up at him. "Why didn't you tell me before?"

Quiet landed back on his shoulder. Kai glanced at her puppy who stretched on the sand before he braved looking into her eyes again. No need to say it. Surely, she understood he'd let her go when she'd fallen for someone else.

She stepped closer and cupped a hand to his cheek. "I mean, after I returned to Port Sunshine?"

He leaned into her touch, then tipped his face to kiss her soft palm. "I didn't want to ruin our friendship. Besides, right away, you told me you weren't looking for romance. But mostly because you had your dreams and more than deserved to achieve them. I didn't want to tie you down."

"Quiet!" Quiet shouted.

And Marina nodded as if agreeing with the parrot. She wound her arms around his neck, careful not to encroach on Quiet's territory. "Darling, you never tie me down. You lift me up."

He grinned and lifted her from the ground just to show how much he enjoyed uplifting her.

Chapter Nineteen

A month later...

Marina tilted her face to the sun, sending thanks to God as she stood beside Kai in the most beautiful place in the world. The sea breeze caressed her skin and teased the veil over her loose-flowing hair while waves lapped the sand a safe distance from the wedding party where, in loving support, those dear to her gathered, including Blake and Professor Tucker.

But most dear of all, Kai. Her heart swelled to the brim, and her groom's eyes peered into hers, their dark depths more luminous than the sparkling ocean. How did she stay away from him and the beauty of her home place for so long? How could she have been blind to his love? To her feelings for him?

His hand touched hers. Yes, this was the way she wanted to go through life from now on, side by side with him. Hand in hand with him. Heartbeat in rhythm with his.

Her cousin stood by her other side, dressed in an aquamarine dress. They'd traded places this time, and now, Marina was the bride and Skylar the maid—or rather, matron—of honor. All the bridesmaids wore the matching necklaces Skylar had made, and so did Marina. But for her hair, she'd woven a wildflower wreath reminiscent of what she now considered her first date with Kai. It didn't exactly match the necklace or the dress, and that didn't matter. She no longer had to follow any protocol on strict clothes and correct answers.

Her veil flowed over her back like a sail of a ship propelling her along for new adventures. Sand warmed her bare toes, and she nearly giggled. Imagine her, getting married in flip-flops! Kai went barefoot, though he paired the lack of footwear with a traditional tuxedo. His only other decoration was the parrot perched on his shoulder, preening.

Mom had been afraid Quiet would interrupt the priest's speech, but so far, the parrot behaved well.

"At this point, why don't you make Buttercup the ring bearer?" Mom had said then.

Marina had chuckled. "Hmm, that's an interesting idea."

Currently, Mom was holding on tight to Buttercup in the front row. Mom had graciously volunteered to take care of the puppy at the wedding, probably so Marina wouldn't make her the ring bearer. Oh, and Buttercup was Marina's dog now. Both Skylar and Dallas had decided Buttercup had gotten too attached to Marina to make the switch.

The guests wore shoes, and Mom's pumps sank into the sand. Poor Mom was at first flabbergasted by the couple's choice of footwear. Lots of the things in Marina's wedding were spontaneous and unusual for her. Before returning to Port Sunshine, she'd always known not only her own next steps but also the next five steps of the people she had to work with.

Despite her concern it might rain, the sun shimmered off the water and bathed them with delightful warmth. Maybe she'd even get her reception outside in Kai's childhood home's backyard, though they had the barn as a backup if needed.

She glanced over her shoulder at her family in the first row, and her heart shifted. She hadn't just escaped her hometown for her career. She'd fled to escape her family. She analyzed many things in her life except that act, and she should have. After so many years of the wrong family dynamics, she'd come to associate her siblings with burdens and responsibilities, something that had weighed on her and pulled her down. But it didn't have to be like that. Seeing again how Kai's family helped each other showed her how it could be. How it *should* be.

Growing up, she'd had no choice. But now she could choose how she interacted with her siblings. It could be mutual support and encouragement, though it might be too late to change her relationship with Gale. Saylor was on board already, and Marina sent her bridesmaid a smile. Hopefully, the others would follow eventually.

The breeze picked up her veil and threw it around a bit, but she didn't bother to rearrange it. It was so different from her first marriage where everything had been carefully arranged a year in advance. Every outrageously expensive detail had to be perfect then. Now Marina understood that it was more to impress Travis's colleagues and acquaintances than to make her happy. She'd been just one of the many beautiful decorations at that wedding.

She moved closer to Kai as she sent thankful thoughts to Travis, wherever he was. She no longer felt the sharp pain anytime she thought of him, only an echo of it. She'd loved him, yes, but she'd chosen to be blind to his faults. She'd spent years working hard to be worthy of the accomplished lawyer he was, striving to please him. She'd been conditioned that way from childhood. As a mentor so deeply admired as well as her husband, he'd been her sun, and her life had revolved around him. But instead of giving her warmth, he'd burned her love to ashes with his infidelities. Had he loved her at all, or only seen an intelligent but malleable partner desperate to escape her circumstances?

Now that she and Travis were no longer together, she'd been blessed to reconnect with Kai and see how different their love was—how different he made her feel. Not only were they on equal terms but also he sincerely admired and loved her. She'd have seen it sooner had her first experience not left her sunblinded. Unlike Travis, who'd been super organized and meticulous, Kai had seemed too reckless, too unpredictable. But also unlike Travis, Kai had his heart in the right place.

In her hands.

He was her opposite in so many senses, and that was exactly what she needed.

What was in store for her now? She had no clue. Probably for the first time in her memory, she didn't have a plan.

She nearly giggled again, which was also unusual for her. Just as it was unusual to smile so much. But it was impossible not to return Kai's infectious grin, not to smile in his presence.

Would she even like working as a private investigator? Would she have enough cases? Would she regret leaving her prestigious, hard-earned, lucrative job? She didn't have the answers to any of those questions. Instead of analyzing everything and charging forward on her own, she'd finally let God guide her.

When it was time to say the vows, she suffered a fleeting panic. They'd decided to say their own vows. Now, her heart stuttered as her mind went blank. Why did she agree to this? She should've written something down.

Lord, what should I say?

Then Kai took her hands, and her panicked thoughts evaporated. She just basked in the sunshine and his love.

"I'll go first, please. I guess some people call me impatient." As he paused, a few chuckles drifted from the chairs. "And I'm impatient. To spend the rest of my life with you, Marina. You're my best friend and often the voice of wisdom in my head. You're my supporter and encourager. But you're so much more. I love everything about you. Your every word, every twist of your gorgeous golden hair and the exquisite scent of it, every glittery speck in your blue eyes, especially when you look at me. I love your inner and outer beauty and the kind way you help people, including me, of course."

A few more chuckles followed, and she couldn't help joining in.

His fingers tightened around hers, anchoring her to him, but also letting her know he'd be the wind in her sails if she needed it. And while she was taking on his name, she knew he'd forever let her stand at the helm of her own life. "I love your tenacity and the way you don't stop until you have it all solved. Even more, I love your mind. But most of all, I love how you've become my world. You know so much about constellations, but do you know you're all those constellations for me? All the stars in the sky. All the drops in the ocean. All the grains of sand. You're it for me. My entire world. Beautiful."

Tears prickled behind her eyes. How did she live without him all these years?

"Beautiful! Beautiful!" the parrot screeched.

Everyone laughed.

Including Marina. "If Quiet means me, I'm glad he's part of the family now. If he means the speech, I'll gladly agree."

"I love you, Marina! I love you, Marina!" the parrot screeched even louder.

Normally, Marina would be mortified. But now she just smiled at Quiet. He must have heard Kai say it frequently to say those words so well. "Love you, too, darling."

Kai continued, "I believe God meant you for me—He even helped our parents match our names, both meaning 'sea.' But as much as I love the sea, I'd give it up for you. You see, you're the only one for me. I've loved you for as long as I can remember, though I couldn't admit it even to myself. I vow I will love and care for you forever. I still want to pinch myself to believe it's real that you love me."

Quiet brought his black beak close to Kai's shoulder as if ready to oblige.

"Um, Quiet, I'm good. Marina, I can't wait to marry you." Kai's grin became mischievous. "And I can't wait to kiss you."

The priest cleared his throat. "Well, we haven't gotten to that part yet. Please wait until I pronounce you husband and wife."

Oh, her turn.

Okay, okay. She wasn't in a courtroom with high expectations. She didn't need to prove anything to anyone. She didn't have to prove herself. The pressure disappeared from her chest. This was her place. Her life.

Buttercup barked, filling in the pause, resulting in a few more chuckles.

Her pets. Her people. Her man. All she had to do was just... be. Well, a few words wouldn't hurt, as indicated by Skylar's friendly nudge when the pause stretched for too long. Kai's lopsided grin, however, never wavered.

Marina drew a deep breath of salty air. "I have to admit I'm speechless."

"And that doesn't happen often," Gale muttered from her seat.

"Quiet!" Quiet shrieked.

Then words flowed. Were they perfect and carefully planned? No. But they were the words she'd needed to say. "I love you so much. You were always my friend, always there for me, and always filling my life with joy. In your eyes, I didn't just find you and your love. I found myself and love for myself. You once asked what I wanted. I'm still not sure career-wise. But without a shadow of a doubt, I know I want a lifetime with you. I vow to always love and support you in all you do." Her heart constricted. "I love you all the way to the Big Dipper and back, and then some."

"That's a long way," Austin said from the line of groomsmen.

"No kidding," Dallas whispered.

But everyone calmed down under the priest's strict gaze.

Then, when the priest finally announced them husband and wife, Kai's kiss took her breath away. Everything in her woke up to life, a life with Kai.

As a euphoric wave swept her up, she started an exciting, unscheduled, but oh-so-marvelous new journey.

Epilogue

Marina's wedding was the first social outing Kennedy Crawford voluntarily attended in many years. The business functions she couldn't avoid in her job didn't count. She squirmed in her wooden seat in Marina's mother-in-law's backyard where they were holding the reception. The mouthwatering scents of barbecue and roasted potatoes floated to her, but she didn't feel hungry. Rather, awkward.

Being among people in large gatherings put her stomach in knots, so she'd gone the opposite way from her socialite parents who'd loved to party. And unlike them, shy and introverted Kennedy didn't have many friends to start with. Any real friends, not those who'd tried to befriend her because of her inheritance. Her rib cage constricted. She didn't want to spoil the happy event, so she ducked her head and hid behind a large glass of lemonade.

Her budding friendship with Marina was too precious to let Kennedy refuse the invitation. Marina was a glorious bride in an off-the-shoulder white dress she paired with a wreath of wildflowers, beaming at her newlywed husband. And he looked back at her with so much love.

Wistfulness unraveled Kennedy's carefully managed emotions. But really, what did she have to complain about? She straightened her back and took a bite from a barbecue rib to keep up the appearance, arranging her features into a cheerful mask. No point in moping, especially at a wedding. She was fortunate to have what she had, and she knew it. And if she'd been lonely, she had only herself to blame.

After all, it was her fault she'd lost her cousin, who'd been as close as a sister. A soul twin.

A knife turned inside her, cutting loose a familiar pain. She welcomed the pain because she deserved it. And because the moment she stopped feeling it would be the moment she'd forget Clara, and Kennedy didn't want that.

"Would you like me to refill your iced tea? Or bring you something else to eat?" Austin's concerned voice reached her as he leaned closer, giving her a whiff of his fresh aftershave.

Right. She'd forgotten she wasn't alone. "No thanks. I'm good." A wisp of hair escaped the updo her stylist had decorated with crystals, and the wind threw it in her face. She tucked it behind her ear with an impatient gesture.

"Okay. How about the next dance, then?" He smiled at her.

Keeping the smile in place got more difficult. "Thanks for asking. But I'll have to respectfully decline."

"Oh. Okay." Disappointment flashed in his eyes, and he deflated in his dashing tuxedo. Great looks and great character sure ran in the Lawrence family. "How about the one afterward, then?"

Seriously?

She suppressed a groan and thumped her ice-tea glass onto the table so fast the liquid nearly sloshed. "I don't dance."

"I understand." He shifted away.

Great. Stifling a groan against the guilt, she hid behind the glass while sipping the cold drink. Sunlight sent golden flecks through the amber liquid. While she didn't know Austin well, everyone in town seemed to like the friendly veterinarian who always had a kind word not only for people but also animals. Her uncle often said one could judge someone's character by the way they treated children or animals.

She shouldn't have been rude. She was irritated with herself, not him. Partly because Clara would never fall in love, never get married, never smile again. All because of Kennedy. Partly because Uncle called this morning and said they needed to talk. At lunch tomorrow.

She stole a glance at Austin. Surprising how he hadn't left his surly neighbor—namely, her—but rather stayed in his chair, sipping tea.

As the groom's brother and a groomsman, Austin showed up without a plus-one. Apparently, someone had thought to punish him by seating him near her, who was also without a plus-one.

Why couldn't she be nicer to him?

Because she'd be ice water to his fire. And not only because of her cerulean-hued party gown where crystals studding the bodice glimmered like water drops while the reddish tones in his fiery hair lit him up. She'd been called out far too many times for her frosty attitude. It was a miracle she'd not only survived in the hospitality industry but also made wise decisions in it. She'd douse his enthusiasm in no time.

"That doesn't mean you should be rude to him. It's just one dance, not a lifetime together." Uncle's voice rang in her ears.

He'd always been her voice of wisdom. And everything important she'd learned, she'd learned from him. Never mind that her parents had sent her to one of the best schools in Europe to study. Also, to be as far away from them as possible after she'd started asking inconvenient questions.

What did Uncle want to talk about? Her stomach clenched, and the barbecue turned sour there. His tone had suggested the conversation wouldn't be easy.

Marina caught her gaze and lifted her lemonade glass in a silent toast. Kennedy did the same with her own. Then Marina shifted her gaze to Austin, frowned, and said something to her newlywed husband.

Kennedy's heart fell into the grass. "Sorry," she mouthed to Marina. Not a great start to a friendship.

Her uncle also often said it didn't cost anything to be kind. She felt like she'd kicked a puppy—or at least the puppy's caring doctor. So she leaned to Austin. "On the other hand, I can make an exception. I'd love to have the next dance."

"Really?" His face lit up.

"Really." Wow, could it be so easy to bring someone joy? How would she know? She seldom brought people joy, something her mother stated too many times.

"I'm glad." He got up and gave her his hand.

She took it, and for an inexplicable reason, tingles erupted over her skin. Weird. She was immune to romance and male charm—wasn't she? His large palm, somewhat callused from physical labor, cradled hers. She liked the feeling. Often, the hands she shook in business were smooth, greasy from lotion, and sporting a diamond ring or two. She'd often had to put on appearances in those meetings, and other people had, as well.

Austin was... was real, down-to-earth, and it made her pause and take notice.

He led her to the space cleared on the grass for dancing. Kai and Marina joined them with the handful of couples already there, having eyes only for each other.

Kennedy placed her free hand on his shoulder, the tuxedo smooth under her fingertips, his shoulder hard beneath it. Hmm. No padding? His fingers curled around her other hand, and he led her confidently but without trying to get too close, not using the opportunity to hold her too tight. He whirled her around when the dance required it, and her head started spinning. Then she made the mistake of looking into his eyes.

"Why do you always look so sad?" Those blue eyes studied her with a genuine interest. Not as if he tried to score, like other guys did with her, but as if he cared.

Not many people on this earth cared about her—not her wealth—and one of those people had a difficult conversation in store for her. Was it connected to Uncle's physical? He was supposed to get results today.

"Do I *always* look sad?" she deflected. Years of practice.

"Well, every time I saw you at the library. At first, I thought it was because you had to study. And I don't know any people who like to study." His gaze flicked to the newlyweds. "Except Marina maybe."

Kennedy shrugged. "It's just my facial expression, I guess."

He held her hand, but he also held her gaze.

Why couldn't she look away? Her heart shifted.

"What would cheer you up?" Concerned notes coated his voice.

"You already did." She meant it. She felt lighter dancing with him, even talking to him somehow made it easier to breathe.

"I hope so."

The music stopped, and a strange disappointment uncoiled inside her. She hadn't wanted to dance to start with.

He led her back to their seats. She nodded to her empty glass, her throat parched. "You know, I'd love more tea."

He brightened again. "Coming right up."

"Thanks."

He returned with a carafe filled with amber liquid and ice cubes and poured some into her glass. They'd melt fast in the sun. But what was much more surprising was how much her resolve seemed to melt in his presence.

Her hand shook and knocked the glass over, sending tea flowing across her dress. Ruining it in a second.

"So sorry." He snatched the glass, his features crumpling.

She reached for some napkins. "Not your fault. *I* knocked the glass over."

"But *I* brought the tea."

Marina rushed to her. "I'll take you to the bathroom. Let's try to save your dress."

"It's okay." Kennedy wasn't going to worry about her ruined dress. She knew too well that some things couldn't be saved.

Her dress was the least of them.

THE END

From Alexa: Thank you so much for reading! Did you enjoy Kai and Marina's story? I hope you'll also want to read the next book in the series and see Austin and Kennedy get their chance at happiness. If so, please click here[1] to purchase their story, *Seaside Cowboy's Marriage of Convenience*.

---

1. https://books2read.com/u/4AA9vA

Other books by Alexa Verde

TO SEE AN UPDATED LIST of all my other books or subscribe to my weekly reader newsletter (and get a free ebook as your welcome gift!) click here[2].

---

2. https://www.subscribepage.com/alexaverdepublishedbooks

Acknowledgments

First of all, thank You to God for putting up with me, and for all the blessings!

A million thanks to you, my readers, for reading my books, for sending me encouragement, and for supporting me.

Many thanks to my street team, Alexa's Amazing Readers, and to my beta readers, whom I love to pieces. Special thanks to Trudy, MaryEllen, Pat, Terry, Margaret, Sarah, Michaela, Carol, Julie, and Kim for their feedback and help with typo-spotting!

Thanks to Linda Klager for suggesting the town name; to Teresa Kirk, Denise Chrisman Ward, Lois Medders, MJ Lockey, Michelle Bauer, Lisa Stillman Barret, Sylvia Vann, Carol Fritz, and Patricia Oaks for suggesting character names; to Sally and Judi for choosing Buttercup's name, and to Pat Dexter for Travis, Cody, and Blake.

Heartfelt thanks to author Jessie Gussman for helping me so much on the way. Jessie, you make me laugh, you make me smile, and you make the world a better place.

I also thank my wonderful editor, Deirdre, for coming through for me every time.